LP   Holmes, Gina. |4
HOLMES   Driftwood tides

01/15   31.99

DRIFTWOOD TIDES

This Large Print Book carries the
Seal of Approval of N.A.V.H.

DRIFTWOOD TIDES

GINA HOLMES

THORNDIKE PRESS
A part of Gale, Cengage Learning

GALE
CENGAGE Learning·

Farmington Hills, Mich • San Francisco • New York • Waterville, Maine
Meriden, Conn • Mason, Ohio • Chicago

GALE
CENGAGE Learning®

LIBRARY OF CONGRESS CATALOGING-IN-PUBLICATION DATA

Holmes, Gina.
    Driftwood tides / by Gina Holmes. — Large print edition.
        pages ; cm. — (Thorndike Press large print Christian fiction)
    ISBN 978-1-4104-7523-7 (hardcover) — ISBN 1-4104-7523-9 (hardcover)
    1. Widows—Fiction. 2. Illegitimate children—Fiction. 3. Large type books.
    I. Title.
PS3608.O494354D75 2014b
813'.6—dc23   2014036030

Published in 2015 by arrangement with Tyndale House Publishers, Inc.

Printed in Mexico
1 2 3 4 5 6 7 19 18 17 16 15

I've written about some pretty flawed fathers, but mine is wonderful. A disabled Marine, he sacrificed so much for his country in Vietnam, and later for his family. Never have I heard him complain. He taught me the value of hard work, perseverance, family, generosity, and a positive outlook. He is one of God's greatest gifts to me. I'll bet he never thought that eye-rolling teenager would grow up to say that. This one's for you, Dad. I couldn't love you more.

"See how very much our Father
loves us,
for he calls us his children, and that is
what we are!"

1 JOHN 3:1

PROLOGUE

The pillow pushed against Holton Creary's nose, forcing him to turn for air. His eyes fluttered, opening just enough to take in the first blush of morning light. Realizing he had at least another solid hour to sleep, he smiled in contentment. Flipping toward his wife's side of the bed, he reached out to pull her close. Molding her warm, familiar body against his was a ritual as old as their marriage. But instead of coming to rest on her hip, his hand thudded against the mattress, jolting him fully awake. Lifting his head, he listened for her pattering about, but he heard only Rufus snoring from his spot on the floor.

The small house was full of the smell of freshly brewed coffee . . . but no sign of her. He peered out the front window, not surprised to see her standing with her back to him, watching the sunrise from the beach they called a front yard. She was wearing her nightgown, his old cardigan serving as her bathrobe. The breeze made the nightgown cling to her legs, which filled him with a momentary possessiveness. If any man should happen to walk by at that moment, the sight of her would stop him in his tracks. That was the downside of marrying a beautiful woman — Holton wasn't the only man with appreciative eyes.

He climbed down the stairs leading to the beach and quietly sidled up behind her. He wrapped his arms around her waist, causing her to jump and turn her head in surprise. A warm smile replaced her startled expression. "You're up early," she said.

"I missed you." He rested his chin on her shoulder, catching a whiff of the perfume left over from the day before.

"Did the cicadas wake you?" she asked.

It was only then that he registered the sound of their screeching. It reminded him of a sprinkler system on overdrive. "Actually, I didn't even hear them until you mentioned it."

She twisted her mouth at him. "In your own world, as usual." The lightness of her tone told him she wasn't picking a fight.

"Right now, I'm all about yours." He hugged her waist tighter.

"I'll never get used to this," she said with

a contented sigh.

Looking out at the sunrise with its layered gauzy pinks and purples, he knew just what she meant. "I forgot how beautiful the beach could be this time of morning."

She spun around to face him. Her light-brown eyes glinted, tiny lines forming around the corners, followed by a smile. "Not just the view. I mean this whole place. You. The gallery. My life is like a dream."

He cleared his throat before his voice could crack from emotion. "I thought you'd be mad at me for coming home so late last night."

She turned to face the water again, reaching back for his hands. She wrapped them around her waist and leaned her back against him. "What good does it do? I'd have better luck punishing Rufus for drooling. I married an artist. It's not fair getting mad at you for being the person I fell in love with."

He ran her golden hair between his fingers. She was more than he deserved. So much more.

"Is it almost finished?" she asked. "Tell me it's about done."

He had spent nearly every waking moment, when they weren't at the gallery, working on the stallion. Until now, she'd always spoken with a twinge of contempt whenever mentioning the piece, like a jealous lover. He knew he was leaving her alone far too much, but tomorrow or the next day it would be finished, and he'd make it up to her.

He kissed the top of her head. "It would have been done yesterday if I hadn't been working on a certain brake issue."

Looking over her shoulder at him, her eyes brightened. "You finally fixed them? No more screeching?"

"Not a peep."

She turned around in his arms and kissed his lips in gratitude.

"If I'd known that was waiting for me, I'd have taken care of it last week."

"If you had taken care of it last week, you'd be getting more than a kiss."

He wriggled his eyebrows. "What can I get for adding an oil change?"

She slapped him playfully. "I better get ready."

He glanced at his watch. "We've got plenty of time. What's the hurry?"

"I was tired last night. I didn't sweep or count the drawer."

Guilt niggled at him. She had slowly taken over all the chores at the gallery that they'd agreed would be his. "I'll run over and do it. You take your time and enjoy the morning."

She laid her soft hand on his cheek, shielding it from the ocean breeze. "Not a chance. I want my husband back. I've got the gallery. You finish the stallion before I decide to set it on fire."

"Deal," he said.

It wasn't an hour after Holton handed her a travel mug of coffee and kissed her through the open car window that a squad car pulled up in front of the house. The moment the policeman took off his hat and slid it under his arm, Holton knew.

After the man informed him Adele had been killed on impact when her car hit another at nearly sixty miles an hour, he said nothing. He was so stunned that his heart froze, unable to respond. Before that could change, he drove to the nearest liquor store and bought the biggest bottle of gin he could find.

CHAPTER 1

The lab had either made a big mistake and none of the results could be trusted, or else her world was about to be turned upside down. It was this Libby Slater thought of as she rushed from the stationery store, bag in hand.

The day had started out pleasant enough. The weather was beautiful, she'd met Rob for lunch, and not one of her clients had dropped a shoe box of receipts on her desk, assuming she'd sort it all out. But then, in the middle of her ordinary day, she'd logged on to her online health account to check the results from Rob's and her premarital genetic counseling workup and gotten the shock of a lifetime.

The results should put her mind at ease, the doctor's note read, but they did just the opposite. Although her fiancé was a carrier for cystic fibrosis, the disease that had taken the life of his younger sister, Libby was not.

This was good news, because apparently it took two to tango. Other than that, all the results were a very positive negative. She would have been relieved if it weren't for her blood type, listed innocently along with the rest of the results: A positive, which wasn't positive at all. Both of her parents had O blood types, and two Os couldn't produce an A child. It had to be an error. Had to.

The screech of sirens ripped Libby from her thoughts. Hunching, she slapped her free hand over her ear and waited for the pulsating red lights to pass. Two city blocks later, her ears were still ringing.

A bus with a giant cell phone carrier ad scrolled across it, dotted by finger-smudged windows, screeched to a halt in front of an empty bench. Pneumatic doors hissed open and passengers hurried off so fast they were almost a blur. After the last passenger filed past, she stepped off the curb to cross the street.

She assumed the approaching cab would stop, or at least not accelerate, but she assumed wrong. Jumping back onto the concrete, she felt a whoosh of exhaust part her long hair. In lieu of an apology, the driver screamed as he flew by. Although she couldn't decipher what he said, the vulgar hand gesture he thrust out the window gave her enough of a clue.

Soon her heartbeat returned to normal, and traffic broke just long enough for her to make a run for it. Having crossed the one-lane freeway of death, life and limb intact, she stepped again onto the relative safety of the sidewalk.

As she trudged forward, she could practically taste the tiny particles of soot and smog falling on her like mist, and couldn't help but wonder if breathing them in was making the inside of her lungs look like a coal miner's.

At last she reached her mother's brownstone. It was unfathomable that Caroline had paid almost a million dollars for what basically amounted to an old row home, even if it was located on the so-called Park Avenue of Casings.

Although the city was located in North Carolina, Casings was about as un-Southern as a city below the Mason-Dixon Line could be. This muggier, less-sophisticated parody of New York was a place she'd vowed to escape the second she graduated from college. Of course, that was before she fell in love with a man who just happened to be as dedicated to his job here as he was to her. She tightened her grip on the bag of wedding invitations she carried and couldn't help but smile at the thought of spending forever with the love of her life. But first they needed to survive this fiasco her mother called a wedding.

She climbed the brick stairs and peered over her shoulder, checking to be sure a mugger hadn't sneaked up behind her before unlocking the door. Inside, the foyer stood dark except for a rectangle of sunlight streaming down from the stained-glass transit window above. The flip of a switch flooded the hall in artificial light.

"Elizabeth?" Caroline's shrill voice echoed from the dining room. "You're late."

Libby rolled her eyes. "I had to pick up the extra invitations," she said, not quite loud enough for her mother to hear. Though, really, it wouldn't matter if she yelled it; the only person her mother listened to was herself.

Her Danskos thumped against the marble floor as she made her way through the corridor and into the dining room. Caroline sat at the long table with a stack of invitations tall enough to invite the entire state. The fact that she'd called Libby at work to tell her to pick up yet more invitations didn't bode well for Libby's vision of a quaint ceremony.

"It's positively barbaric to be doing this ourselves," Caroline said. "They have companies that take care of these things."

It was all Libby could do not to delve right into an interrogation about her questionable blood type. It was probably a mistake, but just in case, she didn't want to put Caroline on the defensive and get stonewalled before she got to the bottom of it.

She sighed as she hung her purse on the back of the chair. "So you've said. And as I've said, I want to know who's coming to my wedding, and I want to be the one who invites them." She eyed the invitations dubiously.

"You don't trust me?" Caroline asked in a sarcastic tone, but her expression was without humor. They both already knew the answer. "We could at least have hired a calligrapher to make them look pretty. Handwriting was never your best subject."

Libby gave her mother a dull look as she took a seat across from her. She hadn't realized how sore her feet were until she was finally off them. She kicked off her clogs and stretched her socked feet. "If I left it up to you and the Internet, my only guests would be the who's who of Casings." None of whom would be in the who's who of her small circle of friends.

A bottle of opened champagne sat in the middle of the table along with two crystal flutes. Caroline slid her tennis bracelet back on her wrist, then reached for the bottle and poured herself a glass. When she picked up the second, Libby shook her head. "Nice try."

Caroline huffed and flipped her blonde hair over her shoulder, revealing a dangling diamond earring — most likely another bauble from one of her long list of admirers. "I just thought it would be nice to celebrate a little while we work."

"No," Libby said. "You thought it would be nice to get me a little tipsy so you could sneak more of your debutante friends onto the guest list."

Caroline brought the champagne to her lips and sipped. "You certainly do think the world of me." She set her glass down and picked up a fountain pen. "Please tell me you didn't park that piece of junk out front."

Libby felt her cheeks flush in anger, but certainly not in surprise, at her mother's superficiality. "No, Caroline. I took a cab to the stationery store, then walked three blocks and almost got run over, all so the snobs you call neighbors wouldn't know your daughter drives a Jeep."

It was Caroline's turn to roll her eyes. "A

Jeep from this century would be fine. Honestly, Elizabeth, you make enough money to afford something less dilapidated. I saw an Audi that you would look so —"

"Stop. Just stop," she said, swallowing the indignation. She'd already fought with her mother three times this week, and what had it accomplished? Nothing but two sleepless nights and a headache. Caroline was always going to be Caroline, and she *was* paying for the wedding, after all. Something Libby had told Rob they never should have agreed to for this very reason. Besides, there were bigger fish to fry tonight.

She reached into her purse, bypassing the test results, and pulled out her guest list. Holding her breath, she set the list of names down on the table and slid it across to her mother like a lawyer offering up a settlement. "I went through this last night, and —"

"I have my own list," Caroline said coolly as she glanced at her. "Don't look so glum. I took your requests into consideration."

Requests? Libby thought. *What a joke.* It was going to be the biggest day of her life, and she had no more say in who was going to be there than the caterer did. "Is Rob at least on your roll?"

Unfazed, Caroline ran a manicured nail

slowly down Libby's list, pausing every so often to consider a name. "Don't be smart with me, young lady. It's my hard-earned money paying for every plate."

Libby looked away, disgusted. If she had the ceremony she wanted, she wouldn't need Caroline's money to pay for it. Caroline wanted the wedding she never had, and through her only child, she was finally going to get it. It wasn't fair; but then, as Rob always said, life wasn't.

"I don't recognize half these people," Caroline said as her finger slid to the bottom of the page.

An all-too-familiar pain began to throb behind Libby's left eye. The sooner this wedding was over, the better. "Of course you don't, because they're my friends, not yours."

Shaking her head, Caroline sighed. "Fine, we'll add them to the master list, but just so you know, this brings the guest count to three hundred."

"Three hundred?" Libby heard herself shriek. "I said I wanted a small wedding."

"It was *going* to be smallish," Caroline said, "but here you've gone and brought me another fifty names. Whose fault is that?"

Covering her face, she took a deep breath, willing herself not to cry. Two more months of this. That was it. She could do this, she told herself. For Rob, she could do most anything.

"Fine," Caroline said after a few seconds of uncomfortable silence. "I'll just cut out the DA's office, but if you get into any legal trouble, you're on your own."

Libby looked over her fingertips. "Why would I — ? Never mind." She reached into the stationery bag and pulled out a sheet of the fancy return labels they'd chosen for the invitations. At least she could get started sticking those on. Any progress was better than none. Her phone rang, and she grabbed her purse off the chair, riffling her hand blindly through it. By the time her fingers touched the phone, the ringing stopped. As expected, her call log showed Rob's number.

"What's he want now?" Caroline asked, sounding more perturbed than usual.

Finally, the perfect segue. Keeping her tone as neutral as she could, Libby decided this was as good a time as any. "We had our genetic counseling, and the results were posted today. I was supposed to tell him what they —"

"Genetic counseling?" Caroline raised a barely visible eyebrow.

"You know Rob's sister, Heather, died

from cystic fibrosis."

Caroline downed the rest of her champagne and reached for the bottle. "Rob had a sister?"

She couldn't tell by her mother's blank expression if she was just trying to get her goat or if she really was that oblivious. "That disease is hereditary. He wanted to make sure we weren't both carriers for it or anything else we could pass on to our future children."

Caroline finished filling her glass and set the bottle down with a clank. "And?"

"Rob's a carrier; I'm not."

"Of course you're not."

"But I did find out my blood type — A positive." She held her breath as she waited for her mother's reaction to the bombshell she'd just dropped, but Caroline had already lost interest and started writing names on the front of the invitation envelopes.

"That's good to know," she mumbled.

Directing her nervous energy toward something productive, Libby began working like an assembly line, carefully affixing address labels to the top left corners of the envelopes. "Yes, it is." She finished her stack, slid it to the right, and grabbed another. "Did you and George get genetic testing before you had me?"

24

Caroline shook her head as she worked. "They didn't really do that when I was . . ." Her voice trailed off. She never could bring herself to say the word *pregnant,* as if the thought of Libby inside her was too repulsive. Unless, of course, Libby hadn't been inside her after all.

"Your blood type is O positive like Rob's, isn't it?" Libby asked as nonchalantly as she could.

Caroline finally finished scrolling out the first invite. At the speed she was working, it was shaping up to be an excruciatingly long night. "That's *all* we have in common." Caroline could barely stand Libby's fiancé, but Libby tried not to take it personally. After George had abandoned them, Caroline pretty much hated all men equally. "How do you know my blood type, anyway?"

"I pay attention."

Caroline squinted at her.

"Wallet," Libby said, sliding another small stack of envelopes over to the finished pile. "You gave blood that one time, and you still carry the donor card." *So everyone can see how fabulously altruistic you are,* she wanted to add. She carefully peeled another label off the plastic sheet and pressed it onto an envelope. "George's dog tags say he's O positive too." For reasons she didn't know, she still kept her father's dog tags tucked away in her jewelry box. The military must have made a mistake. Lucky for him, he never got injured enough to need blood.

"I don't know what his dog tags say. I thought I threw those out with the rest of his junk." Caroline checked the first name off her list with a satisfied smile. "I just know his blood type is the same as mine because he donated for my hysterectomy."

That was it, then; the geneticist had gotten her results wrong. They'd just spent nearly a thousand dollars for results they couldn't trust. Rob was going to be ticked.

Caroline set her pen down and furrowed her brow in Libby's direction. "Why are you interested in everyone's blood type?"

Libby curled her toes. "Two O parents can't have an A child. It's impossible."

Caroline's face turned as white as the tips of her French manicure.

It was in that moment that Libby's life flashed before her eyes . . . and she knew.

The baby books with no pictures of Caroline pregnant. Her mother's claim that she'd lost not only her baby bracelet, but also the umbilical clamp and crib card. Was this why she hadn't minded when, as a preteen, Libby had defiantly taken to calling her by

26

her first name? "Why didn't you tell me?" was all she could manage around the boulder in her throat.

Caroline put on a plastic smile. "Tell you what?" she asked, her voice cracking under the facade. "Don't be silly. The lab made an error. That's all." She was usually such a good liar.

"Fine," Libby said coldly. "I'll get another test tomorrow."

Caroline's expression hardened. "Why can't you ever leave well enough alone?"

Before Libby could answer, Caroline left the dining room in stony silence.

So that was it? She didn't even have the decency to acknowledge the elephant in the room. Typical. Libby walked to the kitchen, poured herself a glass of water, and downed it like a shot, trying to decide what would give her the fastest escape — calling Rob to pick her up or a cab.

Before she could make up her mind, Caroline returned, her spiked heels clicking sharply against the wood floor. She closed her eyes and handed Libby a stack of papers.

Glancing down at the raised seal on the top document, Libby tried to process the unfamiliar names typed neatly on the lines.

With her arms crossed, Caroline tapped

her nails against her tanned arms. "Say something . . . please."

When Libby's gaze fell on the birth date — her birth date — her mouth went dry again.

After parting her thin, red lips, Caroline closed them without saying a word. It may have been the first time Libby had ever seen her mother speechless.

Caroline strode to the kitchen window and pulled open the roman shade. Sunlight flooded the room, casting her face in harsh light, which gave up every fine line. "With you getting married soon, I guess it was about time anyway. I thought about telling you when you turned eighteen, but . . ." Her voice began to crack. "But I chickened out. I was just so afraid you'd find your real parents and you'd . . ." She said more, but all Libby could focus on was the adoption papers she held.

The smell of Caroline's perfume wafted by, and suddenly Libby felt as though she might vomit. The hand that held the papers dropped to her side, while her other hand covered her mouth. This was real. This was really happening.

"I actually thought you should grow up knowing, but your father . . ." Caroline looked out the window, suddenly interested in the Pathfinder pulling into the neighbor's driveway.

Libby's father had left them when she was four. It seemed like only yesterday he had sat her on his lap and, with tears in his eyes, told her to be a good girl and look after Caroline. She thought he was just going to the store and couldn't figure out why he was being so melodramatic about it. She'd tried to fill the void with friends, sports, and of course Rob. But not a day went by that she didn't feel the absence of a daddy in her life. No wonder he'd had no qualms about abandoning his daughter . . . because she hadn't really been his daughter.

"I'm adopted," she said, more as a statement than a question. The brownstone had always been stuffy, but at that moment the air felt as heavy as the news being dropped.

So it was true after all. She shouldn't be surprised. She and Caroline couldn't have been more different. She and all of her family, really. In a gene pool full of girly girls and country-club men, she had always been the black sheep, preferring cutoff shorts and catching frogs to debutante parties and Gucci bags. They had never gotten along. And now it made sense why. They weren't cut from the same cloth.

What would have brought relief in childhood felt heavy and cold now. Caroline was far from a storybook mother, but she was all Libby had ever known. Feeling unsteady, she leaned against the counter. She thought she was on the verge of tears until she heard herself laugh.

Caroline whipped around. "There's nothing amusing about this, Elizabeth."

She knew the laughter was inappropriate, especially since she wasn't feeling happy in the least — confused maybe, scared, angry . . . and sad. Very, very sad.

Her laughter slowly died as she searched Caroline's eyes for any sign this all might be some sort of terrible joke. But Caroline didn't joke.

Her gaze darted back to the adoption papers — *her* adoption papers — and her biological mother's name: Adele Davison. The place where her father's name should have been was conspicuously blank.

"Who's my father?"

Caroline licked her lips nervously and slowly shook her head.

The child's name — *her* name — had been Grace. And she had been born in Wilmington, North Carolina, not Casings as she had always believed. Her head swam as she tried to process the fact that nothing

30

was what she thought it was. Not even
herself.

CHAPTER 2

The GPS led her straight to the Crearys'
driveway. With her heart in her throat, Libby
parked her Jeep beside a dinged pickup and
stared at the run-down shack with a yard
consisting of tall weeds pushing through
waves of sand. The structure itself was a
gray, shingle-sided box built on stilts, with a
small porch and plywood stairs leading
directly from the beach. The closest neighbor was a distant mansion.

Her Internet search for her birth mother
had turned out to be fruitless. Adele Davison had no web presence to speak of, but
Libby was able to pull up a marriage an-
nouncement in an Oahu newspaper for
Adele and a Holton Creary. It was dated six
years after Libby's birth, which meant, of
course, he was not her father. The man was
a renowned driftwood sculptor, and luckily
for her, he had a half-baked website that
listed a Nags Head address. It would stand

to reason that the husband would have to lead to the wife.

Slipping off her sunglasses, Libby pulled down the rearview mirror and checked herself one more time for good measure. She looked healthy and together. Maybe she wouldn't win a beauty contest, but she was definitely daughter material. At least she hoped so. She bared her teeth to make sure she had nothing caught between them, then cupped a hand over her nose and mouth and puffed. Satisfied her breath still smelled of spearmint, she double-checked that the adoption papers were safely tucked inside her purse. Carefully, she slipped them out and unfolded them.

It was strange to think that Grace had once been her name. Stranger still to see the empty line where her father's name should have been.

It was possible, she supposed, that her biological mother really didn't know her father's identity. She could have been drunk, high, or otherwise out of her mind. Maybe she'd been raped. But Libby doubted it. Her bet was that her bio-mom knew full well his identity but didn't want him involved for whatever reason. Hopefully her reluctance to name him didn't reflect on his character, or lack thereof. But even if he was a modern-day Jack the Ripper, Libby felt she had the right to know. Had the right to at least try to see if either or both of her parents could learn to love her.

She tucked the documents back in her purse, blew out a breath of nerves, and climbed out of her Cherokee. The bright summer sun beat down on her shoulders as the roar of ocean waves drowned out the pounding of her heartbeat. Glancing at the water, she wiped her damp palms against the sides of her jean shorts and drew in a lungful of briny air. To her right, seagulls cackled, circling ocean prey. Giving them a fleeting glance, she willed her wobbly knees to carry her forward.

The wood railing swayed at her touch and the stairs creaked under her weight. In her purse, her phone alerted her to a message. She didn't have to look to know it was Rob, asking how things were going.

At the top of the stairs, a bench swing hanging by rusty chains jangled in the breeze. She couldn't help but wonder how many nights her birth mother had spent there, sipping sweet tea and staring out at the ocean. Did she wonder if her daughter was looking up at the same sky? The thought made her heart beat harder. Beside the swing sat a pot of dirt, growing sandspurs identical to those in the yard.

Biting her lip to the point of pain, Libby rapped her knuckles against the door, half-expecting the rickety thing to fall over. The paint had long since been worn away by wind, sun, and sand. Only a remnant of white remained, clinging in patches to the splintered wood.

Inside, she could hear glass breaking and a man's voice grumbling obscenities.

Apparently now wasn't a good time. She had turned to leave when a loud bang shook the planks beneath her feet. It sounded like something — or someone — had hit the floor hard.

Alarmed, she hurried to the window.

"Hello?" She cupped her hands around her eyes, trying to see in, but the pane was so clouded by dirt it might as well have been a curtain. All she could make out was a blur of color lying on the floor. Frantically, she twisted the doorknob, gasping in relief when it turned.

And that was how Libby Slater met her stepfather — lying facedown on the carpet, surrounded by a shattered tumbler, at least a half-dozen empty gin bottles, and an overturned bucket of KFC.

■ ■ ■ ■

A strange gurgling sound came from the man Libby assumed was Holton Creary — renowned driftwood artist and husband of her biological mother. She dropped her purse and made her way to him through the obstacle course of broken glass, empty gin bottles, and fried chicken, praying he wasn't already dead. She pushed a bottle aside with her foot, knelt on the floor, and shook him. He reeked of alcohol, ocean, and body odor. "Are you okay?" she asked.

He didn't answer. She was grateful he wasn't a big man — medium height and wiry. She pushed him onto his side with relative ease. His lips were an unnatural shade of blue. She had been certified in CPR during her lifeguarding days, but with her mind racing, she couldn't remember the ratio of breaths to heart pumps. Fifteen to two? No, that was for a child. Thirty to two . . . or was it fifteen to three? She wasn't sure, but anything was better than nothing.

Pressing two fingers into his jugular, she almost fainted in relief when a soft, steady beat pulsated against her fingertips. His chest, however, wasn't rising and falling. With a gentle shove, she moved him onto his back to have a better look before deciding whether or not to force air into his lungs.

Lifting up his bleach-speckled Grateful Dead T-shirt, she hoped clothing had been masking shallow breaths. His chest was definitely not moving. She placed one hand on his forehead and the other under his chin, tilting his head back to open his airway. The last thing she wanted to do was to expose her lips to whatever was all over his, but it wasn't like she could let him die, stepfather or not.

She used the hem of his T-shirt to wipe his mouth. A hand grabbed her wrist, and a scream ripped from her lips.

Eyes the same shade of smoky gray as hers glared up at her. She was so startled that she fell onto her bottom. Something bit the back of her thigh, and she screamed again. As she yanked the small shard of glass from her skin, her phone started ringing. She glanced over at the purse she'd dropped near the door.

"What did you do to your hair?" Holton slurred. "I liked it better blonde."

"I, uh, heard you fall," she stuttered as she stood.

His lopsided grin reminded her of Rob's. "I knew you'd come back," he said.

Something warm trickled down the back

of her thigh. She wiped at it with her fingertips, surprised to find them smeared with red.

"You're bleeding." He tried to push himself up but collapsed again.

Her phone finally fell silent, followed by a short beep to let her know she had a message.

"It's just a cut," she said.

His color returned to warm beige, but she figured she'd better have EMS look at him anyway. Using a Colonel Sanders napkin she grabbed off the floor, she wiped the smear of blood from her hands and leg.

She retrieved the phone from her purse, but before she could dial 911, the phone rang again. Rob, of course.

Pressing the phone to her ear, she said, "Not a good time, babe."

The TV blared in the background. "What are they like?"

"Not now," she said, dabbing her balled napkin against her thigh. There was only a small dot of red this time.

"What's going on?" he asked, sounding alarmed.

Not having the time or patience to play fifty questions, she told him she'd call him when she could and hung up.

Holton rubbed his face against the carpet

like he had an itch, barely missing a hunk of jagged glass. She needed to get him off this floor before he sliced his throat.

"I'm calling an ambulance," she said, more to herself than to him.

He propped himself up on his elbow as his head swayed like an infant's. "Since when does my girl go to the hospital over a little cut?" He jabbed his finger in her direction and slurred, "You're tougher than that."

She wasn't sure who he thought she was, but then again, he was so drunk he probably didn't know who *he* was. "I'm not calling about me — I'm calling about you."

He bolted to a sitting position with a sudden burst of sobriety. "What? Why?"

"Uh, you stopped breathing."

He screwed up his mouth like she was crazy. "No, I didn't."

"Yes, you did." She started dialing.

He smacked the phone out of her hand before she could finish. It hit the paneled wall, then the floor.

"Hey!" She hurried over and picked it up, relieved the screen hadn't shattered.

"You know how much an ambulance ride costs? We don't have that kind of money." He scratched at the dark scruff on his chin.

Probably about the same as a new phone, she thought. She glanced around the tiny living room. Yeah, there was no doubt that finances were an issue. The focal point was a rusty woodstove, which, judging by the pile of ashes surrounding it, served as more than just bad decoration.

Mismatched rug remnants covered the unfinished plank floor. In front of the torn futon couch sat a small, ancient-looking TV complete with bunny ears, resting on a pressed-wood stand. Hanging on the wall behind the couch was one of the few things in the place not covered in a layer of dust — a picture of a pretty, middle-aged blonde. Forgetting everything else, Libby's heart stopped.

The woman had the same heart-shaped face as hers, the same ivory skin, and the same pouty lips. Their eyes were different, and of course Libby had dark hair, but there was enough of a resemblance to erase all doubt. There was no question in her mind that this was her birth mother, or that, in his drunken state, Holton thought that Libby was her.

She wanted to get a better look at the photograph, but right then wasn't the time. "Don't you have health insurance?"

He swatted at his nose like he was trying to knock it off his face. "You always carried the insurance, but you're d—" The color once again drained from him. He picked up an empty bottle beside him, tilted it back into his mouth, licked the lip, then dropped it. It landed with a thud on the carpet but didn't break.

She shook her head in disgust. She would think that almost dying might have been his first clue that he'd had enough of that stuff for one day. "Who are you?" He let out a lion-size belch, then grinned like he'd done something to be proud of.

In his inebriated state, she didn't think he was in any position to hear the truth, so she went with, "Your guardian angel."

He bellowed a hearty laugh like she'd said the funniest thing he'd ever heard.

"Where's Adele?" The first utterance of her biological mother's name felt strange but wonderful on her lips.

He reached for another empty bottle, peered inside it, and dropped that one too. It clanked against the first and cracked down the center. "I thought you were her," he said. He snatched a drumstick from the floor and held it out to her. A piece of yarn, the same color as the carpet, dangled from it. "You eaten?"

Her stomach grew queasy at the sight. "I'm good."

Setting it back on the carpet, he looked

around like he was realizing where he was for the first time. "Where's Rufus?"

"Who?"

His eyes grew wide and wild.

What if Rufus was her half brother? Did this drunk leave him in the bathtub alone or wandering by the ocean? "Who is Rufus?" she repeated.

He stumbled to his feet and out of the living room, yelling, "Rufus!"

Panic-filled, she followed him down the narrow hall into the smallest kitchen she had ever seen. Dirty dishes were piled everywhere, including on the linoleum floor curling at the seams, and the room smelled like gym socks.

"Who is Rufus?" she repeated, more insistent.

"Dog," he spat, as if she ought to know.

She exhaled in relief. He, however, had worked himself into a frenzy. "Rufus!" he yelled again. He nearly knocked her over as he stumbled back through the living room and thrust open the front door.

The fear of him falling down those steep stairs caused her to jump into action. She ran ahead of him and blocked the stairway. "You stay here. I'll find him."

He opened his mouth to object but leaned over the side rail and vomited into the sand below instead. It was all she could do not to do the same. When he finished, she led him back inside and laid him on the couch. "Rufus," he mumbled.

"I'll get him," she said. "You stay put."

He gave a reluctant nod, then curled up into the fetal position and closed his eyes.

She didn't even know what the dog looked like, but on a remote stretch of beach, she figured there shouldn't be too many wandering canines.

At the bottom of the stairs, she slipped off her sandals by the house so she could better navigate, but five steps in, the bottoms of her feet threatened to blister from the scorching sand, so back on they went.

Walking close to where the waves broke along the shore, she let the mist of salty spray keep her cool. "Rufus!" she called.

In the distance, a brown pelican sat on a log between sand dunes, stretching its wings. As Libby neared it, it flew away.

"Rufus!" she called again, holding her hand over her eyes like a visor. A wave broke over her feet, spraying her with a rush of cold foam. Stepping over countless broken shells, sand crabs, and dried kelp, she made it almost to the neighbors' mansion and was about to turn around and try the other direction when she heard a succession of yaps.

Following the sound, she made her way through a break in the sand fence. Again she called for the dog.

A small white poodle raced toward her and practically jumped into her arms. She picked him up and rubbed at his tight, white curls. There was no collar on his neck for a name tag, but this had to be him. He licked the bend of her arm as she carried him back up the beach. Even as small and light as he was, her arms still ached by the time she got back to the Crearys' place . . . and she had two more messages from Rob.

She was hoping Adele would have returned from wherever she had been, but the only vehicles in the driveway were her own Jeep and Holton's pickup. Hopefully he was still alive and hadn't wandered off somewhere himself.

Holton now sat on the couch with his head in his hands.

"I found Rufus," she said proudly. Her gaze drifted down to a large hound crunching chicken bones on the floor. With a feeling of dread, she looked at the poodle she carried. "You're not Rufus, are you?" He barked at the real Rufus, whose tail wagged like mad in response.

She set the impostor down and let the dogs sniff each other. Only then did she notice that the poodle wasn't even a male. She should have thought to look.

"Rufus doesn't like other dogs. Better get yours out of here," Holton slurred.

He pushed himself from the couch and started picking up bottles from the rug, swaying so much each time he leaned over, she thought he would fall again. It was then she noticed his left ring finger was bare. Did that mean he and Adele were divorced? Somehow the thought left her both devastated and relieved. Finding her birth mother might not be as simple as she'd hoped, but this was not the life she would want for her anyway. Why they might have split up was obvious enough, but other questions begged to be answered, such as when and how.

"You're no angel," he said, walking his handful of bottles to the kitchen. "So who are you really?"

She had fantasized about meeting her birth mother a hundred times — practicing what she would say and what the woman might say back — but this? With a loud clang, bottles spilled from Holton's hands into an already-full garbage can. This she hadn't prepared for. It was possible Adele had never told him she'd given a daughter up for adoption. "Where's your wife?"

He turned and looked at her with those gray eyes still veined with red. "This a joke? If it is, it ain't funny."

"I'm not joking."

He walked back to the living room and threw the last two gin bottles into the now-empty chicken bucket. "You friend, family, or bill collector?"

Although she hesitated too long, he didn't seem to notice. "Friend," she finally said. Not knowing what else to do with her hands or the rest of her, she started helping him pick up.

Their eyes met when they both reached for the same napkin.

"You really don't know?" he said.

She did then, and her blood turned to ice.

CHAPTER 3

With a heart as heavy as lead, Libby set off carrying the poodle back to where she found him — much to the relief of the mansion lady. The walk back was long, and the sun seemed to be sapping her of what little energy she had left. When she reached the pier, her phone rang. She slipped it out of her pocket and put it to her ear. "Rob, I'm still not —"

"This is *not* Robert, thank you very much," Caroline said.

Libby was still angry with her mother, and she had every right to be — now more than ever — but the familiar voice was still music to her ears. The only thing holding her tears back was not having Caroline's or Rob's shoulder to cry on. "Caroline, I'm glad you called."

"I must have dialed the wrong number, then," she said with a hint of sarcasm. "My daughter is never glad I called."

"Not now." Just once she wished Caroline would behave like an actual mother.

"Did you meet her?" If Libby didn't already know that her mother was incapable of the emotion, she might have suspected jealousy by her tone. "I hope she's everything I'm not."

Leave it to Caroline to make this about her. Libby paused to look out over the ocean. The whitecap waves appeared twice the size they were the first time she'd made the trek down this beach. A lump formed in her throat, and she had to force the words out around it. "She's gone." She never would have imagined it could hurt so much to lose someone she'd never even met.

"Gone where?" Caroline's voice took on its customary irritated tone.

"*Gone* gone. You know, to heaven." The phone fell silent, and she looked down to check if she'd lost the call. "Are you there?"

"Of course I'm here, Elizabeth. I'm sorry to hear that." She didn't sound particularly sorry, but then sympathy wasn't exactly her forte. "How are you doing?"

"How do you think I'm doing?"

"The motherly thing to say would probably be some nonsense like time healing all wounds, but you deserve better than a cliché. What about him? Her husband, the woodworker?"

Libby gave the ocean a final look. A small flock of seagulls swooped toward the pier. She sighed into the phone as she continued down the beach toward Holton's shack. "He's not a woodworker. He's a driftwood artist."

"Sounds lucrative."

"Not everything's about money."

"And not everything's an argument. So you've met him? What's he like?"

Deciding that Caroline didn't need to know about his drinking problem or the condition in which she'd found him, she simply said, "He's really talented."

"Does he know about you?"

"I'm not sure."

"Someone may have been keeping a pretty big secret."

That's what parents do, she wanted to say. Instead she went with, "I know." She paused, knowing what she was about to say made no sense. "Caroline, I think I look like him." It could have been her imagination, but his eyes did look an awful lot like hers. The crashing ocean waves filled the silence. "Did you hear me?"

"I heard you, Elizabeth. You said they married years after your birth. I know you miss having a father, but that wouldn't make sense. She probably just had a certain type of man she was attracted to. My aunt Janelle only dated men with a dimpled chin. Some women just have a thing."

Libby kicked at the sand, feeling a mixture of sadness and relief. Caroline was right; she was grasping at straws.

"So what are you going to do?"

It was the million-dollar question — one she hoped her mother could help her answer. "I don't know." She paused to kick gently at the sand. "What do you think I should do?"

"What do *you* think you should do?" The one time she actually wanted Caroline's advice would have to be the time she withheld it.

In the far distance, a purple kite drifted and dipped in the current. She stared up at it, mesmerized. Was it like her, being blown this way and that, untethered, or did someone, somewhere, hold the string?

"Are you asking me what you should do or what *I* would do?"

Libby forced her gaze from the kite and back onto the water. "What I should do, I guess."

"You *should* tell him who you are and ask if he'll help you."

She could be honest like Caroline said,

50

but what if he freaked? He could slam the door in her face, and then she might never get any information. The gamble was huge. "What would you do?"

Caroline was silent for a second or two and then said, "I would try to find out all he knows about Adele's past before I told him who I really was."

Libby exhaled. That was easy for her to say. She'd once seen her mother bluff a professional cardplayer into folding on his full house when all she'd been holding was a pair of sevens. Libby, on the other hand, couldn't bluff a toddler in a game of Go Fish.

"Libby," Caroline practically whispered, "I should have told you sooner about her. It's unforgivable."

"You couldn't have known," she said, letting Caroline off the hook she probably deserved to dangle from.

After hanging up, she pondered her mother's advice as she walked beside the broken waves foaming along the shoreline. By the time she reached the shack, her calves were sore, her eyes were gritty, and Holton seemed to be on his way to sobering up.

CHAPTER 4

Alcohol was the antidote for reality. Too bad the antidote needed an antidote. Holton held his aching head, trying to keep down what little was in his stomach. He was tempted to swear off booze once and for all, but he knew this too would pass and he'd be back at the store tomorrow, stocking up on aspirin, Pepto-Bismol, and the cheapest gin money could buy.

The misery of a hangover was nothing compared to the pain of having to deal with life stone-cold sober. The thought made him reach for another bottle. As he held it to his lips, a single drop of gin slid down his tongue. He tapped the bottom of the bottle in a vain attempt to coax out another drop or two.

The girl stood in front of the portrait of Adele hanging on the wall, looking lost in thought. "I can't believe she's really gone." Pursing her lips, she blew out a breath, then lowered herself onto the couch as if unable to bear her own weight any longer.

Intending to sit beside her, he instead stumbled over his own feet and fell onto the couch.

With a grimace, she slid herself over, putting a few more inches between them. He ran his tongue over his teeth and cringed. No wonder she backed away. His mouth tasted like the bottom of a chum bucket. No doubt it smelled the same. If he could find a way to back up from himself, he would.

"How did she die?" she asked, wiping at the corner of her eye with her index finger.

Her reaction to the news of Adele's passing made his head ache more. Obviously she had known his wife, and judging by the tears, she'd known her well. No matter how hard he racked his brain, though, he just couldn't place her.

"I killed her." Leaning his head against his palm, he realized too late that nothing supported his elbow, and fell sideways onto the armrest. He quickly pushed himself back up.

Jerking her head toward him in surprise, she said, "Excuse me?"

It took him a moment, in his present state, to remember what he had just said. He'd told the girl he'd killed Adele. It was a shocking thing to say, and although it was how he had always felt, it was the first time he'd ever said it out loud.

Slipping a finger under her nose in an obvious attempt to shield herself from his rotten breath, she waited for him to explain.

Instead, he leaned his head back on the couch and stared at a water stain snaking its way across the ceiling. It had been there since he and Adele had bought the place. They never bothered painting over it because they were only supposed to live there until they could save enough to build a proper Cape Cod. It turned out to be just one of many dreams that would never come true.

The girl raised her eyebrows at him impatiently. He didn't want to answer her. Didn't want to do anything except make her go away so he could sleep off his agony.

"What do you mean you killed her?" she insisted. With her gray eyes, petite frame, and delicate features, she was pretty in a girl-next-door kind of way, he thought as his eyelids drooped in her direction . . . and young enough to be his daughter. How would Adele have come to be friends with someone this age? The girl would have been in her teens when Adele was alive. It didn't make sense, but in all fairness, nothing much did when his brain was marinated.

"I didn't shoot her or anything if that's what you're implying."

She rubbed her wet eyes against the shoulder of her T-shirt. "You're the one who said you killed her."

Not wanting to carry on this conversation and not able to keep his eyes open another minute, he closed them, and sleep mercifully overtook him.

She was there, with her beautiful blonde hair, standing at the ocean's edge, laughing and kicking at the foam. He watched her long white nightgown flow in the soft evening breeze as moonlight glistened off the inky water. Looking over her shoulder, she nodded, indicating that he should join her.

He tried to move, but his feet felt as if they were being held in place by quicksand. With a wave of her hand, she motioned again. With all his might he tried to force his foot forward . . . but it was no use. He might as well have been wearing concrete boots.

Her smile died. She turned back and began walking into the water — ankle, then waist high, and still she kept walking.

"Don't go!" he tried to cry out, but his

mouth refused to surrender the words. If she disappeared into the water, he'd never see her again.

"Addy," he finally forced out, and was jolted awake. Covered in sweat, he found himself not on the beach but lying on his ratty couch. Quickly he closed his eyes, hoping to return to his dream. Praying this time he could save her.

CHAPTER 5

In her freshman year, Libby was required to read Kurt Vonnegut's *Cat's Cradle*. She couldn't claim to be a fan, but one line never left her: "Of all the words of mice and men, the saddest are 'it might have been.'"

Caroline had been a good provider, but she lacked the nurturing gene. The softness and warmth of a mother had always been painfully missing from Libby's life . . . and now they always would be.

Looking down at Holton snoring away on the couch, she tried to imagine what he could have meant by his drunken confession. He made a strange gurgling sound as he rubbed the drool from his lips, then flipped to his other side and resumed his heavy breathing.

He had probably been driving under the influence and hit a tree or something. Needing someone to help her make sense of it all, she walked to the front porch to call

Rob. After brushing sand from the top step, she took a seat and dialed.

Rob's number rang and rang and finally went to voice mail.

When the recording directed her to leave a message, she said, "You wouldn't believe what happened. Holton's a —" Her phone alerted her that Rob was trying to get through, so she switched over.

"Why did you hang up?" he demanded. "Are you okay?"

A warm breeze rolled off the ocean, carrying the scent of brine and blowing her ponytail into her face. She pushed it back over her shoulder. Picking at a piece of splintered wood jutting from the railing, she said, "She's dead, Rob. My mother's dead."

"Oh, Lib, baby, I'm sorry. When? How?"

Rufus whimpered at the screen door to be let out. She didn't know if he needed to go potty, but she wasn't about to take a chance of having to chase him down again. Wiping her eyes, she said, "Five years ago. I don't know how. Holton said something about killing her, but he's plastered, so I don't know what to think."

She watched a tiny pair of black-beaked birds skittering away from the incoming surf on their stick legs. When the wave retreated, it had washed away the peppering of shells, leaving behind only a sheet of glistening sand. If only her questions and longings could be erased as easily.

There was so much she needed to know. What kind of woman was her birth mother? Why had she given Libby up? Did someone know who her biological father was? Did Holton? Her mind raced with more questions than she had time to entertain.

"Libby, you still with me?"

Snapping to, she said, "Sorry, yeah."

"What's he like?" he asked. "Is he nice? Did he know about you?"

"He's a blazing alcoholic on skid row. I don't think he knows about me, but I'm not sure yet. Other than the fact that my mother's deceased, I really don't know anything."

"Are you okay? Do you need anything?"

She blew a strand of hair from her eyes. "Just answers."

"I wish you'd come home. It doesn't sound safe there. What if he really did kill her?"

"If he did, I doubt he'd be confessing it to me. Besides, I can take care of myself."

"That's probably the last thing she said too."

Maybe he was right. After Holton's drunken confession, she probably should be afraid, but she wasn't. He seemed about as threatening as a bowl of oatmeal. "I'll be fine. We'll talk later."

Rufus continued to whine behind her. She put a finger to her lips, and his tail wagged in response.

"Wait," Rob said.

She turned and stared out at the ocean waves lapping at the shore. "What?"

"I miss you."

"I know," she said. "I'll be home soon."

Inside Holton's shack, Rufus's overgrown toenails clicked against an exposed area of floor as he trotted to his water dish. Holton snored loud as ever as a fresh stream of drool worked its way from the corner of his parted lips.

Unsure if she should wait him out or go home, she glanced down at the time on her phone. It was a long drive, but she still had a few hours before it got dark. She could give it a little while and see if he woke. A loud crack made her jump, and for a split second she thought it was a gunshot. Her gaze darted to where Holton slept, as soundly as ever. She hurried to the window and, with the side of her hand, rubbed an area of glass clean.

Through the smudged circle, she stared out at the horizon — and the wall of clouds closing in at an alarming rate. She decided she'd better leave before the sky turned black, but before she could even make it off the porch, the clouds opened up in a torrential downpour.

Rufus barked at her, then the door. Irritated, she opened it. "You want to go out in this? Be my guest."

Poking his nose out, he sniffed the air, whimpered, then turned and ran into the kitchen.

Inside, Holton slept facedown on the couch, snoring, with the knuckles of his right hand dragging on the floor. As she sat watching him sleep, an overwhelming sadness overcame her.

Everyone she knew had at least one parent who adored them. What did she get? Abandoned not once but twice, then left to fend for herself with an ice queen mother, and now this bozo? It wasn't just unfair, it was cruel.

The sound of the rain battering the house, along with Holton's snoring, threatened to put her in a coma. She walked down the hall looking for his bedroom, figuring she could maybe find something to cover him up with.

The bedroom door stood open, revealing a room barely big enough for the single bed and chest of drawers occupying it. A corner wall shelf displayed miniature driftwood sculptures no bigger than her hand, all beautiful stallions in differing poses — trotting, lying down, nuzzling. Even having seen some of his work online, she was still taken aback by the skill and heart of these particular pieces.

She grabbed the pillow and quilt off the bed and brought them out to him. When she laid the blanket over his legs, he lifted his head just long enough for her to slide in the pillow. "Thanks, Addie," he mumbled, then went back to snoring.

Leaning over the couch, she studied the picture of her birth mother. Her smile was different than Libby's, brighter somehow, and there was a gentleness to her mother's eyes that she wished she had inherited. Her heart ached knowing that sweet smile and gaze would never be fixed on her. So sad, too bad.

She walked to the front window and looked out again. Walls of rain hit the ground and the side of the shack with hurricane-like intensity. The driveway and yard were already flooded. An overturned plastic chair bobbed in the newly formed pond in the front yard. Thunder rumbled angrily as the sky lit up with flashes of purple and white. There was no way she was going anywhere until the rain let up.

She figured she might as well pass some time by cleaning up. It beat sitting there watching him drool. In the corner of the kitchen sat a broom that looked like something a wicked witch would ride, along with one of those manual carpet sweepers everyone's grandmother seemed to have.

By the time the weather broke, the place looked halfway decent, she had a pot of coffee brewing, and Holton was at last opening his eyes. He furrowed his brow at her. "Who are you?"

CHAPTER 6

Across from the girl, who introduced herself as Libby, Holton started to push himself up from the couch but stopped, grabbed his aching forehead, and lowered himself back down. The old, lumpy sofa sat about as comfortably as a pile of rocks.

"I hear tomato juice is good for a hangover," she said. Her eyes were red, and she looked as tired as he felt.

"You read that tidbit on the Internet?" His words vibrated through his skull as the lingering scent of fried chicken turned his stomach.

She gave him a sharp look.

Slowly, his gaze moved off her and around his house. The ashes around the woodstove had been swept up, the carpet vacuumed, and the layers of dust covering the TV were gone. It hadn't been this clean since Adele had been alive. Why would a stranger clean his house, unless she wanted something from him . . . or was crazy? Since he didn't have anything worth wanting, that just left the insanity motive. Eyeing her suspiciously, he said, "You've been busy."

She blushed. "I was stuck here during the storm. Cleaning was more exciting than watching you drool."

It was his turn to be embarrassed, though he wasn't about to show it. "I don't drool," he said, knowing he probably had. It wasn't like he'd never woken up in a puddle of his own slobber after he'd been drinking. He'd just never done it before in front of a female . . . pretty sure. His drinking had gotten out of hand after Adele died, but what did it matter anymore? What did he?

A familiar voice whispered softly into his soul, *It matters to me.*

Ignoring that voice was getting increasingly harder to do. Jonah had tried to outrun God and failed, but Holton thought he'd been doing a fair-enough job of drinking him away. Too bad sobriety —

"Or listening to you snore," the girl added, interrupting his thoughts.

He gave her a look like she was crazy. And she probably was. Without trying to be too obvious, he studied her pale face, her slightly upturned nose, and the way she nervously rubbed a thumb across the palm

65

of her small hand. There was something naggingly familiar about her, just out of memory's reach.

A loud gurgle fractured the silence. He pressed a hand into his stomach, trying to quiet it as his cheeks caught fire.

The girl flashed a hint of a smile. "That's not you. I'm brewing coffee."

Relieved but trying to play it cool, he turned toward the kitchen. "You make it a habit of breaking into people's houses to make coffee and clean?"

She crossed then uncrossed her thin legs. "Not often."

Pain stabbed him in the center of his forehead, and he squeezed his eyes shut. After a few seconds the pain ebbed and he felt his face relax. When he opened his eyes again, small flashes of light floated across his line of vision, and the girl was leaning forward, looking alarmed.

"Are you okay?" she asked.

"You didn't answer my question." He pinched the bridge of his nose, trying to ward off a headache. "Who are you?"

"Addy . . . was a friend of mine."

No matter how close to his wife this girl thought she was, she certainly hadn't been close enough to call her Addy. Adele had never let anyone other than family use the nickname. "You can't be more than what —" he squinted at her — "twenty?"

She opened her mouth as if to correct him, then closed it again.

They sat there for a moment, just blinking at one another until the silence grew thick. Finally he broke it. "Did you know her from the gallery?"

She hesitated, then nodded. "My, uh, mom used to take me there."

Slowly he stood and made his way to the kitchen. A piece of battered chicken skin that had been stuck to the back of his sock fell to the floor. Rufus lifted his chin from the carpet, sniffed the air, then walked over and cleaned it up. When the girl wrinkled her nose, Holton pretended not to notice.

"Art fan, are you?" he called from the kitchen. He glanced into the sink, where he'd last seen his coffee mug, but it was empty. Opening cabinet after cabinet, he tried to locate something for them to drink from. Finally he found a mug whose handle had been broken off and another with a chip in the rim. He set them on the countertop he hadn't seen the surface of in years.

"Isn't everyone?" the girl asked from behind him. She reached up, opened the cupboard above the fridge, and pulled out a Tupperware container he didn't know he had, full of sugar.

He pulled a spoon from what was once again the silverware drawer. "If that were the case, I'd be in a lot better financial shape," he said as he dipped the spoon into the container. "So, what is it I can do for you?"

"How did she die?" she asked.

He sighed, slid the coffeepot from the burner, and gave her the short answer. "Car accident." He poured them both a cup, then opened the fridge, hoping he still had enough milk left. He pulled the half gallon out, unscrewed the lid, and sniffed. On the edge but not quite over it, which, come to think of it, was a lot like him. He poured some milk in the handleless cup and offered some to her.

She waved a hand, indicating she didn't want any. "You said you killed her."

"No, I didn't," he said, though he knew he had.

Her gaze hardened and she cocked one eyebrow. Adele used to give him the same look, and it always managed to send shivers down his spine. "Yes. You did," she said.

Listening to his spoon clink against ceramic as he stirred his coffee, he wished the girl would just go away and take her questions with her. "Guess I feel responsible."

He shoved the container toward her. "Sugar?"

She shook her head. "Why?"

"Some people think it tastes good."

Rolling her eyes, she said, "Why do you feel responsible?"

"Why do you ask so many questions?" Careful to hold the cup by its rim so he didn't burn his hands, he brought the coffee to his lips and took a sip. She might talk too much, but her java was nearly as good as her cleaning skills. If his ship ever came in, he might hire someone like her to help keep up the place. He rubbed the back of his sunburned neck as he looked at her. Her manicured toenails were painted the same shade of blue as her fingernails, which were the same shade of blue as her designer T-shirt. On second thought, a nice old German lady who didn't speak English would be more his speed — or better yet, a mute.

"I cared about her," she practically whispered, wrapping her hands around her cup like she needed to warm them.

If she cared so much about his wife, why didn't he remember her? He studied her from over the top of his cup. The truth was, Adele had a lot of friends, hobbies, and a complete life he'd known nothing about because he hadn't been around as much as

69

he should have.

When he pulled a chair from the small table and sat, Libby did the same. The pain in her eyes was too fresh to look at, so he busied himself flipping through a stack of unopened bills some three months old. If he didn't sell something soon, he was going to need to buy some candles and a bucket to carry water with.

She blew steam from her cup, brought it to her lips, then set it down on the table without drinking. "What day did she die?"

It was a strange question to ask. What did it matter what day? "September 14."

"What time?"

He stared hard at her, hoping to intimidate her into ending her interrogation. Not catching the hint, she simply blinked back.

"Around 9 a.m.," he finally said, sounding almost as annoyed as he felt. He took another sip of his coffee, wishing it were something stronger.

She stared down at her cup for a moment, then glanced up at him with a smile that looked more bitter than joyful. "I would have been on my way to class, probably stopping off at Hardee's for coffee, listening to some stupid song on the rad—" Without finishing the sentence, she squeezed her eyes shut.

Her reaction seemed a little over the top for an old acquaintance he didn't remember Adele ever mentioning. "So, what did you need from my wife?"

Her eyes flashed open. "Need?"

"Need, want, whatever. Why are you here?"

Her face and neck blotched red as she looked around like she'd lost something. "I, uh, I'm . . ."

His patience with the girl had just about worn out. He needed to get her out of here so he could resume his pathetic excuse for a life. "You're what? Spit it out already."

"Job."

"You need a job?"

She tucked her lips, looking ashamed. If she needed money, she had to realize by now that she wasn't just barking up the wrong tree, she was at least ten forests away from the right one. "Look, Lizzy, as you can see, I'm not exactly running a booming corporation here. I'm lucky to —"

"Everywhere I go it's the same old thing." Her words flew out clipped and fast. "They won't hire a new grad without experience, but how can I get experience if no one will hire me? I was hoping you might let me do, like, an internship or something." She leaned forward and seemed to be holding

71

her breath.

"Internship?"

"You know, let me help out and get something I can put on my résumé. You don't even have to pay me."

That was good since he could barely afford to pay Tess and have a little himself to live on. But she wasn't asking for money, so that excuse was off the table. He knew Tess would welcome an extra set of hands, but the price of having yet more estrogen in his life was a high one. And this girl talked way too much. "I don't really need any more help. I already have an assistant, and I can barely afford to pay myself or —"

"Please," she said, her voice cracking. "Addy said when I graduated she would hook me up. I really need this." She clamped her hands together as if in prayer and reminded him of Rufus begging for table scraps.

Adele had always been a bleeding heart, taking in strays they couldn't afford to feed, giving away their only set of dishes to a single mother, agreeing to help anyone who asked. "So, you're an artist?"

She curled her fingers around her cup again and looked everywhere but at him. "Artist? No, not really. I'm more interested in the business of art, I guess."

He frowned at her. "You guess?"

"I like art, but my degree's in finance."

"Finance?" He'd heard a lot of stupid stuff in his life, but a finance major thinking she could land a job by interning with a washed-up driftwood sculptor took the cake.

"Look, Lizzy —"

"It's Libby, and just forget it." She pushed her chair back from the table and stood. "If you don't want to honor your wife's promise, that's fine. Nice knowing you."

She *would* have to throw his honor into the mix. He watched her walk to the front door and snatch her purse off the floor. She turned around and pointed a finger in his direction. "Oh, and by the way, you're welcome for saving your life."

Saving his life? Not only was she a talker, his least favorite trait in a woman, she was also melodramatic — something he disdained. Maybe if he did this one thing, Adele would see from heaven and smile down on him and maybe, just maybe, she'd stop haunting his dreams. "Liz — Libby, simmer down. I didn't say no. I just . . ." He sighed. The last thing in the world he needed was a college-grad prima donna to babysit. "My studio's behind the house. Monday, 7 a.m. sharp. No pay. There's a room above the studio if you want it, and when the summer's gone, so are you."

CHAPTER 7

"Libby!" Rob called from the living room.

"What?" she yelled from the bedroom. She reached into her suitcase, moved the bottle of hairspray to the outer pocket, and zipped it back up. Her packing was coming along well. Now she just had to convince Rob she wasn't going to run off with some muscle-bound beach guy.

She'd already let her boss know she was quitting. She tried to give Cameron two weeks, but as she'd expected, it had been refused due to the threat of client stealing. Offering the notice did, however, buy her two weeks of severance pay. That, along with her savings, would more than cover her rent for the summer with a little left to actually live on.

"What are you doing in there?" Rob called. "Come out here and kiss the future partner of Smith and Johnson."

Walking to the living room, she sat beside

him, pushing his legs out of the way with her hip. "If you don't let me finish getting ready for tomorrow, I'm going to partner with Smith and Wesson."

"Come on, be nice, baby. I'm going to miss you." He grabbed the chenille throw off the back of the couch and draped it haphazardly over his legs.

He puckered his lips, moving them up and down like a fish. She leaned in and kissed him. He tasted like the fruit punch he'd been drinking. "Don't go," he whispered.

She ran her hand across his freshly shaven cheek. "It's only two months, and then we'll be together forever." She just hoped she wouldn't have to keep reassuring him that long.

He pulled up his T-shirt and scratched at his chest hair with the corner of the TV remote. If only the law partners could see him now. "I don't see why you need to do this two months before our wedding."

"You'd prefer my deathbed?"

"You know what I mean. Why can't it wait until after the honeymoon? Like you needed anything else on your plate right now."

She sighed. "The rate Holton's going, in two months, I'll find out he's dead too."

Rob picked up his juice-filled coffee mug and took a sip. "You're probably right. Oh,

I forgot to tell you, I talked to my dad, and he said he'd be honored to walk you down the aisle."

His words were nothing less than another slap to her ego. As if her life weren't pathetic enough. "I wish you hadn't done that." She knew he meant well, but she'd rather walk down the aisle alone than have a pity stand-in. "Caroline will do it."

He frowned. "She'll do something to mess it up. She's never liked me."

Laying her head on his chest, she soaked in his warmth and familiar scent. "You can't take it personally; she's never liked me, either." It sounded harsh, but it was true. Caroline would be the first to admit she didn't have a maternal cell in her body. Her husband had thought fatherhood would give his life meaning, and she'd finally agreed just to placate him. So Libby wasn't the result of a couple wanting a child to share their lives with, but a failed remedy. She couldn't help but wonder if her parents would still be married if she hadn't come along.

"I wish you'd let me go with you. This guy really could be a homicidal maniac."

She slid her fingers through his soft curls and massaged his scalp the way he liked. "He's more pathetic than scary. Besides,

I'm a grown woman. I can take care of myself."

"That's what you said about New York."

She pulled his T-shirt back down and pushed herself up, letting out an aggravated sigh. "And I did."

"You call getting mugged taking care —"

"I wasn't mugged." She'd left her purse on the subway and surprise, surprise, someone stole it. It could have happened to anyone, but Rob saw it as proof that she needed his protection. What she needed then, and now, was just a little breathing room. She walked to the fireplace, picked up the candle, and blew it out. The smell of smoke, along with a small curl of gray, dissipated into the air. "I'm going. You're not. And that's the end of this conversation. We've got today. Let's just enjoy it."

"Easy for you to say," he said glumly.

The front door slammed and they exchanged startled glances.

"Hello?" Caroline's shrill voice rang out.

Libby glared at Rob. "I'm going to kill you," she whispered.

He licked his lips and looked down. Caroline was the last person she needed to deal with right now and he knew it. No doubt they were going to double-team her to try and guilt her into staying. She let out a sigh

78

of frustration as she wondered again how Caroline had obtained the key she wasn't supposed to have and refused to give back.

A shock of blonde appeared in the doorway. Her mother was dressed in a lime silk scoop-neck top and black pants. As usual, she was fully accessorized, with an oversize hot-pink bag, sequined black heels, and a chunky pink-and-green necklace that had to weigh as much as she did. Caroline gave Rob her usual look of disapproval before moving her gaze to Libby. "What is he doing here?"

Before either of them could answer, Caroline began her rant. She crossed her arms and tapped her long, squared-off fingernails against the silk of her blouse. "Has he been here all night? You two aren't married yet. What's so difficult about showing self-control for a few more weeks? How's it going to look for me if my only daughter gives birth seven months after she gets married?" She grunted and shook her head, making her earrings jingle. "I'm not ready to be a grandmother, and I am certainly not raising another child."

Libby just stared at her. Rob had stopped by that morning, but she wasn't about to dignify the accusation with an explanation. "Yeah, we get it. You hate being a mother."

She darted another look at Rob. "I'll talk to *you* later."

His brows knitted together. "What? Why? I thought we'd all go out for breakfast for your last day. That's why I called your mom."

Libby walked to the kitchen with two sets of feet following behind like a couple of yappy dogs nipping at her ankles. Two months far away from both of them was sounding better and better. "It's almost lunchtime, and I know exactly why you called her."

"When were you going to tell me?" Caroline demanded, her nose flaring indignantly.

Reaching her fingertips toward the ceiling, Libby took her sweet time stretching. "Tell you what?"

Caroline let out an impatient grunt. "Don't play stupid with me, Elizabeth. Robert told me everything."

When Libby raised an eyebrow in his direction, he suddenly became interested in a fly keeled over on the windowsill.

Giving him the sternest look she could muster, she said, "My mother and I need time alone."

He looked to Caroline to save him. "But I thought —"

Libby gave him her back. "You thought wrong."

CHAPTER 8

Libby stepped out of her mother's Porsche into the warmth of the summer sun, then into the cold, refined dimness of the Cotton Well Country Club. The air-conditioning was running full force, which almost made sense of the fire crackling in the stone fireplace at the center of the room. The smell of burning oak mingled with that of beef and fresh-baked bread. The furniture was made of what looked like intricately carved mahogany with red velvet cushions and accents. The tabletops were covered in white with matching linen napkins.

The maître d' tugged on the hem of his tight black vest and led them to Caroline's usual table. While he pulled out her mother's chair, Libby helped herself to her own. She set her purse on the empty seat beside her, plucked the fanned linen napkin from her empty water glass, and laid it across her lap.

A waiter with slicked-back hair and a navy jacket appeared at the table. Caroline tilted her head toward him. "Charles, would you bring my daughter and me lemon water — make sure it's bottled this time, please."

"Of course, Mrs. Slater."

"Miss," she corrected.

He smiled and winked as if the exchange were an inside joke.

Caroline slid her menu to the edge of the table. "Sundays they have a seafood gumbo that's to die for. They grow their own vegetables and herbs right out —"

"I don't care about the food, Caroline," Libby said. "Let's just get this over with. I've got somewhere else to be, as you know."

Caroline fiddled with the back of her left earring as Libby listened to the fire crack and pop. The maître d' seated an older couple across the room, near a wall of windows overlooking the man-made lake.

Two glasses of water, with lemon wedges perched on the rims, were set before them. When the waiter paused, looking expectant, Caroline shooed him away with a wave of her hand. With a red face, he backed up several steps, as if he were leaving the presence of a queen, before turning around. When at last he was out of earshot, she turned her attention back to Libby. "What

83

in the world are you thinking? I didn't give you those adoption papers so you could dump your fiancé, kill your career, and run off to live with a bunch of hippies."

"First off, you didn't just hand them over — you were caught in a lie and backed into a corner. Second, he's not a hippie; he's an artist. And third, I did not kill my career. I quit a job I never liked anyway, and I certainly didn't break up with Rob. I'm just trying to figure out who I am. You of all people should understand that. After all, isn't that what you've been claiming to be doing ever since . . ." Her throat tightened, blocking the rest of the sentence from escaping.

Caroline threw her hands up. "Go ahead and say it — ever since your father abandoned us. Why can't you bring yourself to talk about it? It's been twenty years, for crying out loud."

The waiter cautiously reapproached, and this time Caroline impatiently waved him over. "We'll both have a cup of the gumbo and a side salad with avocado vinaigrette."

He nodded and started to walk away. Libby grabbed his pleated sleeve. "Bring me a blood-rare porterhouse and a baked potato with so much butter and sour cream I'll need a ladle to fish the potato out of it."

Caroline gasped. "Ignore her. She's suicidal."

The waiter looked between them, nervous and unsure.

Libby locked eyes with him. "Bring me what I asked for or nothing at all."

Her mother rolled her eyes and waved him off. "Keep it up and not even Robert will want to marry you."

Sliding the phone from her front pocket, Libby hoped for a message that needed to be answered, anything that would get her out of another lecture. She was shocked and a little disappointed not to have one, let alone half a dozen, from Rob. Fear crept into her that she might lose him over this, but that was irrational. He loved her. She loved him. She slipped the phone back into her pocket. "You keep it up and everyone's going to figure out what a control freak you are."

They sat across the table listening to Natalie Cole sing about not being able to say no from the overhead speakers and staring each other down. Finally Caroline's gaze broke away. "Three years after George left us, you wouldn't stop asking about him, so I tracked him down to this shoddy little neighborhood in Burland." She pressed her lips together in disgust.

Libby slid her fingers around the napkin on her lap and began twisting the edges back and forth, not wanting to hear the story but unable to say so.

Caroline ran the tip of her middle finger around the rim of her glass. "We walked right up to the porch and rang the doorbell." With a hardened expression, she shook her head. "He poked his head out, looked down at you. He kept looking back over his shoulder like he was afraid his new wife would see us. Then do you know what he said to me?"

Libby balled the napkin up in her hand as she shook her head.

" 'My life's not complicated, and I want to keep it that way.' I was so worried that you were going to start crying and try to get him to pick you up or something, but even as a little girl, you understood what he meant. You looked to the window at the three sets of curious little eyes watching us, then turned around and walked back to the car without so much as spitting in his direction."

Libby remembered that day with the clarity of a dream. If she'd had any innocence left after George abandoned them, it was taken that day. The world hadn't felt safe since. "Why are you telling me this now?"

Caroline drew her hand away from her glass and ran it over the tablecloth as if to work out wrinkles that didn't exist. "Just to remind you that he's not worth pining over. No one can replace what he stole from us. Those three sets of eyes watching us through the window were the daughters he had with his new wife. Twins and another little girl. Apparently they were worth the trouble to him. We weren't."

Libby swallowed back the pain as she had done so many times before. If she wasn't worth it to him, then he certainly wasn't to her. Not anymore.

"It was his loss, Libby. Not ours."

She gave Caroline a bitter smile. "I'm better than a cliché you don't really believe, remember?"

"That one's true," Caroline said, reaching out as if to take her hand, but withdrawing again when Libby didn't reach to meet her. "I hear not all men are like that," she added with a twinge of sadness. Caroline's own father had been a workaholic who died at his desk when he should have been at her tap-dance recital. "Besides being talented, what's he like?"

"Holton?" Libby plucked the lemon wedge off her glass and bit into it. The sour taste matched her mood. She set the spent wedge on her bread plate. "I'm sure Rob told you all about him."

Caroline squeezed her own lemon wedge into her water, sniffed it as if it were a fine glass of wine, and took a sip. Ice cubes clanked against each other as she set the glass back down. "He didn't tell me anything except that you were going to Nags Head for the summer for some kind of art internship farce, and if I wanted to say good-bye, I had better come this morning. He made it sound like you'd gotten cold feet about the wedding and you probably were going to stay there."

"Rob can be a little paranoid. You know that," Libby said.

Caroline shrugged her thin eyebrows. "What I've been saying all along. So, is the artist all the things you wish I was?"

Libby ignored the barb. "He's handsome —" she paused to take a sip of water — "and he likes dogs." *Plus fried chicken and near-death experiences,* she almost added.

"And your mother? What did he tell you about her?" Caroline reached for a piece of bread, then stopped abruptly as if someone had slapped her hand. "What was she like?"

All the emotion from the day she'd met him came rushing back. "I don't know yet."

Caroline grabbed the piece of bread she

wouldn't allow herself before. "I wish I could have thanked her for giving you to me." She tore off a corner of the bread and popped it into her mouth.

"Thanks," was all Libby could come up with. It was a surprisingly touching thing for her mother to say . . . and completely out of character.

"How did he react when you told him who you were?"

Libby choked on the question. "Listen, can we not talk about this until I work it all out? I don't really know what he's like yet. I don't know anything about him, her, or anything else yet."

Caroline tore off another piece of bread and this time smothered it with butter.

"Look," Libby added, "I'm not even done packing. I have to get Caesar some food and litter and take care of a million other things. Can I just call you later and we'll talk about it then?"

"You won't call me," Caroline said, emotionless.

The waiter set salads before them and disappeared again. Libby picked up her fork and pushed an artichoke heart to the side. "Thanks for having faith in me."

Caroline's expression darkened as she stabbed a cherry tomato. "Oh, I forgot to tell you that the bridesmaids' dresses came in."

"How do they look?"

She wrinkled her nose. "That canary-yellow was even uglier than in the catalog. You would look like a fried egg on the altar with your white gown surrounded by that horrid color." She shook her head. "They were positively awful. I told you they would be. I returned them and went back to our original choice."

Libby dropped her fork. Those dresses had been her original — and only — choice. "You mean *your* original choice. Why would you do that without asking me?" A million raw emotions nipped at her, each retreating so fast she couldn't identify a one and was too afraid to try.

"You've been busy with this new father obsession of yours. I figured you'd want me to take care of it."

Libby pushed her chair back and stood. "No, you didn't. Once again, this is you trying to control every minute aspect of my life. I'm sick of it. For the hundredth time, this isn't your wedding; it's mine."

Caroline leaned back in her chair and crossed her arms. "Well, excuse me, Miss High-and-Mighty. I was just trying to help. You're obviously stressed out. Do you think now is the best time to go to Nags Head? If it were me, I'd wait until after the wedding. How must Robert feel with you running off like this? And your job. Do you know how lucky you were to get a position like that right out of college? I could probably make a few calls and get them to reinstate you. I'm sure I must have a connection or two over there. I'm sure —"

"Enough!" The blood rushed to Libby's head, making her temples pound. "This isn't about my stupid job. It's not about Rob, and it's definitely not about you. This is about me. For once in my life, something is about me."

The two couples now in the restaurant, the maître d', and the waiter stared at her. She scanned their faces in defiance. She had nothing to be ashamed of. She locked eyes with the maître d'. "This is about me," she repeated.

CHAPTER 9

The sun began its ritual rise from slumber, yawning and stretching along the vast horizon. Coffee in hand, Holton leaned against the splintered railing that overlooked the endless shoreline, absorbing the palette of orange, pink, and purple making up the morning's canvas.

Foam lapped against glistening sheets of sand, only to retreat again, leaving in its wake an array of tiny crabs, seaweed, and broken shells. Sunlight set wisps of clouds ablaze and cast golden hues across the sky and ocean. His ocean. One of the few things that still held power to draw a smile from his lips.

Even after ten years' worth of sunrises here, the miracle of morning never ceased to affect him. For it was only in this twilight, where the hazy purple horizon met ripples of frothy blue, that he could believe again that God was good. That he delighted in giving beauty, not taking it away. And this time of morning, this place, reminded him of the good times between him and Adele. So many of them happened right here where the water met the shore. But good times or bad, she was never far from his thoughts.

The only times he could get her off his mind were when he was working, drinking, or sleeping. Even then she plagued his dreams. Reaching out to him from the wreckage of mangled metal, shattered red plastic, and deployed air bags. Through the ambulance sirens constantly ringing in his ears, he could still hear her screams. He should have been the one who died that day. And in his own way, he supposed he was.

He slid three ibuprofens from his front pocket and choked them down along with the last gritty swallow of coffee. A warm gust bowed the sea grass bordering the dunes below, drawing his eye to the sand fences he'd fashioned himself from galvanized iron and pickets. They proved as effective in preventing erosion as Henry's store-bought rolls, and only cost him twice as much. Didn't matter, though; he had the satisfaction of proving to the punk he could do it, and that was worth any amount of money and just as many blisters.

He set the mug on the railing and paused

to draw in a lungful of fresh salt air before starting down the beach for his morning walk. A deep bark stopped him before he'd taken his third step. He glanced up at the hound dog fussing at him from the porch. "Well, come on!"

Before he could blink, Rufus was at his side panting, looking up at him. "I didn't forget you," he lied. "I was letting you sleep in."

Rufus hurried ahead, ears flopping in the wind. He ran toward an incoming wave, barking and wagging his tail, inviting it to give chase. Not having another dog to frolic with at the moment, the ocean was as fine a fill-in as he could hope for. When the wave broke over the sand, he turned tail and ran away.

Holton shook his head. Even at nine years old, Rufus was no less a puppy than the day Adele found him on a deserted stretch of beach, hiding under an old, abandoned catamaran. He paused his game of tag to sniff the sand. With his knee, Holton pushed him gently to the side to see what unfortunate critter he had discovered this time. The dog looked up at him in question, a hunk of seaweed dangling precariously from his snout.

Holton squatted beside him. Five coral-colored points poked through sand. "Well, I'll be. You found a starfish, Rufus."

In all the years he and Adele had lived here on the Outer Banks, he had never been able to find a live one. Ever curious, she wanted to know what it felt like to touch one that still held life. What he wouldn't give to do the same to her. He turned it over to its smooth side. Sure enough, hundreds of tiny tube feet wiggled at him. Turning it back over, he closed his eyes and ran his finger over the spiny surface. "Wet sandpaper," he whispered to the sky. "That's what they feel like, sweetheart."

He waited for the latest wave to recede, then tossed the starfish back out to sea. Rufus lunged into the waves, hoping to retrieve it. As if he'd forgotten that water was wet, he couldn't get back out fast enough.

Holton shook his head at the dog. "You should probably learn to swim if you want to play fetch in the ocean."

"You should probably not stand me up," a woman's voice said from behind him, "if you want me hauling wood for you today."

Startled, he turned to see Tess glaring at him. As usual, she wore her long, red braid draped over her freckled shoulder, a faded bathing-suit top, and cut-off shorts.

Brushing the sand from his hands, he said, "What are you talking about?"

Rufus ran to her and jumped up and down impatiently, wanting to be greeted.

She patted the dog's head, then waved him away. "I waited at the studio for you for thirty minutes."

He frowned at her. "Why?"

Digging a hand into her slender hip, she said, "Are you kidding me?"

A seagull glided in from the ocean, swooping in on an unlucky crab as a foghorn sounded somewhere in the distance.

Holton glanced at the horizon, hoping to get a glimpse of the boat, but could see only the reflection of the rising sun on the water. "Do I ever kid?"

"Not nearly enough. We were going to photograph the studio against the sunrise for the website, remember?"

He felt something like panic as he tried to recall the exchange. He vaguely remembered her saying something about the website. In his hungover state, he would have agreed to dressing up like Carmen Miranda just to get her to leave him alone. "We were going to do it tomorrow," he said, trying to sound surer than he felt.

She rolled her eyes in disgust. "That's what I get for trying to have a discussion with you after five."

"What's that supposed to mean?" As if he didn't already know. So he drank too much. So what? It's not like he had anything better to do with his evenings. Besides, when he was trying to keep the room from spinning, he wasn't missing Adele.

"Never mind," she said. "I don't want to have this conversation again."

"Makes two of us."

She picked up a broken shell and tossed it into the water, probably wishing she could do the same to him. "As far as I know, gin has never brought anyone back from the grave."

Patting his thigh, he called Rufus to him. "Thought you said you didn't want to have this conversation."

"I don't."

"Good." A gust of wind kicked up sand into his face. He tilted his head down to keep it from pelting his eyes.

When the wind died, he watched Tess knead her temple and decided he'd better change the subject in a hurry unless he wanted to lose his assistant to another migraine. "I'm on my way to Rotten Reggie's. Why don't you let me buy you breakfast?" He had been eating at Reggie's for at least ten years. Where else could you get two eggs, two pieces of toast, and a cup of hot java — all for three bucks?

Considering the offer, she shielded her eyes against the rising sun. "You're broke."

Just what he needed, another reminder that he was a failure. "I'm poor, but I ain't *that* poor."

"I don't know. I'm not really in the mood for Emma Jane and her cleavage."

"Now you've got a problem with Emma Jane?" Good grief, the woman could find fault with anyone.

"I have no problem with desperate widows," she said, scratching her shoulder. "She sure has a problem with me, though. If you would just ask her out already, she could get it out of her head that I'm her competition."

Holton closed his eyes and sighed. Tess seemed to have an issue with every woman he came in contact with. "She may be a flirt, but she's a good seed."

"Why don't you dig a hole and plant her, then?" She smacked at her other shoulder as if a mosquito had bitten her. She was in one of her moods again, and obviously nothing he could say was going to change that. It was probably that time of the month. It seemed like it always was lately.

And then a thought occurred to him.

"Think you might be going through the change?" he asked, before his mind had a chance to filter his words.

Her green eyes narrowed as her nose flared. "The what?"

His cheeks caught fire when he realized he had once again said what should have remained a thought. "Never mind."

"Are you talking about menopause? I'm only forty-one."

He could feel heat working its way up his neck. "Forget it."

"I'm still of childbearing age, for your information. And why is it you men think anytime a woman is ticked it has to do with hormones? Maybe, just maybe, I'm irritated because you made me drag my butt out of bed two hours early, then stood me up."

Apologize, the little voice in his head told him. *She's probably right. She always is. Maybe you did say you would take the picture this morning.* When his mouth refused to form the words, he went with, "Want breakfast or not?"

She buried her bare toes in the sand, then wiggled them out again, making them appear unattached from the rest of her foot. "Since you already blew the sunrise shot, I guess we might as well eat. But I'm buying."

In all the years she had known him, how could she not get that a woman's offer to pay felt to him like an offer of castration? "No, ma'am," he said.

Something like a mixture of affection and pity glinted in her eyes. Having no use for either, he looked away.

When they started up the beach, Rufus shot ahead, kicking up sand and heading off to do whatever it was he did all day.

"So, I was thinking," she said, stopping to point out a tiny set of sand fiddler antennas poking up through the sand a few feet ahead of them. The antennas disappeared as soon as he spotted them. "Maybe we could start working again on the stallion."

It was the piece he had been working on when Adele passed away. It had looked like it would be a sort of magnum opus, until he gave up on it. Tess thought he'd simply lost interest, but the truth was, every time he tried to finish it, he ended up breaking down in tears. He didn't understand it and didn't care to. "We've got an intern," he said, knowing that would effectively change the subject.

She stopped and stared at him. "An intern? You're joking."

"No joke," he said, walking on. "Her name's Libby. She's spending the summer."

She caught up and squinted at him. "Seriously?"

"Seriously."

"Why?"

He could have told her about Adele's promise, but he couldn't mention his late wife's name without Tess getting all weird on him. It was no secret that she thought he should move on. He would if he could.

In a way, he was glad Tess didn't understand. The only way she could was if she had gone through that kind of loss herself. He wouldn't wish that on anyone, especially not her. "She used to come in the gallery when she was a kid. We promised her this when she graduated."

"Is she pretty?" she whispered.

As they walked, seagulls circled over them, squawking for handouts. "I guess."

Tess's neck blanched the way it always did when something ticked her off. Why she should feel threatened by every attractive woman in the world, he had no idea. It's not like she was an ugly duckling herself. He could think of half a dozen men who would ask her out if she didn't send off an "only good man is a dead man" vibe.

"Just because another woman is pretty doesn't mean you're not," he finally said.

She looked at him askance with a hint of

a smile playing on her lips. "You think I'm pretty?"

"You've got a mirror. You're pretty; she's pretty. So what?"

Instead of thanking him for the compliment, anger flashed in her eyes again. "Isn't a college kid a little young for you?"

Here we go again, he thought. "Yes, Tess, she's a little young for me. I'm old enough to be her father."

"Grandfather," she mumbled.

"Excuse me?"

She turned her head toward the surf, ignoring him.

"Hey," Holton said, stopping, "you got something right there." He touched the corner of his eye, indicating she should do the same.

With a frown, she rubbed at the corner of her own, mirroring him. "What is it? Did I get it off?"

He squinted at her, moving in closer for a better look. "No, it's still there." He licked his finger and rubbed at her skin like Adele used to do to him. "Oops. Just a wrinkle."

She furrowed her brow. "That's not funny."

A man jogged by, wearing a T-shirt wrapped around his neck like a tie. He nodded a greeting as he passed.

"You said I didn't joke around nearly enough. There you go."

She smiled mischievously. "Who says you can't teach an old dog new tricks?"

He gave her an annoyed look, but inside he was relieved to be bantering with her again. That meant all was well, and the workday wouldn't be spent walking on eggshells in brittle silence.

"So tell me about her." She wrapped her arm around his the way she sometimes did when she was in a good mood. He never told her just how uncomfortable it made him feel — or unfaithful to Adele.

She leaned into him and gave his arm a gentle squeeze. "What's her major?"

His muscles stiffened. "Finance or something."

She dropped his arm. "Finance?"

He nodded.

Scrunching her face in question, she said, "What does a finance major think she's going to get out of a summer internship with us?"

He shrugged. "You've been saying you could use another set of hands. I got you an intern to help. Be happy."

"It sounds a little fishy."

"All I know is that she needs experience and we need the help."

She let out a long sigh as if she had been holding it all her life. "You don't need anyone or anything."

He wanted to say that wasn't true. That he, in fact, needed her. That's what she seemed to need to hear, and it was true. He couldn't do what he did without a reliable assistant. But he just couldn't make himself admit it out loud. "Not true. Right now, I need breakfast."

CHAPTER 10

The summer sun beat down on Libby's shoulders as the roar of ocean waves drowned out the pounding of her heartbeat. This was it. She had never been much of an actress, but she would have to give an Oscar-worthy performance if she hoped to pull off this charade.

Tufts of sea grass poked through the sand and gravel surrounding Holton's studio. The large barn, which stood a hundred yards or so behind his house, looked as if it might have been used at one time for farming purposes. Though what anyone would be able to grow this close to the ocean, she couldn't begin to imagine.

Although it was considerably larger than the house, it was in no better shape, with several of the window openings covered in plastic where the glass was broken or altogether missing. The paint had completely worn off with the exception of an occasional streak of faded yellow.

Gathering her courage, she drew in a deep breath of the briny air and walked toward it.

"Hurry up!" a man barked.

Startling at the harshness of his tone, she fought the impulse to run back to her Jeep. Making her way to the side of the building, she forced her lips to stretch into a smile.

A door with a crack snaking down its glass pane stood ajar, wedged open by a heavily chipped garden gnome. She stepped inside, squinting against the darkness. Dusty white sheets covered the barn floor, and the open space smelled of glue and sawdust. Peering past a row of driftwood mirrors, lamps, and tables, she searched for Holton.

"Hello?" she called.

"Tess, where have — ?" A tuft of black hair streaked with silver poked out from behind a stack of driftwood. His frayed Bermuda shorts stopped at his knees, and a black T-shirt clung to his wiry frame. "You're not Tess," he said accusingly, as though she claimed to be. "Oh, it's you. You're fifteen minutes late."

Paralyzed, she stood taking in his familiar features and reminding herself to breathe.

"Hey, earth to space girl. I'm talking to

you." He tapped his flip-flop-clad foot impatiently.

"I'm sorry. It was a crazy morning. My phone battery died, which meant my alarm didn't go off, and then my cat got out."

He went back to fishing through his pile of driftwood. He appeared thinner than when she'd first met him, and older somehow. Apparently sobriety didn't agree with everyone.

Rufus emerged from the same pile of wood that had hidden Holton. He trotted over and pushed his cold, wet snout into the bend of her knee.

"Go on, dog." With a wave of his hand, Holton shooed him away.

Tail between his legs, the meaty hound slunk over to a corner and lay down. He rested his chin on the dusty cement and peered at her with a look of misery.

Despite their rocky start, she suddenly felt a kinship with the dog. After all, for most of her life, no one had wanted her around either. She walked over, knelt beside him, and scratched behind his soft ear. "Nice to see you again, Rufus." Smiling at Holton, she said, "It's hard to stay mad at him, isn't it?"

"Like him so much? Take him with you when you go." He grabbed a towel off a bench table, slung it over his shoulder, and mumbled just loud enough for her to hear. "Tess was supposed to be here to greet you. She listens about as well as that dog."

Libby felt her whole body droop. His welcome was about as warming as a brain freeze.

He grabbed a piece of driftwood from the top of the pile and held it out to consider it. To her, it looked like an arm with gnarled fingers reaching for a handout.

He twisted his mouth at the wood, looked at the half-finished table beside him, and mumbled.

She stood and brushed the dust from her knees. "Maybe I should wait for her outside?"

He laid the piece of wood back on the pile. "If I wanted you outside, I would have told you. We're not going to start having the tail wag the dog around here."

Irrational as it might be, a pang of sadness gnawed her. "I have no idea what you said. Maybe I could just put my stuff in my room?"

"She'll be back in a few minutes. Wait for her over there." He nodded toward a rickety wood director's chair standing in a dusty corner beside a stack of white plastic buckets.

Feeling like a child in time-out, she squatted to take a seat. Before her full weight bore down on the chair, it collapsed with her on it. Her rear hit the floor with a thud, and pain shot up her back.

Rufus bayed in her direction as Holton shot her an annoyed sideways glance. "Did you break it?"

Pressing her fingertips into her aching tailbone, she said, "I don't think so."

"I meant the chair," he said, walking over.

Anger flashed like lightning through her. "I'll buy you a new one. Two bucks ought to about cover it."

Leaning down, he held out a callused hand to her. She made no move to accept his help. Her birth mother must've been pretty hard up to go for someone like him.

He threw his hands up. "Have it your way. And the chair's worth at least five."

"Take it out of my pay. Oh, wait, there is none." As she prepared to push herself up, a woman's silhouette appeared in the doorway, sunlight streaming around her.

A petite redhead emerged from the shadow and hurried over. "What did he do to you?"

"Nothing," Libby said. "I just fell."

Giving Holton a dirty look, the woman barked, "Why aren't you helping her up?"

With a huff, he looked at Rufus as though expecting him to explain everything. "I tried." He cleared his throat and resumed the offensive. "Tess, meet your new intern. Intern, meet Tess."

With an exaggerated eye roll, she helped Libby stand. "Don't mind him. He gets like this when one of his pieces won't cooperate. You'll get used to it."

More like when he doesn't have a bottle in his hand, she thought. Brushing off her bottom, she cringed at the soreness and the inference she'd ever get used to this kind of treatment. "Listen, if this is a bad time . . ."

Tess adjusted the straps of her bathing-suit top. "It's always a bad time when he's working. Don't let him bother you, though. Underneath that teddy bear personality lies a heart of stone."

Despite herself, Libby cracked a smile. Holton may be awful, but his assistant she was beginning to like. She watched Tess walk over to Rufus and pat him on the head.

"I'm sure I'm the first to tell you, but welcome aboard. Do you need a minute to recover, or do you feel up to helping me carry in some wood?"

Propping up the broken chair the best she could, Libby leaned it against the wall. "I'm fine."

Squinting against the sun, she followed Tess outside to a battered pickup. The smell of the ocean was as thick as the sound of crashing waves. Tess grabbed the truck bed's handle and yanked. It opened with a screech. A small piece of driftwood fell, landing on Libby's foot. It was too small and light to hurt.

"Sorry about that." Tess snatched up the piece and flashed a smile. "By the time we're done with you today, you'll be wearing a full-body cast."

They made three trips to the barn, dumping their loads onto the pile Holton was choosing from. Each time Libby passed, she studied him, racking her brain to figure out what Adele could have possibly seen in him.

When she turned, she saw Tess watching her watch him. Her cheeks grew warm and she averted her gaze.

When they walked back outside for the last load, Tess said, "He's good-looking, don't you think?"

Almost swallowing her tongue, Libby choked out an "Excuse me?"

Tess brushed a forearm across her perspiring hairline. "Women gawk at him all the time, but as soon as he opens his mouth, his nine plummets to a four."

Libby wasn't sure if she detected a twinge

of jealousy in Tess's voice, but the look on her face stayed neutral enough. "A, I'm happily engaged; and B, I don't think of men his age that way. I guess he's okay for an older guy."

"He's more than okay." The blush in Tess's cheeks spoke volumes about her feelings for him.

"Are you two a — ?"

"Nah," Tess said, cutting her off. "He's very much still married to his late wife, if you know what I mean." Laying her hand over her eyes to shield them from the sun, she cloaked her face in shadow.

"Oh." Libby tried to sound disinterested. "Did they have any kids?"

Tess laughed. "They passed a law making it illegal for him to bear children." She laughed again. "Holton as a father — what a horrifying thought."

"Yeah," Libby said, faking a smile. It was all she could do then not to probe further. If she came out and started an interrogation, it would raise too many suspicions and more than likely make it look like she had a crush on her own stepfather. Besides, she had all summer to figure it out.

Brushing the debris from her hands against her cutoff shorts, Tess said, "Let's get you unpacked and settled. Then, if you want, I'll show you around."

Libby carried her suitcase up the stairs leading to the loft above the barn as Tess followed her with a smaller bag. The room smelled as musty as a basement, but it held a simple sort of charm. She'd been set up with a small coffeemaker, a microwave, a dorm-size fridge, a window unit air conditioner, and a tiny bathroom.

Catching a glimpse of her reflection in the mirror above the dresser, she saw that her long hair was peppered with sawdust and already her pale skin had started to turn pink. "He doesn't seem to like me much."

Strawberry-blonde eyelashes blinked back at her. "He doesn't like anyone much, except Rufus."

"He didn't seem that crazy about him, either," Libby said.

"Don't let him fool you. That man would kill someone over that mutt." Tess helped her lift the suitcase onto the bed. "Speaking of the ogre, I better get down there and help him before he throws a tantrum and smashes something. He's got an artist's temperament all the way." She picked up a book from the shelf beside the bed, studied the spine, then set it back down and headed for the stairs. "We'll break for lunch in about an hour. Does that give you enough time to get situated?"

Libby scooped a pile of shirts from her suitcase. "Plenty. Hey, Tess?"

She turned and raised her eyebrows.

"Thanks for getting the room ready for me. It's lovely."

Looking back over her shoulder, her hand touched down on the stair rail. "Don't thank me. Thank Holton. I didn't have a thing to do with it."

A mason jar full of daisies rested on the shelf. Libby picked up a stem. "The flowers, too?"

The back of Tess's head disappeared as she descended the stairs. "You'll like him a lot more if you listen more to his actions than to his words."

CHAPTER 11

After a hard day's work scouring the beach for wood and listening to Holton's rants, Libby was more than ready for a good night's sleep. She lay on the small bed in the studio loft, listening to Taylor Swift on her iPod. Dying sunlight streaked through cracks in the rustic wood walls, suspending tiny dust particles in the musty air. She watched them float about as she considered the option of just telling him who she was. Already she had gotten enough of a taste of his grim personality to fill her belly, but she still hadn't learned a thing about Adele. That, she reminded herself, was why she was there.

It was only eight o'clock, but the fatigue that came with physical labor, combined with sheer boredom, made her eyes droop. She was on the verge of sleep when a soft rap on the stair rail snapped her eyes open.

"You decent?" Tess's voice carried from

the bottom of the stairs.

Looking down, Libby noticed her T-shirt had ridden up her stomach. She pulled it down and sat up. "Yeah, I'm good. Come on up."

Still wearing the same cutoff shorts she had on earlier, Tess now had a men's button-down on over her bathing-suit top, tied at the waist.

"What's up?" Libby asked, trying to shake the grog from her voice. When she flipped on the lamp sitting on her bedside table, she could see by Tess's puffy red eyes that she'd been crying. "What's wrong?"

"Holt's drunk again." Tess flicked her braid off her shoulder.

Why she felt the need to tell Libby this, or why it should make her cry, Libby couldn't imagine. The man probably got toasted every night. "He's not driving, is he?"

Swiping at her eyes, she said, "No. He's down on the beach, yelling at kids about the dangers of bonfires. He's going to get himself beaten up or arrested again. I tried to get him out of there, but as usual, he won't listen to me."

Arrested *again*? Great, so not only was her stepfather an alcoholic; he was a convict too. She didn't know what Tess expected her to do about it. He was a grown man,

116

after all.

As if Tess could read her mind, she asked, "Do you think you could go talk to them?"

Pulling her flip-flops from under the bed, Libby asked, "The police?"

"No, the kids he's getting into it with. They're about your age. You're a cool-looking girl. Maybe if you asked them to help you get him inside. Tell them he's your dad or something, or that it's his birthday. They're pretty loaded themselves, and with his mouth . . ." Her voice trailed off as she looked toward the window.

The only thing she dreaded more than talking to drunk twenty-year-olds was talking to an unruly mob of them. But what choice did she have? Tess was clearly worried for a reason. "Sure," she said. "I can try."

She followed Tess outside. The sound of breaking waves and distant laughter filled the cool night air. The sky was clear and inky blue, giving an unobstructed view of the stars above and a nearly full moon, which made the ocean below shimmer in its reflection.

As they approached, the smell of burning wood filled the air. Black silhouettes moved around the flickering firelight. One shadow stumbled forward with his finger pointed.

His words came out so slurred they were barely discernible. "I not tellin-you-gen— get off the beach."

Two guys maybe Libby's age, maybe a little younger, took turns kicking him in the rear as the rest of the group howled with laughter and cheered them on.

Stepping into the light and heat of the fire, Libby was filled with dread. "Hey, everyone. I'm just here to pick up my dad." *Dad* — even under the circumstances, the word felt surprisingly nice on her lips. It had been nearly twenty years since she called anyone that.

"Your dad's a drunk," one of the girls slurred. Her long blonde hair hung over her shoulders down to her waist. Half of her face glowed red from the fire, the other side cast in shadow.

"Yeah, well," Libby said sheepishly as she took Holton by the shoulders. He reeked of gin, and his skin was hot and dry. "Let's get you home."

He yanked away from her. "Get yer hans off me, Libzy."

The group was now watching them intently. One kid said, "He wants to stay here with us and hang out. Tell her, old man."

Not that they could see her expression in the dim light, but Libby smiled apologetically just in case as she took Holton's arm. "Come on, Dad, birthday celebration over."

"Oh, man, it's his birthday?" one of the guys said. "Seriously, dude, stay and have a beer."

Holton furrowed his brow in confusion. "It's my birthday?"

She tried to steady him as she turned him in the direction of the road. "No, it's mine. Remember?" It wasn't her birthday, either, but she hoped the small mob might offer them extra grace if they thought it was.

She closed her eyes and shook her head at the group, trying to turn their anarchy into sympathy. A few kinder chuckles met her.

Holton stumbled into her, almost knocking her over. "It's your birthday? Well, happy birthday." The side of his face scrunched as his mouth opened. It took a second for her to figure out that he was trying to wink at her. *"Daughter."*

"You're hot," a young guy said, also sounding lit. She could only see a spiky-headed shadow. "How old are you?" he added.

Ignoring his question, Libby started leading Holton away like a lost toddler.

"Hey, man, how old's your daughter?" the guy yelled.

Holton stopped and turned around, his

head wobbling on his neck like an infant's. "How old are you?" he asked her.

She almost opted to tell the truth since he was too drunk to remember the discrepancy of the age she'd claimed to be earlier, but then remembered Tess was still nearby. "Twenty-two," she lied.

He stumbled forward, throwing his hand up like he was waving good-bye to old friends. "This girl's seventeen. Go near her and I'll arrest ya."

"Jailbait," one of the guys said, sounding more than a little disappointed.

"Old enough to see, old enough for me," another male voice rang out, followed by a female voice calling him a pig.

Holton's feet plowed trails in the thick sand as Libby and Tess helped steady him along. When he tried to barrel through a dune rather than go around it, Libby pushed her weight into his shoulder to force him to the left.

When they got to the stairs leading up to his shack, she wrapped his shaky hand around the rickety rail and walked behind him with both palms flat against his back. She wasn't sure if she could keep him from tumbling backward, but at least she might help break his fall if he did. His steps were slow and wobbly, and she couldn't help but wonder how he hadn't broken his neck before now.

Eventually they made it up to the porch. She struggled to keep Holton upright as Tess opened the door, then stepped out of the way to hold it. Libby led him inside. The place smelled of pizza and hound dog. An empty Domino's box lay upside down on the rug, along with a chewed-up paper plate and several empty gin bottles. So much for the scrubbing she had given the place.

When Tess led him to the small couch, he curled up on it and closed his eyes. She grabbed the blanket draped over the back of the chair and covered him. Carefully she tucked it around him, as though she had done it a million times.

Feeling like a voyeur witnessing a private moment, Libby watched Tess sit beside him and brush his unruly eyebrows into place with her thumb before kissing his forehead.

"He needs to get it together," Tess said. "This is the second time this month I've had to save him from getting his butt kicked." She slid down on the couch toward his feet and began untying his sneakers. "He wasn't always like this. Before his wife died, he was so much fun to be around."

Libby's heart stopped. Tess had known

Adele? It took everything in her to keep from lunging into interrogation mode. "I didn't realize you'd known her. What was she like?"

With a shrug, Tess dismissed her question.

Disappointment filled her, but there was plenty of time left that summer to probe. She leaned against the wall. "Do you think maybe you're enabling him by taking care of him when he gets this way?"

Tess slipped off his sneaker and set it on the carpet. "You sound like my sister. She thinks I could do so much more with my life if I didn't have to worry about him."

"What do *you* think?"

Setting his socked foot gently back on the couch, she said, "I think I'm doing what I love, and not many people can say that. Especially not my sister."

Considering this, Libby watched the kindness in Tess's expression as she pulled up Holton's slouching sock.

"Collecting driftwood is what you love?"

Tess removed the other sneaker and set it beside its mate. "Doing that is just one part of the job." She pulled the blanket down over his feet and turned around on the couch. "Walking along the beach all day in the fresh salt air, helping Holton create these amazing works of art, satisfies me. Maybe my sister's right. Maybe I should want more out of life, but I'm content. I've worked the corporate scene; I hated it. I love calluses on my hands, glue under my fingernails, being covered in sawdust and sweat. That stuff makes me feel alive."

Tess stood and looked down again at Holton, who was now snoring. She laughed. "I even love that."

Libby wrapped her arms around herself. "The snoring or him?"

A somber expression settled over Tess's face. "Both, I guess."

"Does he know?" Libby asked.

Tess just smiled.

CHAPTER 12

Libby's first week had been spent shadowing Tess, scouring out-of-the-way coves and beaches for driftwood. Her arms were sore, legs sorer, and her sunburned skin was finally starting to change from red to brown. Holton stayed out of their way, barely talking to either of them. The internship lasted until a week before her wedding, so that left a mere six weeks. She hadn't learned much more about Adele than the picture on Holton's wall had already told her.

Caroline still hadn't called to check on her, which was no big surprise — out of sight, out of mind as usual.

At the start of week two, Tess told her that she had taught her all she had to teach her. "My job's pretty simple, as you can see," she said as they sat at the picnic table behind the studio barn, eating burgers and sipping Diet Coke. "Tomorrow you'll start assisting Holt directly."

Libby crunched a piece of ice that had managed to make it through the straw. She dreaded working with him, but it was the only way she would find out what she needed to.

"You're afraid of him, aren't you?" Tess asked, licking ketchup from her fingertips.

As a rogue seagull circled them like a vulture, Libby laughed like this was preposterous. "That old grump doesn't scare me."

Tess's full lips curled upward. "Sure he doesn't. That's why every time he looks at you, your face turns as red as the sun."

"I'm sunburned. I'm always red." She shooed a fly away from her paper plate and moved her chair into the shade of the table umbrella.

After shoving a few fries in, Tess covered her mouth. "Everyone's a little afraid of him, myself included. Of course if you tell him that, I'll have to destroy you."

Libby shrugged. "Not me." And it was the truth. She wasn't afraid of him — she was afraid of finding out that he really was nothing more than the jerk he appeared to be.

Suddenly Tess's gaze fixated over her shoulder and her expression hardened to stone. Libby turned to see what she was looking at. A man in his midtwenties strolled up the sidewalk toward them. He wore flowered Bermuda shorts, leather flip-flops, and a pair of mirror-lensed Ray-Bans. His mop of blond curls hung in his eyes and he brushed them away. Against a deep tan, a shark tooth dangled from a braided hemp chain hanging against a bare, muscular chest. To Libby, he looked like a typical rich kid who spent his afternoons napping and surfing while Mom and Dad paid his parking tickets.

Tess groaned and set down her burger. "Here we go," she mumbled.

"Hey, ladies." He plopped down beside Tess like they were old friends and draped his arm over her shoulder. "And I use that term loosely."

She sneered, picked his arm up like it was something detestable, and flung it off her. "What do you want?"

In his lenses, Libby's reflection stared back at her. "Who's the new girl?" he asked with a toothy grin.

Looking away in obvious disdain, Tess said, "A summer intern, not that it's any of your business."

He picked a fry off her plate and popped it into his mouth. "Interning with Creary, eh? Now there's a waste of a perfectly good summer."

Tess looked at Libby and rolled her eyes,

126

then turned her attention back to the interloper. "What do you want, Henrietta?"

He smirked at her, then shoved his hand toward Libby to shake. "I'm Henry, the younger, more talented version of Holton Creary. Have you got a name?"

As much as Holton had gotten under her skin her first week there, this guy was the epitome of all she despised. Caroline would love him. Knowing just how to handle his type, Libby gave him her sweetest smile and took his hand. "Nice to meet you, Henry. I'm Libby."

Her mouth dropped open when he brought her hand to his lips and kissed it.

Despite his good looks, he made her skin crawl. Discreetly, she slid her hand under the table and wiped it off on her shorts. "Henry, I don't know how to say this, but you've got a —" She touched her nostril, indicating he had something on his.

His reaction was exactly what she was going for. His cocky smile turned to a grimace. He stood and held his hand in front of his nose, hiding what wasn't really there. "It was a pleasure to meet you, Libby. Tess, tell Holton I've got some bad news for him. Chelsea is replacing his consignments with mine." He made his free hand into the shape of a gun and pretended to shoot her.

As he left, Tess shook her head, wearing a hint of a smile. "You've got Holt's sense of humor."

Having lost her appetite, Libby pushed away her half-eaten burger. *What sense of humor?* she wanted to ask. Instead she opted for a safer question. "Who's Chelsea?"

Her smile died. "The busiest art dealer in the Banks. An account we can't afford to have lost."

Libby waited for her to explain as Tess picked a poppy seed from her bun.

"That slime is going to throw Holt into bankruptcy. He's like a knockoff dressmaker. He mimics our pieces but then produces them in half the time and for half the price. That's the fourth account we've lost to him this year."

"What a creep," Libby said. "I wouldn't buy a glass of water from him if I were passed out in the desert."

"If you were passed out, I don't think you'd be buying anything from anyone." She rubbed her temple like she was fighting a headache.

Libby took a sip of her soda, which was already getting warm and flat. "You know what I mean. Finances are bad, huh?"

Tess picked up what was left of her bun,

revealing a soggy red center and a slice of pickle. "Beyond bad. Don't tell him I told you, though. He's already slashed his prices, but every time he does, Henry takes his down further."

Libby thought about her mother's makeup line and the financial trouble she had been facing some years ago, and an idea came to her. But before she shared it, she needed to find out more. "How is Henry able to produce the same pieces cheaper and faster?"

"He cheats," Tess said. She waved her bun under the table and whistled for Rufus. The hound looked up from his spot beside Tess's truck and slowly pushed himself up like the food offering was almost more trouble than it was worth.

As Tess fed the dog, Libby let her mind reel. "What do you mean, he cheats?"

Tess wiped her hands on her napkin, then balled it up. "He doesn't use all-natural material. He uses just enough real driftwood to make it look authentic, but if he needs a shape of wood he doesn't have, he manufactures it. It's not fair. Most people can't tell the difference. We've cut prices so much to compete with him that we're almost paying to make them."

Libby watched Rufus lick up a dollop of

ketchup that had fallen to the ground. "He needs to stop slashing his prices, then," she said. "He needs to go the other direction and double them."

Tess gave her a look like she'd lost her mind.

"It sounds counterintuitive, I know. But, believe me, it works. My mom's in the cosmetics business. She was trying to compete with cheap drugstore lines, but she was losing her shirt. If you charge more, people think they're getting more. You can't under-price a Walmart mentality, so you don't go after the same type of customer. Let him have the tightwads. Go for the people with money. They'll pay triple if they think they're getting better quality, and in this case, they are. It's all in the marketing. Trust me."

Libby could see Tess's wheels turning. "That actually makes sense, but I don't think there's enough people around here that have that kind of money."

"Who says you've got to sell locally? Why not sell through your website?"

Tess shook her head. "We only get about two hits a day, if that."

"You need to do a little PR work. Update the site. Make him known as the best of the best at what he does. You'll attract interest from all over the world to buy one of his pieces if they're getting something that's one of a kind." She took another sip of her soda.

Tess's eyes lit up. "It's worth a try," she said. "So how are you going to mention it to him?"

With a mouthful of soda, Libby almost choked. She swallowed, then coughed to clear her throat. "Me? He hates me. He won't listen to any of my ideas."

"He doesn't hate you." Tess started turning the umbrella handle, closing it up. "He's just desperate enough to listen."

Libby was all nerves as she explained to Holton her theory that price determined perception. Sitting in front of a half-finished driftwood cocktail table, he wore a layer of sawdust and a frown. When she finished, Tess leaned her elbows on her knees and pretended to look surprised and impressed by the pitch.

Holton glared at her for what felt like hours, until she couldn't stand it a second longer. "Well, I guess I should probably get going back to —"

"You're not going anywhere," he said.

She figured he was preparing to give her a speech about how a college kid didn't know

131

the first thing about the business of art, and how she should keep her stupid ideas to herself. Instead, he surprised her by shaking a finger in her direction. "I just figured out who you remind me of."

Her heart leaped into her throat. So he had noticed the resemblance between her and Adele at last. If her cover was finally blown, well, at least now she could stop pretending and just get on with it.

"That chubby little girl in that movie with the elves," he said with a satisfied smile. "You know, the one with the frizzy hair."

When she gave him a horrified look, his eyes grew wide.

"You're not frizzy or chubby," he said with a frown. "That's not what I'm saying. You're a stick. I just mean in the face. The eyes or something." He looked to Tess as if she could bail him out; then, getting no help, he turned back to Libby. "She was a cute little girl. Stop looking at me like that." He turned to Tess again to save him.

Her arms were crossed and eyebrows raised. "Don't look at me to dig you out of that hole."

His gaze ping-ponged between them. After a few seconds of uncomfortable silence, he threw his hands in the air. "I give up." He stood and slid his chair against the wall with his foot.

"So?" Libby asked, exasperated.

He scrunched his face at her like he was disgusted. "So *what*?"

She stood and pushed her own chair against the barn wall. "So, what about my idea?"

Plucking his trusty shoulder towel off the workbench, he shrugged. "Oh, that. I think you're nuts." He threw the towel over his shoulder. "And I'm going back to work."

She might as well have been speaking to Caroline. She yanked the towel off his shoulder, making him whip around to face her. "My idea is a good one. The least you could do is pretend to consider it."

He snatched the towel back out of her hand so fast she felt the burn on her palm.

"I don't owe you anything." Reaching into a large plastic bucket full of milky water, he pulled out a piece of wood that had been soaking to soften it.

He was right, of course. He didn't owe her anything. So what if his wife had given her life? Parents didn't owe their children anything. Just thrusting them into the world to fend for themselves should be enough. On the verge of tears she knew she wouldn't be able to control for long, she whispered, "Fine, have it your way. What do I care if you go under?"

His mouth screwed up as he glared at Tess. She responded by studying the floor. "I'm not going under," he snapped. "What makes you think that?"

She knew that she had already betrayed Tess's confidence, but she could at least try to do some damage control. The woman had been nothing but nice to her. "It doesn't take a rocket scientist to figure it out. You live in a shack that looks like it's going to collapse into the next tide, and your studio is being held up by beams that look like they've been chewed through by termite-infested beavers." She paused to catch her breath and find something else of his to pick apart when a stifled giggle rose from Tess's direction. She looked over to see her covering her mouth.

"It's not funny," she said, feeling betrayed. Whose side was she on, anyway? It was her idea to share the stupid plan with him.

Another chuckle came, this time from Holton. Libby looked at him, and unlike Tess, he made no attempt to hide his mockery. At the same time, they both broke out in laughter . . . and tears sprang to her eyes.

The laughter stopped suddenly. Tess rushed over to her and put an arm around her shoulder. "What's wrong? Why are you crying?"

Embarrassment and anger washed over her as she tried to wipe away the tears that refused to stop falling. "It's not funny. It's a good idea." Her voice began to break up. "It worked for my mother, and now she's rich. Really rich."

Holton walked over and put a hand on each of her shoulders. His expression was somber and kind, and for a moment she got to see the father he was capable of being. "Your idea isn't a good one, Libby. It's a great one."

She rubbed her palm against her eyes, horrified by her lack of emotional self-control. "Then why were you laughing?"

He smiled at Tess.

A small grin pulled at her lips. "Termite-infested beavers?"

She searched her memory to recall if she had said that and decided she probably had. "Oh." It was embarrassing that she had let something so stupid upset her so much. It was then that she realized she did care about Holton and what he thought of her. She cared a lot.

CHAPTER 13

Libby left Holton and Tess to their afternoon walk and went upstairs to her room. She couldn't wait to call Rob and tell him about the glimpse of a father she had seen in Holton. Pulling her phone out of her pocket, she had a second thought and slid it back in. It had been over a week since she'd seen him. A face-to-face on Skype would be better.

She set her laptop on her mattress and signed in. Rob's computer rang and rang, and just when she was ready to close out, his face popped onto her screen. Thick black lashes blinked at her. "Hey, baby!" he said, wearing a smile as big as Texas. Behind him, the picture his mother had taken of them last Thanksgiving sat on his office shelf.

Her heart fluttered in a way it hadn't in a very long time. Apparently absence really did make the heart grow fonder. "It's so good to see your face," she said. "I've missed you."

He leaned toward the screen, and for a second she thought he was actually going to kiss it. "You have?" He was all vulnerability.

She nodded. "But before you ask, not enough to come home."

"Can't blame a guy for trying." His secretary beeped in on his intercom. "Mr. Beddow, Miss Slater is here to see you."

Confusion filled Libby as she wondered how Lisa knew she had called via the computer.

With a look of exasperation, he leaned his head back on his chair. "Please tell her I'm on a call and ask her to wait in the lobby."

It dawned on her then that there was more than one Miss Slater. "Caroline's there?"

He huffed. "Yeah, she's been on my back ever since you left. All the wedding planning is now on my shoulders. Lucky me."

"There's nothing left to plan. We should be all ready to go."

"We're talking about your mother here," he said glumly.

Leave it to Caroline to find more details to worry about. It had to be the event of the century, not for Libby's sake but for reputation's. "I'm about ready to call the whole thing off and just elope." It was something she had threatened a thousand times, and Rob had always met the idea with enthusiasm.

Not this time. "Don't talk that way," he said, pulling at the shirt collar that dug into the flesh of his neck. It was the shirt she'd bought him for his birthday that was one size too small. She had offered to exchange it, but he wouldn't hear of it, calling her gift perfect. That was Rob, making everything she did a perfect fit, even if it wasn't always.

Taken aback by his sudden one-eighty on the elopement offer, she studied his expression on the screen. "I thought you were all for running off?"

He picked a pen out of the stein on his desk and jotted something down. He was always doing that — capturing thoughts, he said, things he would never remember later if he didn't. The memory of an Alzheimer's patient is how he liked to describe himself, and Libby had found that description to be fairly accurate over the years. She wished she could look over his shoulder to see what he had written.

"So, what are you two doing today?" she asked.

He shrugged and rolled his eyes. "Probably spending five hours tasting cake icing."

She grabbed her pillow off the bed and hugged it to her chest. "We already picked out the cake. It's some twelve-tier monstrosity that has so much butter in it, everyone's going to be in line for the bathroom all night."

Rob grinned at this. He was so beautiful when he smiled. She wished she could reach through the computer and kiss him.

"We've changed some things up."

Libby raised her eyebrows in question. "Should I be worried?"

"No," he said, "you should be happy. I'm trying to make this the wedding you wanted instead of the one she hijacked."

Twisting the corner of her pillowcase, she tried to make sense of it. Caroline had been such a bully, insisting on choosing everything from the church to the flowers, and even the color of the napkins, that Libby had grown weary and finally conceded on just about every area. Why her mother should have a sudden change of heart about the wedding, she could only wonder. "How do you know what kind of wedding I really want?"

"I listen to you, and believe it or not, so does Caroline."

His secretary beeped in again. "Miss Slater says she's tired of waiting."

He lowered his voice, speaking through gritted teeth. "Tell her I'm almost finished."

"Now there's one thing I don't miss," Libby said. "You've got me really curious." *And more than a little afraid,* she wanted to add. Rob may have been listening all along, but his interpretation of the facts wasn't always spot-on. Last Christmas, when she had asked for a watch, he presented her with a smaller version of his own. It looked about as feminine on her as a three-piece suit.

"One month and three weeks to go." He leaned his face on his palm and looked at the screen like a lovesick school-boy. "You still want to marry me?" He shifted in his seat, moving his head into a finger smudge on her computer.

She paused a second too long, but only because she was contemplating Caroline listening to her, not because she was having second thoughts. "Of course."

The dreamy look on his face was replaced with hurt. "You don't sound so sure."

"I'm sure," she said, trying to sound convincing. "Of course I'm sure. Hey, guess what?"

"What?" he asked unenthusiastically.

From experience, she knew that when he was feeling aggrieved, he wouldn't really hear a word she said, so there was no use in even sharing. Her excitement ebbed. "Never mind."

"Tell me," he said, still wearing the same wounded expression.

"Holton and I had a kind of, sort of father-daughter moment."

"Great," he said flatly.

There were a million things she wished he were mature enough to hear at that moment. That his behavior was threatening to cause what he feared most. That she loved him and only him, but she was so afraid that she was going to have to spend the rest of her life trying to convince him of something he would never believe . . . or that his never-ending well of neediness would never be filled, no matter how many compliments and reassurances she poured into it. One day that neediness might even suck the life out of their marriage, but it didn't have to be that way. If he could just learn to trust in her, trust in himself and his own lovability, they'd be okay. But those were all things she had already said a million times, in a million different ways, and it always ended with him apologizing but not really getting it. "I'm going now," she said, feeling drained. "Have fun with Caroline."

"Libby, don't —" But she shut her computer before he had a chance to finish.

Her phone immediately rang, and of course his name showed up on the screen.

She tapped Accept and put it to her ear. "What?"

"If you don't want to marry me, just say so."

Opening her mouth, she was prepared to convince him, yet again, that she did want to spend her life with him, but no words would come. She just couldn't bring herself to repeat it one more time.

Silence met her, followed by a click.

CHAPTER 14

The sun was still hot and high and the tide had yet to make its evening retreat when Holton began his afternoon walk with Tess. They had been taking these daily treks together for at least two years, though he couldn't remember how the tradition began. Even after spending day in and day out working with her, he still enjoyed her company, particularly outside the stress of the studio.

Soft sand worked its way between his bare toes as they strolled along the shore. "So, how about Libby's crazy idea of raising prices instead of lowering them?" he asked, testing her. The idea was pretty out there, but like he told the girl, it had merit. They had tried everything else. He'd already forfeited Adele's gallery to foreclosure and the house was next, so there really was nothing more to lose by trying it.

When, after a few seconds, no answer

came, he turned to see Tess still standing in the same spot, scowling at him with Rufus by her side. He impatiently waved them both over.

Rolling her eyes, she approached. "I hate when you walk away from me like that."

He knew she wanted an apology, but he had a hard-enough time saying he was sorry when he had actually done something wrong. "We were talking about the intern's idea."

"I liked it," she said, stopping to pick up a shell and examine it. She was always crafting something out of them, though he had yet to see a finished product.

When she stopped, he decided he had better too, lest he tick her off again. She shoved a small conch shell into her pocket, then re-rolled the left leg of her cutoff shorts until it was even with the right. His gaze fell on her legs. Tess, with her athletic build, hadn't had an extra ounce of fat on her to spare, but in the past months it seemed to him she had still managed to lose weight. "You need to put some meat on those bones."

She cocked a thin, red eyebrow at him. "I haven't lost a single pound in all the years you've known me. In fact, I've probably put on about five in the last three. You know, for an artist, you're awfully unobservant."

Without reply, he trudged on. This time she and Rufus stayed by his side. "I'm plenty observant, thank you very much. I observe that you never wear anything but bathing suits and cutoff shorts anymore."

"That's all I've ever worn as long as you've known me. And what would you have me wear strolling along beaches, picking up driftwood all day?"

A hard piece of shell stabbed his heel and he paused to flick it off. "That's not all you do."

She pointed to a pelican stretching its wings along the pier. The bird tilted its head back and opened its beak as if a fish might drop out of the sky.

When it flew away, they continued on. "No, it's not," she said, "but I didn't think you knew that. And you're one to talk anyway. If I'm not mistaken, those are the same shorts you've had on all week. Are you waiting for them to grow legs so they can wear themselves?"

He looked down at his frayed khakis and yanked off the longest thread. "Just got them worn in."

Humor glinted in her eyes as she intertwined her arm with his, leaning into his shoulder. "Oh, they're worn all right," she said. "And you might want to pick up a few

145

razors. You're starting to look like Grizzly Adams."

He touched his prickly chin, surprised to feel more of a beard than a five o'clock shadow. "Chicks dig facial hair."

Kicking at the sand, she said, "As if you care what any chick thinks."

He stopped and stared out at the waves, listening to them roar like thunder. "Speaking of caring what you think —" he pushed a clamshell around with his big toe, unable to look her in the eye — "there's something I've got to tell you."

Silence sat thick between them.

"They're foreclosing on my house," he finally managed.

He hated her look of pity more than he had hated reading the letter of intent from the bank.

"I know," she said.

He frowned at her. He'd been so careful to keep his financial mess a secret, hoping to get everything straight without having to worry her. "How did you — ?"

"When you're drunk, you talk."

He groaned, horrified at the thought of what else he might have admitted to when he was three sheets to the wind. "What did I say?"

She stooped to rub behind Rufus's ear.

His tail wagged like mad and he let out a low, appreciative moan. The tide glided in over her sandals, leaving a foam outline in its wake. "You haven't paid the mortgage in months, and the property tax is behind too."

Shame filled him. When Adele was alive, she had been the one to handle the finances. When she'd complained about money, he accused her of being a worrywart penny-pincher. Secretly, he'd thought he could have done a better job with the bottom line, but the proof turned out to be in the pudding. "I'm sorry," he said. "I should have told you."

"You did."

"You know what I mean." He started down the beach again as a breeze blew off the ocean, cooling off his sweaty brow. With the back of his hand, he swiped away the dampness. "That's not the worst part. I'm not sure I can pay you this month."

After a moment of silence, he turned to see that once again she hadn't followed. She threw her hands up in exasperation. This time when he waved her to join him, she didn't move. Instead he walked to her. "Sweetheart, I don't think I can keep you on."

She smiled sadly. "You called me sweetheart."

He cleared his throat. "I only meant —"

"You can't let me go," she said. There was pleading in her voice, which managed to make him feel even worse than he already did. Another warm, foamy wave washed over their feet, this time bringing in an offering of seaweed. She picked a strand off her foot and tossed it onto the wet sand. "I have to be out of my apartment by the end of the month. If you get rid of me, I have nowhere to go. Don't make me crawl home to my parents with my tail between my legs."

Studying her freckled expression, he said, "I don't understand."

"I knew you couldn't afford to pay me anymore. I've known it for a while. Since I don't have another job, I'm going to have to move into the loft with Libby until we get things back on track." She took her sunglasses from the top of her head and slid them on. The tint made it hard to read her eyes. "You still own the studio outright? Please tell me they're not foreclosing on that, too."

It was the only thing he did fully own, besides his truck and the clothes on his back. "Far as I know, that's not in danger."

A group of seagulls cackled above them. One broke off from the pack and dive-bombed the ocean. He emerged with a wriggling fish in his mouth, which he promptly dropped. Another swooped in to catch it right before it hit the water.

"How long do you have before they kick you out of your house?"

He shrugged as if it didn't matter. The truth was it mattered more than anything else in his life at the moment. Adele and he had bought that property together in the hopes of one day knocking down the old shack and building their dream home. Losing it to the bank felt like he was letting her down yet again.

It was only a question of time now, though. The mortgage company had been leaving voice mails for months. Even his half sister in Washington State had called to let him know that they'd been harassing her too. As if his own feeling of personal failure and the threat of being on the street weren't punishment enough, they had to humiliate him on top of it.

"I could ask my parents for a lo—"

"No," he said before she could finish. She was fiercely independent, and he loved that about her. His poor financial decisions shouldn't rob her of that too. No, he'd rather be homeless. "Thank you, but no."

They walked in silence for a few minutes, each of them deep in their own thoughts.

As they reached the pier, he stopped and set his hand on one of the splintered piles. "You shouldn't have to give up your apartment for me, or anything else. You've put your whole life on hold working with me. It's time to face the fact that I'm going under. The last thing I want to do is take you with me. You've got your whole life ahead of you. Mine's all behind me."

"So that's it? You're just going to quit?" Her hands had begun to shake.

"I'm not quitting," he said, though he knew he'd already done that long ago. "Summer's end, when Libby goes back to school, if they don't kick me out before then, I'll take the barn room. I'll just keep doing what I do and eke out enough to get by."

She slipped off her glasses and rubbed her eyes. Sunlight shone on her face, and for the first time he noticed the flecks of blue mingling with her otherwise-green eyes. They were pretty. She was pretty. Not in the same way Adele had been, but she had a certain something that in another life he might have gone for.

"Listen to yourself," she said, her cracking voice giving away her emotion. "You'll eke out a living? Is that what you want for the rest of your life, just to get by? I know you

150

loved your wife, Holt — everyone loved her — but this isn't what she would want for you. If I leave, then what? You just spend your days alone in the barn working on tables and drinking the night away until you turn yellow and die?"

Why not? he wanted to ask. "I'm tired. I don't have any more fight in me."

She slipped her glasses back on and turned toward the sea. "If Adele were still alive, would you be giving up so easy?"

Stepping into the shadow of the pier, he let the waves break against his bare legs. He licked his lips and tasted the salt of the ocean. "We bought that little house together."

"I know," she said softly.

He smiled at the memory of sleeping in that tiny bedroom beside his wife. She loved the location but hated the house. They both did, but five years after her death, he was still living there and had learned to love it.

A wave broke fast and hard over Tess, nearly toppling her. He reached out and grabbed her arm in time to keep her from falling. She moved away from the pier and he followed. When he stepped out of the shade, the sun seemed doubly bright and he squinted against it.

"Thanks," she said, looking embarrassed.

"Listen." He scratched at the sea salt drying on his legs. "I've loved having you work for me, but maybe it's time to move on, for both of us."

She let out a long, deep sigh. "If I thought you would really move on if I left, I wouldn't walk; I'd run. But we both know that's not what's going to happen." Suddenly she jerked her head left, then right. "Where's Rufus?"

Holton scanned the beach. In the distance, a man who was surf fishing caught his eye. The fisherman's pole was held at a forty-five-degree angle by a PVC pipe buried in the sand. Sure enough, lounging beside him was a brown-and-tan hound dog. Holton pointed, and Tess's shoulders came down a few inches.

"Henry replaced us with the Chelsea account," she said.

A lump formed in his throat and he tried to swallow it down. That was the account that could have at least kept the barn lights on. "I'm finished," he said, feeling completely defeated.

"You can't let that weasel win."

He laughed coldly. "Already has. Doesn't matter, anyway. He's not the only one underselling us."

She slid her fingers into his, and they

continued their walk. "Let's at least try Libby's idea. We'll give it until they evict you from your house. Maybe we can make up the money and you can pay them off before then."

He shoved the fingers of his free hand into his mouth and whistled for Rufus. Over his shoulder, he watched him come running. When Tess paused to pick up a sand dollar, he dug a jagged shell from the sand, imagining what it looked like when it was whole and full of life. It was too small a fragment, and too damaged, to even guess what it might once have been. He tossed it into the next incoming wave. "I don't want you to have to give up your apartment."

Rufus appeared beside them, panting and wagging his tail.

"It's too late," she said. "It's already rented out next month. I have to move into the studio."

Good old dependable Tess. He didn't deserve her loyalty, but he was grateful for it just the same. She would never know how much. "And if we can't make a go of it?" he asked.

"Then I move out of the barn, I guess, and you move in permanently . . . and drink yourself to death."

"We'll give it the rest of the summer," he

153

said wearily. "I don't think it's going to work, but I'm willing to try if you are."

Like sunshine breaking through a cloud of gray, she smiled and threw her arms around his neck, and for a split second, he thought she was going to kiss him.

She smelled like tangerines today. It was a good smell, a hopeful smell. She leaned back and stared up at him. "We're going to do this."

Uncomfortable with her closeness, he gently pulled her arms off him and started walking. "We'll see."

CHAPTER 15

Holton had been twenty-five when Adele came back into his life. His girlfriend of three years had just broken up with him over what she saw as a lack of ambition on his part. Apparently she was tired of eating at fast-food restaurants and driving around in his rust bucket of a car and had wanted him to set his art aside and get a real job.

Trying to appease her, he went to work with her father's printing company. The old man slapped him on the back and promised that he could work his way up from the bottom if he stayed focused and gave it his best. Two eight-hour days of filing receipts in an office full of fluorescent light and stale air had sucked the life out of him. He walked out on the job and the girl.

Swearing off dating, he threw himself into his so-called hobby of charcoal sketching for more than a year, and had enough success to at least feed himself and pay rent on a tiny studio apartment above a tailor shop downtown. He was content with the solitude and freedom . . . until he once again laid eyes on a beautiful young woman with hair the color of barley.

Opening night of the Festival of the Arts, she stood in front of a charcoal sketch he was particularly proud of. Trying to make out the illegible signature scrawled across the bottom right-hand corner, she leaned in and squinted.

Maybe it was the champagne that allowed him the bravado to approach her after the way he'd treated her, or maybe it was the ambition his previous girlfriend had accused him of lacking. He squeezed the shoulder of the man he was speaking to and left him to talk to her. "Can't find something better to stare at than this piece of garbage?" he asked.

Until that moment, he figured she had somehow heard that he would be among the exhibiting artists that night, and might even be expecting to see him there. But the alarm in her eyes told him that wasn't the case. Pulling her sequined jacket closed, she backed away from him as if he were some kind of pervert. "I like it," she said with an air of superiority.

With a snort, he said, "Oh, come on. You

can't be serious."

She turned around, probably searching for someone to rescue her. "I *am* serious. I'm thinking of buying it, in fact."

Her reaction to seeing him again wasn't what he had hoped for, but selling something that night definitely was. He was sick of eating ramen noodles. With an eight-hundred-dollar price tag, this piece could keep him in steak and potatoes for a few weeks. "You think it's really worth what the guy's asking?"

She glanced down at the price, then back to him. "I think he should have charged more. It's a brilliant piece."

"How much more?" he asked, sipping from his champagne glass.

Looking annoyed, she smoothed her black skirt and said, "I'm going to go claim it before someone else does. Please excuse me."

Gently, he grabbed her arm. "Wait," he said.

She looked down at his hand on her arm, then gave him a look that made it clear she didn't appreciate being touched.

When he let go, he was sure she would take off. He was pleasantly surprised when she didn't.

"You used to like art," she said in a tone

that hinted of resentment — or perhaps regret.

"I still like art," he said. "Just not everyone's idea of it."

"Well, I like his idea of it," she said.

Turning to face it again, he rubbed his chin as if considering it for the first time. "What do you like best about it?"

Her gaze moved back to the drawing. "What's not to like? The horses aren't harnessed, they're not saddled, they're just free." She became animated and her eyes gleamed with passion. She seemed so much more sure of herself than he remembered, which only added to her attractiveness. "And the ocean — just look at it. It's as wild as they are." She reached toward the sketch, almost but not quite touching the boulder cliff being battered by the sea. "It's what we all want, I think. To be that way."

He couldn't say for sure, but it might have been at that moment that he fell in love with her. "Is there anything you would change about it?"

Tilting her head to the side, she studied it again. "I'd put it in oils," she said quickly, as if she had already asked herself the same question. "The contrasting colors of white horses against a gray ocean, grayer sky, and

158

beige sand would be beautiful. Don't you think?"

A cocktail waiter walked by with an empty cork tray, and Holton set his half-full champagne glass on it. "What makes you think the horses are white, or the sky is gray? Maybe the horses are brown and the sky is blue."

She laughed as though it were preposterous. "Of course the sky isn't blue. How would that be possible with the waves that tumultuous? It's a stormy day, obviously."

"It's not," he said, studying her profile. He didn't remember her features being so delicate. "The waves can beat the rocks with the sun shining. I see it all the time."

"I grew up on the ocean and I've never seen waves hit that hard unless it's storming."

"Is that right?" he said, amused.

She pressed her lips together and raised her eyebrow in a way he had always found charmingly cocky. "That's right."

"Well, for your information, the horses are black, the sky is the lightest blue, and the sea is —"

She turned to him and let out an exasperated sigh. "You interpret the artist's intention your way and I'll interpret it —" Her eyes grew wide as understanding passed over her. "You're him, aren't you?"

He simply smiled then, and would smile for the years he spent with her by his side. He would smile through the heartache of childlessness. He would smile through financial hardships and health scares. He would smile through the hardest of times because even if they had to fight tooth and nail for everything they'd built together, he never had to fight for her love. It was given to him freely and completely. Unlike her predecessor, Adele loved him just the way he was.

He would only stop smiling when a police officer showed up on their doorstep to inform him that she had died. At that moment he was sure that he would never smile again.

But he found himself smiling now as he brought the finest driftwood table he'd ever made to Ark Antiques and Collectibles, his last cash-paying account. With a little chutzpah and charm, he knew he could convince them that Libby's plan to double his prices was a sound one. They would buy the piece, and others would follow. He might not be able to save the house at this point, but maybe he could keep on Tess and the lights. If losing Adele had taught him anything, it was that stuff could be replaced;

people couldn't.

The husband-and-wife team met him out back to look at his latest offering. Their initial reaction was exactly what he wanted. It had been a long time since hope had risen within him, and it felt good. Maybe if things went well, he could even afford to give Tess a raise. She hadn't had one in three years and if anyone deserved one, it was her.

Carmen smiled brightly as her fingers traced the ornate tree he'd fashioned as the base of the table to hold up a beveled glass top. "You've outdone yourself, Holton. This might be your best work yet."

Her husband, Roberto, wore just a trace of a smile as he looked it over, which was a trace more than he usually wore. "Definitely your best, Holt. The tree looks like you plucked it right out of Eden."

Carmen stood back and crossed her arms. "Did you bleach the wood to get it that white? The color is amazingly uniform."

He shook his head, feeling a surge of pride. "Nope. I've been collecting these pieces for years. Just finally had enough to do it."

"Wow," she said.

"How much you asking on this one?" Roberto said, stepping back to distance himself as he always did when it was time to negotiate a price.

"Five," Holton said, feeling the pit in his stomach.

The couple exchanged an unhappy glance.

"Only five hundred?" Carmen said. "That's a little low even for you. What's wrong with it?"

"Absolutely nothing," Holton said, feeling suddenly sick to his stomach. "Which is why I'm asking five grand." He knew they wouldn't agree to that much — they had to make a profit, after all — but he was prepared to let it go at twenty-five hundred after a little back-and-forth.

Roberto started coughing as if he were choking on the price.

Carmen jerked her head back. "Five thousand dollars? Are you kidding?"

He could feel his face flush as he widened his stance. "Nope. Like you said, it's my finest work, and it took two full weeks to put this together. I think you could price it at seven and we'd all walk away happy."

Carmen laughed coldly. "I could get Henry to do something similar for a fraction of that."

"He's a hack and you know it," Holton said. "This piece is one of a —"

"Come on, man." Roberto shook his head. "They're all one of a kind. That's the nature

162

of driftwood."

"Henry's pieces aren't. They all look the same because he manufactures half the wood with plaster molds." He wasn't entirely sure what Henry used; he only knew it wasn't real driftwood. He could get the stuff to bend in ways impossible for real wood. And he whipped the pieces out at a breakneck speed. Of course, if you were copying, you didn't have to deal with the time-consuming process of creating.

"People don't care," Carmen said, taking two steps back. "They don't care how long it takes you to make them. They don't care if you bleach them white or pick them off the sand that way. They don't care if other people have one. They just want something interesting to stack magazines on."

Her husband crossed his arms and shook his head, indicating no deal. "We're not going to be able to do that kind of money."

"Fifteen," Carmen said. "We'll list it for two, and we'll be lucky to get that."

Two weeks, he wanted to repeat. *It took me years to find the wood, and two forty-hour workweeks to put it together.* But like they said, no one except him cared.

"Better take it before she makes it twelve," Roberto said.

"Think about it, Holton," Carmen said.

163

"Henry told us we're the last shop buying from you."

Holton's face blazed with anger. So that was why they were lowballing him. They knew he was backed into a corner. Never mind that he had always brought them his best, even when he had a dozen other accounts. Whatever happened to loyalty — or just common decency, for that matter?

"The offer stands at fifteen," Roberto said almost apologetically.

He told them where to put their fifteen hundred dollars and promptly lost his last paying account. He dragged the table home with him, intending to photograph it with the hopes of selling it online. But when he walked up to the porch and saw the notice of default taped to his front window, telling him he had ninety days to pay all that he owed in full, he decided to go with plan B.

CHAPTER 16

When Libby had finished her pint of takeout lo mein, she licked the soy sauce from her lips and hugged her pillow to her chest, mentally replaying her conversation with Rob. They'd been through this a hundred times, and he always called right back to apologize, or at least allowed her to when she'd been the one at fault. But it had been hours and she still hadn't heard from him.

She dialed his number but hung up before it could ring. What would she say? That she was sorry? Sorry for what? For hesitating and then not qualifying why, knowing he would assume the worst. He always did. But that wasn't her fault, and she was tired of being made to feel as though it were.

She flopped back on the bed, noticing the feel of the springs through the mattress for the first time. The thing was probably as old as Holton. The brief thought that Adele might have slept on it gave her a strange sort of comfort. Flipping onto her side, she stared at an oval-framed still life of a pear and vase. It looked suspiciously like a paint-by-number deal. Had her mom been an artist wannabe and this was the best she could do?

She glanced at her phone again. Maybe if she gave Rob a few days, it might really sink in this time that he needed to do some changing. She loved him, but he never could seem to believe it. Never mind that he was sweet and generous, or that he loved her in a way most women could only dream of being loved. Never mind that he was the most beautiful man she'd ever laid eyes on. And never mind that she told him repeatedly how much she adored him.

She set her phone down on her pillow, climbed out of bed, and walked to the small window on the other side of the room. The studio overlooked the ocean. It wasn't the nicest building, but it was great real estate. It would only be a matter of time until this sparsely populated stretch of beach was built up like everywhere else. Maybe she and Rob should invest in a piece of it before the prices became unaffordable. Of course, they would have to make up first.

Her stomach sank anew with worry. If they couldn't work this out soon, there might not be a wedding after all. Maybe in the end, it would be Rob who got sick of her. Maybe she was the one being unreasonable. Was it such a big deal that the guy needed reassurance of her commitment? Would she rather have a man who couldn't care less? No, she'd rather have a man who trusted her. That's what it came down to, and that had to be the foundation of a successful relationship.

She watched a sailboat skim across the waves until it disappeared into a tiny white dot on the horizon, then walked back over to the bed. Her cell phone screen had gone to black from inactivity. When she slid open the keyboard, it came to life with her sunflower wallpaper, but there were no missed calls or messages. When she sat, the bed squealed under her weight.

Call or don't call?

Don't call. Definitely don't call.

Although she'd settled on not calling for a minimum of three days, under no circumstances, she found her fingers dialing his number. It went straight to voice mail. Pressing the phone tight against her ear, she listened to his familiar message with longing.

He had such a beautiful voice, with just a hint of a Southern accent, so masculine yet refined. Before her mouth could take over and leave a message pleading for his forgiveness, she forced herself to end the call. It hit her then that the feeling of desperation she was experiencing must be how he felt most of the time. What a horrible way to go through life. If only she could put his mind at ease once and for all. Though she knew that somehow, someway, he would need to learn to do that for himself.

Just then Caesar came to mind. It was the perfect reason to call him without groveling. What if she and Rob were really broken up and he no longer wanted to watch her place or her cat? He might be upset enough to take off in a huff, leaving Caesar to fend for himself. The poor baby would starve to death. Now she had no choice but to call. Relief mixed with joy filled her as she hit Redial. Once again, no answer.

Another ten minutes after sending him a text, her phone remained silent. She should go home and check on Caesar. But it was already nearly five. By the time she drove home and back to Nags Head, it would be late, and she had to wake at dawn to be in the studio on time. Plus, she hated driving at night. The astigmatism in her right eye sometimes bent light in the dark. More than once, she'd thought she had seen someone standing in the middle of the road and slammed on her brakes. Nothing would be there, but she'd come close a few times to being rear-ended.

She didn't think Rob, even at his worst, would abandon his responsibility, but then, they had never broken up before. She loved her cat too much to take that chance. Calling her friends would be out of the question. Only two were close enough to ask such a favor, and both of them had dogs.

Caroline would have to do it. She groaned at the thought of asking her mother for a favor. She always made even the smallest request feel like such a hassle. Surely she could act like a mother this once, though.

The phone rang only twice. Caroline answered a little too eagerly, like she had been expecting her call.

"Hey, it's Libby." She twisted her bedsheet around her index finger like a strand of hair. The sheet was the type of soft that only came about by hundreds of washings.

"You don't always have to say who you are. By now I should think I'd recognize my own daughter's voice."

Libby examined the wilted daisies next to her bed. They desperately needed to be thrown away. She pulled the least-mangled one out of the murky water and laid it beside the jar. Maybe she should press it as a memento of her time here.

She brought the mason jar to her nose, winced at the sewage smell the water had taken on, and set the jar back down. "I need you to do me a favor," she said, already preparing herself for a lecture. With Caroline, there was always a lecture.

A pause was followed by a suspicious "And that is?"

"I need you to check on Caesar for me."

Another pause. "I thought Robert was watching him?"

She cringed. She hated sharing her personal business with her mother, but lying was out of the question. Caroline could sniff one out even a hundred miles away. "We had a fight."

"I know," she said coolly.

"You talked to Rob?" She shouldn't have been surprised. They seemed to be spending an odd amount of time together lately.

"Yes, of course," she said, as though her omniscience were a given.

Libby walked to the bathroom and pulled a file from her makeup bag. Although her fingernails were neat and short, she began to obsessively work the file back and forth over already-smooth areas. "What did he say?" she asked, trying her best to sound disinterested.

A stifled mumble sounded on the other end of the phone, as though her mother had covered the receiver to talk to someone else. No doubt another one of her adoring boyfriends.

"Caroline?" Libby said, irritated.

Her voice became clear again. "Sorry, what was your question?"

Working the file hard over her pinkie nail, she managed to scrape off a layer of skin. With a yelp, she looked down at a tiny area of raw pink skin. "You said you spoke to Rob." She waved her hand, trying to cool the burn.

"Oh yes," Caroline said casually. "He said you two broke up. So, how's the fake internship going?"

Libby gave up the pretense and just came out with it. "What did he say exactly?"

Her mother sighed dramatically into the receiver. "Exactly? I don't know exactly. I don't hang on his every word like you do."

It was all she could do not to hang up the phone. It was like the woman was trying to tick her off. "Give me the Cliff's Notes."

"Something about him asking if you still loved him and you not answering. Same old."

She picked up her toothbrush from the

sink counter. "Was he very upset?"

"Upset? Not particularly. He said something about maybe needing to move on with his life."

She leaned against the vanity, feeling sick to her stomach. "He said that?"

Caroline mumbled something she couldn't hear, then uncovered the phone again. "You said you needed me to do something for you?"

"I need you to keep Caesar."

Her response came back as quick and fast as a drop shot. "Absolutely not. You know I'm allergic to cats."

A sudden infusion of anger replaced her hurt. She tried never to ask her mother for anything. As a girl she hadn't asked her to help pick out a prom dress, take her for a driving test, or even pick up deodorant when she was out. She learned early on that everything was an imposition. "You're not allergic to cats. You just don't like them. Please," she forced out between clenched teeth as she walked back to the bed.

"Yes, I am allergic. I'll board it, but it can't stay here."

The thought of poor Caesar locked in a cage for six weeks, even at the frilly sort of place her mother was likely to patronize, made her want to cry. "Never mind," she said as she sat down on the mattress. "I'll pick him up."

"If you think that's best," Caroline said. "So, have you learned anything about your — ?"

Before she could finish her sentence, Libby hung up. Phone still clenched in her fingers, she fell sideways onto her pillow. Somehow she had survived childhood without a father, and essentially without a mother either, and just when she thought she'd come to terms with her relationship with Caroline, the woman's indifference had once again managed to blindside her. Every once in a while, it still did.

And now she'd lost Rob too. She had no one in the world left. A burst of indignation washed over her and she pushed the pillow stuffing down, allowing her to breathe easier.

Fine. If Rob wanted to abandon her just because they got into a fight, she didn't need him. And if Caroline didn't want to be a mother, she didn't have to be. She had checked out long ago anyway. Maybe it was time for Libby to do the same.

CHAPTER 17

Tess agreed to ride along with Libby to pick up Caesar from her apartment, but only if they drove her pickup. She said if she wasn't the one behind the wheel she tended to get carsick. Besides, the person driving got control of the radio.

Libby was more than happy to give up rights to the FM dial if it meant not having to go alone, and she didn't even own a tape for the prehistoric cassette deck.

She slid onto the leather bench seat beside Tess and buckled herself in. "Thanks for coming with me."

"Thanks for asking me." Tess adjusted the rearview mirror and slowly backed out of the spot. "I was bored out of my skull. To save money, I gave up cable last month, and Angry Birds gets old after your five hundredth game. Besides, I love a road trip about as well as anything. I think if I didn't love art so much, I'd probably drive for a living."

Libby looked for a drink holder to put her can of Coke in. Finding none, she set it between her thighs. The cold felt good against the warmth of the night. "I did tell you it's a two-and-a-half-hour drive, didn't I?"

"Twice now," Tess said as she turned on the radio. A twangy country voice rang out from the door speakers. "I love the classics. How about you? You a country music fan?"

"I guess I like the stories more than the music." The suspension apparently needed some work because she could feel every bump in the road.

"Sorry," Tess said, patting the dash. "She's a little rough around the edges."

They drove along for a while, listening to the country station as Libby watched the side of the road slowly turn from sand to grass and the horizon began to disappear into billboards and concrete.

Tess took her eyes off the road just long enough to glance over. "So, tell me about your fiancé. You don't talk about him much."

Libby looked down at her engagement ring, a one-carat princess-cut diamond surrounded by a band of white gold, and her heart sank. "Actually, I think we broke up, which is why I need to pick up my cat. Rob was taking care of my apartment."

Gripping the wheel at twelve and two, Tess groaned. "Oh, honey, I'm sorry. Open mouth, insert foot."

Libby kicked off her flip-flops and drew her bent legs up to her chest. "No, it's fine. He's a good guy, just kind of clingy sometimes. If he could only see himself the way I do, he wouldn't be so insecure."

At the end of a car commercial, Carrie Underwood began to sing about a Louisville slugger and a cheating boyfriend. Tess turned the radio knob, and the cabin fell silent except for the humming of the truck and the whapping wipers. "You guys are a little young to be thinking about marriage anyway. I mean, you just graduated."

She hated perpetuating the lie but couldn't set the record straight quite yet. "Maybe so, but it still hurts."

Tess reached over and gave her hand a motherly squeeze. Her palms were even more rough and callused than Holton's. After a few minutes of silence she said, "Do you think it's true what they say: that's it's better to have loved and lost than never to have loved at all?"

Libby pulled a pack of Wrigley's from her purse and offered Tess a piece. When she refused with a wave of her hand, Libby unwrapped a stick and popped it into her mouth. Since Rob was always chewing the stuff, it tasted like one of his kisses. "I think it's far sadder to never have loved than had your heart broken."

Tess stared ahead at the road. "I don't know. I think if you've never loved, you might long for it, but I don't think it really hurts. It's like when you're a little kid, before you have any notion of love. You're not missing it. You're not even thinking about it. But it hurts like crazy losing someone you love."

She knew Tess was speaking of romantic love, but she couldn't help but think of Adele. What she wouldn't give to have loved her before losing her. "It does hurt," she agreed, "but at the same time, I think when you never experience love, real love, you have a hole in your heart. You may not be able to pinpoint what's missing, but you still feel it. I think once someone fills that hole, even if they leave you, the hole stays filled."

Tess glanced in the rearview mirror, then at her. "So Rob filled a place in your heart that needed filling?"

"He's the best person I've ever known. He brings his mother flowers every week, collects blankets for the animal shelter, and

I've seen him give his last five dollars to a homeless man." A sudden bout of sadness overwhelmed her, and she looked out the window to distract herself. Their headlights reflected off the wet road, breaking up the blackness with streaks of gold.

Putting on her right blinker, Tess checked the side mirror, then the rearview, before veering into the exit lane. The reflective green-and-white sign named a town and road Libby had never heard of. It dawned on her then that Tess had no GPS and hadn't asked for directions. "Do you know where we're going?"

Tess flipped the radio back on. "Holton calls me a human map. I've been to your neck of the woods a few years back for an art convention."

"Just once?" Libby needed the navigation system in her own neighborhood. She never understood how people could drive some-where once or twice and get there again purely on memory. To her, it was like listen-ing to a foreign-language instruction tape once, then speaking it fluently. It seemed superhuman somehow. Of course, others had always said that about her mathemati-cal abilities too. People's brains were just wired differently, she supposed.

She studied Tess's profile. "You and Holton — have you ever . . . ?" She paused, letting the unfinished question hang in the air.

Tess stared straight ahead at the road. The wipers began to squeal against the glass when the rain slowed to a mist. Tess turned them off and glanced her way. "Ever what?"

Heat rose up Libby's neck. "You know, dated or whatever."

Cracking open her window, Tess let in the warm evening air. "Holton doesn't date. I told you, he's still hung up on his late wife."

Libby breathed in deep and long. Adele must have been a good person to have a man still hung up on her five years later . . . even if it was Holton Creary. "Do you wish he did — date, I mean?"

"Why are you asking?" Tess said defensively.

"Just asking."

"Just asking because you care about my love life, or are you thinking you might be interested in him now that you're free?"

The ludicrousness of the question caught Libby off guard. She began to laugh, nervously at first, and then she couldn't stop. Tears rolled down her face as she looked over at an unhappy Tess. "If you only knew," she managed around her laughter.

Wearing a scowl, Tess's bottom lip slightly protruded. It was the same face Rob made when she had made a joke at his expense. Maybe it was a mixture of physical fatigue and road hypnosis that made her feel delirious, but whatever it was, Tess was not appreciating it.

Wiping her eyes, Libby held her breath to get herself to stop laughing. A few chuckles escaped until she was finally able to get ahold of herself.

"He's a good-looking, talented man," Tess snapped. "It's not that funny."

"Sorry." Libby exhaled the last of her amusement. "He's old enough to be my father." *And sort of is,* she wanted to add.

The corners of Tess's lips curled up in a hesitant smile. "Yeah, I guess a fortysomething man must seem ancient to a twenty-two-year-old."

"Not quite as ancient as it used to," Libby said. "I remember when I was in elementary school thinking that eighteen was old. And when I was eighteen, I thought twenty-five was old. Now that I'm about to turn twenty-five, it doesn't seem quite so —" As soon as the words left her mouth, she realized her mistake.

When Tess looked at her, she couldn't meet her gaze. Caroline had always said that she was the world's worst liar. Judging by Tess's expression, that hadn't changed.

Lips disappeared into a thin white line as Tess flipped on her blinker. Jerking the steering wheel to the right, she pulled onto the shoulder of the road. She threw the truck into park, applied the hazards, and turned to face Libby. "Why are you lying about your age?"

Blood shot to Libby's head as her pulse pounded against her eardrums. "I'm not. It was just a mistake."

Narrowing her eyes, Tess slowly shook her head. "We're not going anywhere until you tell me the truth. If you're twenty-five — and now I'm sure that you are — then you didn't just graduate and you're not really an intern. So what are you?"

"I am," Libby pleaded, staring down at her wringing hands.

Looking up at the roof, Tess breathed, "I knew it," before glaring at her. "I told Holton that you don't talk like an art enthusiast. You don't know any of the lingo, none of the principles . . . You didn't even know what *patina* meant."

Libby sat on her hands to keep them from shaking. "Yes, I do. It's the green stuff that gets on copper pots over time." She didn't admit to only looking up the word after Tess had mentioned it for the third time.

Tess stared at her for an uncomfortably

long time. " 'The green stuff'? That's what I mean. Who are you really?"

A car sped by them, hitting a puddle and sending a wave of water over the back of the truck.

"The truth," Tess said coldly. "Are you some kind of overzealous bill collector or what?"

Frantically, Libby tried to spin a story in her mind that would explain it all away, but nothing would come.

"Well?" Tess said, crossing her arms.

"I'm not a bill collector, and I'm not interested in Holton romantically." Her head began to swim. "I'm . . ." She drew in a deep breath, knowing the jig was up. "I'm his stepdaughter."

Tess searched her face for the truth, or maybe some family resemblance. "He doesn't have a daughter, step or otherwise," she finally said.

"Yes, he does," Libby said. "He just doesn't know it yet."

CHAPTER 18

Like clockwork, Holton's internal alarm went off at five every morning. But this morning, when he opened his eyes, he didn't have to turn on his bedside lamp to find his slippers. Instead he squinted against the sun. Disoriented, he rubbed his eyes and checked the watch he'd worn to bed: 6:39.

His head ached as though someone had bashed him upside it. Pressing against his throbbing temples, he looked around his tiny bedroom as waves of nausea washed over him . . . along with memories of the night before. Having taken Libby's advice, he lost his final account and then came home to see a big black-and-white notice of default stuck to his window.

Now, as he sat on the edge of the bed with his head in his hands, he couldn't remember how he'd gotten home, or where he had even done his drinking. He just hoped he hadn't driven drunk.

He trudged to the kitchen and opened the freezer to see if his car keys were still frozen in a block of ice. It was a measure he had learned to take each night before he started drinking, so that in his inebriated state he wouldn't kill anyone. Atop the ice trays sat a plastic bowl, which, thankfully, still contained his keys, frozen solid within a rectangle of ice. He grabbed the container, threw it in the sink, and turned on the hot water. Glancing down, he noticed a chunk of broken wood on the floor beneath the table . . . and remembered how he had spent the rest of his night. Not since losing Adele had he felt that utterly hopeless.

Sure enough, when he entered the living room, a mallet sat in the corner, surrounded by hunks and bits of broken driftwood. As he knelt beside what had once been a table, his bare knees pressed into splinters of wood that had worked themselves into the rough carpet. The table was one of the finest he'd ever made. It had taken him two weeks to make and only five minutes to destroy.

But it didn't matter now. Nothing did. He was finished. Soon he would have to move into the barn apartment, and Tess and the intern would have to move on with their lives.

After seeing the last of his dreams fade into the sea, Holton set a new goal for himself. He would drink himself to death before the sheriff showed up at his door to kick him out. The only thing left to do was tell Tess she was fired and tell the girl she needed to go home, wherever that was.

With a heart as heavy as an anchor, he pulled the cell phone from his pocket and dialed Tess's number. She answered on the first ring as she had so many times before.

"Morning, Holt," she said cheerfully.

He opened his mouth, but no words would come.

"Hello?" she said. "Holton?"

Most people said his name enunciating the *n* at the end, but she placed emphasis on the *t* instead, breaking it into something that sounded like two separate words. He loved the way she said it. He'd never told her that. Never told her a lot of things that he maybe should have.

"Are you okay?" she asked.

Unable to bring himself to say what needed to be said, he hung up. He'd text her instead. It was the coward's way out, but he couldn't bring himself to listen to the pain in her voice, or hear it in his own. She had been his best friend for half a decade, and he knew he wasn't just failing himself. He had failed her, too. Not since Adele had anyone believed in him so completely. But it was time for Tess to put her faith in something worth believing in.

His large thumbs fumbled to type with the small black buttons on the screen. Not coming to work today. Need you and girl gone before I get there tomorrow. You don't deserve this, but you're fired. Sorry.

He hit Send as he looked around for a bottle that wasn't empty.

CHAPTER 19

Morning came all too soon. Libby intended to wake up early so she could practice how she would tell Holton who she really was, if the right opportunity presented itself that day, but after repeatedly hitting the snooze button, she barely had time to get her teeth brushed and throw her hair into a ponytail before charging down the stairs.

"Sorry I'm late," she said breathlessly as she got to the bottom of the stairs. But the place was eerily silent. Doing a quick scan of the studio, it was obvious she wasn't the only one running behind. Breathing a sigh of relief, she figured she might as well get started setting up for the day. Looking around for the five-gallon bucket Holton used to fill the steamer with, she spotted it sitting on a rumpled dust cloth beside the paint-spattered sink.

She filled it with water and lugged it over to his work area, leaving a trail of liquid behind her. After setting it beside the long wooden steam box, she eyed the pile of driftwood he worked from. There were plenty of the larger pieces, but he would definitely need more of the smaller ones. Tess must have realized the same thing and left early to start collecting.

She pulled open the barn door. The fact that it wasn't locked told her that indeed someone had already been there. As the doors creaked open, blinding sunlight hit her, along with a soft breeze rolling in off the ocean. The sound of a truck engine starting up caught her ear, and she turned to see Tess's truck parked on the gravel beside the studio. Hurrying over, she hoped to catch her before she set off. As she neared the driver's-side window, the soft sound of whimpers filled the air. Tess's shoulders shook violently as she gripped the steering wheel, eyes swollen and red.

Alarm filled her as dreadful possibilities raced through her mind. Maybe Holton had been killed in an accident like Adele. Did he drive drunk? Did he kill someone else? She hadn't even told him who she was yet and she'd already lost him.

"What's wrong?"

Tess hyperventilated her answer. "He's —

giving — up. Fired me — wants you — go too."

Stunned, Libby grabbed hold of the open window. "What? Why?"

Tess's words were so broken, it was difficult to decipher them.

Libby locked eyes with Tess and lowered her voice to a calm whisper like Caroline used to do to her when, as a teen, she'd had one of her hormone-induced meltdowns. "Slow down your breathing. It's going to be okay." But even as she said the words, she doubted their validity. Tess wasn't the damsel-in-distress type. If she was this upset, something was worth being upset about.

Resting her forehead against the steering wheel, Tess said, "I can't do this anymore. Just can't." A fresh bout of tears streamed down her cheeks.

Not knowing what else to do, Libby reached through the open window and patted her back in an attempt to calm her.

After a moment, Tess wiped her eyes against her bare shoulder and forced a smile that looked more like a grimace. "It was nice to meet you, Libby. If I were you, I'd forget I ever met him."

"Don't go," she started to say, but Tess was already throwing the truck into gear.

Feeling numb, she watched the truck screech off, kicking up sand and gravel.

When it disappeared down the road, she walked to the ocean and sat at the water's edge, hoping to clear her mind and make sense of what had just happened. Tess said Holton had fired the both of them. Sure, he was having a hard time financially, but he seemed willing enough to take her advice and give raising his prices a try. She couldn't imagine what could have changed between yesterday and today.

Tess was clearly shattered, and no wonder. It was obvious she was in love with him. He might be too blind to see it, but no one else was. Having a master's in art ed, she could be making a decent living for herself teaching. Instead she rented a crummy apartment and worked for practically nothing just to be near him.

Tess said he'd given up, but as far as Libby could tell, he'd already done that long ago. A wave washed over her bare feet. When it receded, she dug her toes into the wet, gritty sand.

A little girl with blonde ringlets passed by, holding her daddy's hand. She swung a red castle-mold pail at her side and stopped every few inches to pick up a shell and show it to him before dropping it into her bucket.

Libby's heart ached at the sight of them. Had she done the same thing with George once upon a time, or had he always had one foot out the door?

Why did the men in her life have to be so selfish? They had no problem creating babies — or adopting them — but when the going got tough, they just bailed. And wasn't that what Rob had done by moving on with his life when all she had wanted was a little breathing room? Now Holton was giving up too. Even if his decision had nothing to do with her, it stung just the same. The banner over her entire childhood had been rejection, and it had followed her into adulthood.

She traced a frown into the wet sand just as another wave rolled in to erase it. Maybe it wasn't their fault. Maybe the blame lay with her. If she were better somehow, maybe each of them would still be around. If she had been prettier, had a better nature, smarter, whatever . . . her birth mother wouldn't have given her up for adoption to begin with. She might have grown up like a normal, happy child with a father and mother who loved and wanted her. The emotional scars would only have come, as they should have, from an unrequited crush or not making the track team or . . . whatever.

A seagull landed to the left, jerked its head toward her, and blinked at her with vacant eyes outlined in red. The smudge of black on an otherwise-yellow beak disappeared into the sand. When it emerged, he carried what looked like a shriveled french fry. She watched him fly off with it, disappearing into the skyline.

Maybe she had somehow poisoned her relationships with Rob and Caroline, but what could she have done as a baby to make her unlovable to her biological parents? Did she kick too much in utero? Cause Adele too much weight gain or indigestion? Although her mind told her it wasn't her fault then and probably wasn't now, her heart had trouble believing it.

Suddenly she ached for the one person who had caused her a fair share of pain but at least had never left her. She slid her phone out of her pocket and dialed Caroline.

She picked up on the third ring.

"It's me," Libby said.

"Well, good morning," Caroline said with a hoarseness in her voice that told Libby she'd just woken. "You're up early. Is everything okay?"

The question brought tears to her eyes. And then, like Tess's, they refused to stop.

"What is it? What's wrong?" Caroline asked, suddenly alert.

"It's Holton," she managed around her tears. "He fired me, I think. Tess said he's quitting. Giving up."

"Elizabeth, you're not making sense. Who is Tess, and what is Holton quitting?"

"His assistant. I think she's in love with him. She knows who I am."

"She knows he's your stepfather? Does he?"

Libby sniffled. "No. But there's something I haven't told you — he's an alcoholic. Not just a couple of cocktails a night either. I'm talking about facedown-in-the-gutter, nightly drunk." Although she knew she would probably live to regret telling Caroline the truth about Holton, she desperately needed to talk to someone. "I think he's been mourning the loss of my mother for years. I don't know what to do."

Caroline was silent.

"I need some advice."

"I think you should come home," was her predictable response.

"Just leave him here to die? And I haven't found out anything about my mother."

"Then stop the charade, tell him who you

are, and ask about her. Then come home and let's get on with our lives. He's chosen his life, Libby. Don't throw away yours on someone who doesn't care. You can't make Holton quit drinking or get his life together. It's time for you to start worrying about you."

What she said made sense, and really, what choice did Libby have now but to tell him? He wanted her to leave anyway, so it was now or never. Drying her eyes against the back of her hand, she said, "Okay."

"Be careful," Caroline said, then added what Libby needed to hear more than anything else at that moment: "I love you."

CHAPTER 20

The perspiration beading on Libby's forehead had little to do with the warmth of the
morning sun. Standing on the porch of
Holton's shack, she took a deep breath,
wiped away the dampness, and knocked.
Without warning, the door thrust open, and
Holton's back was to her as he walked away.
As expected, he had a glass in his hand, and
the smell of gin hung heavy in the air.
"Hope you ain't here for the severance pay,"
he said, leaving her in the doorway as he
made his way to the couch.

"I need to talk," she said, wringing her
hands together as he plopped down onto
the couch. He waved her over to sit.

Reluctant to give up the possibility of a
quick exit, she maintained her position by
the front door.

He frowned at her. "Guess you saw the
default notice plastered on the house for
the entire world to see."

She hadn't seen it, but of course she'd already known about it from Tess. Giving him a sympathetic look, she said, "I'm sorry. You know you could fight it. Lots of people these days are in the same boat and —"

"I'm not fighting anything. Not anymore." He leaned his head back on the couch and stared at her with deadpan eyes.

"What happened between yesterday and today?"

Ice clinked as he drained his glass with one gulp. He picked up a bottle of gin from the end table and unscrewed the top to refill. "Took your advice and lost the last account." He held his glass up as if to toast her.

The revelation took her breath. She had been so sure her plan would work. After all, it had for Caroline.

He pointed the bottle at her. "And they practically laughed at me."

"I'm sorry," she whispered, trying to process that it wouldn't be her confession that would send him over the edge, just some well-meaning business advice.

His shoulders drooped and he nodded as though commiserating with her. "Hey, we gave it our best."

"What about online sales?" she asked.

His mocking laugh was quickly aborted.

"We get two visitors a day to the site. Pretty sure Tess is one of 'em."

The weight of guilt made her knees feel as though they would buckle, and she finally accepted his offer to sit. Moving a rumpled T-shirt out of the way, she sat beside him on the sofa. "I can't believe it didn't work. I was so sure."

He seemed to forget he already had a glass in his hand as he tilted the bottle over his mouth and took a long swallow, grimacing at the taste. He held it out to her as an offering. As disgusting as the sight of him was, she was half tempted at that moment to take him up on it. She studied the defeated look in his eyes and wondered if Adele had ever seen him this way and, if so, if she had known just what to say to snap him out of it. "You can't give up, Holt."

"Already have." He topped off his glass.

"What would Adele think?" It felt like a low blow, but desperate times deserved desperate measures.

"Everything's messed up because of me." He took another gulp.

"We can fix this," she said, wanting to grab the glass from his hand. "You've got to stop looking at the obstacles and start focusing on what you can do about them. We just need a plan."

The side of his mouth curled up into an almost-smile as he glanced over at her. "You know, you kind of remind me of her when she was younger."

"Yeah," she said with a smile, "her and that frizzy-haired girl in the elf movie." It surprised her that he only saw the resemblance between them when he was drinking.

"There's something I need to tell you," she said. It was now or never. She finally had the perfect segue.

He ran a hand through his disheveled hair. "I know what you're going to say."

"I don't think you do."

"You don't want me to let you go. It messes up your internship and you'll have to start over somewhere else."

"That's not what I wanted to talk to you about."

"You don't have to worry." He looked down at his glass. "If you don't tell it ended early, I won't."

"I'm not who you think I am." The moment she said it, it felt as though a hundred-pound weight had been lifted from her shoulders. Suddenly she couldn't wait to unload the other hundred pounds.

He stared at her so long, she was sure he was toying with her until he said, "I can't

198

believe she's gone." Apparently he had been too wrapped up in his own misery and thoughts to process her admission.

At first she thought he was talking about Adele, and then she realized he meant Tess.

"You didn't have to fire her, you know. I think she'd live in a box if it meant being with you."

"I know," he whispered. "I know she would." He started to push himself up to stand, but fell backward. He shook his head as though disgusted with himself. "Help me up," he said, putting out his hand for her to pull.

She doubted tiny her could do much to help him, but she stood, locked her knees, and reached down her hand anyway. His weight nearly toppled her as he slowly rose to his feet. "Let me make you some coffee."

He shook his head. "If you really want to help me, take Rufus to Tess."

She scrunched her face at him in question.

"I'm leaving him to her." He looked around his small house. "If you see anything you want, help yourself." He grabbed the brass lamp off the table and held it out to her. "If you don't like the looks of it, you can always scrap it."

She looked down at the lamp as under-

199

standing hit her like a sack of bricks. Psychology 101 — giving away possessions was a sign of suicide. "Do you have a gun?"

"Do you?" He sat back down on the sofa.

When he reached for the bottle, she was quicker and grabbed it away from him. "Answer me. Do you own a gun?"

"Pawned them both a couple months back." Before she could react, he snatched the bottle back out of her hand.

"Are you going to hurt yourself?"

He let out a mirthless laugh. "Nice detective work, Sherlock."

"Why?"

"Why not? Got nothing to live for. Lost Adele. Lost my house. Lost Tess. Lost everything that matters."

Her heart ached for him, but his despair was completely unnecessary. So he was going through a tough time. Everyone did, sooner or later. But you didn't answer a temporary problem with a permanent solution. "It doesn't have to be that way."

Still holding the bottle, he shrugged. "Some people don't deserve to be happy. Don't deserve to live."

"Listen to yourself, Holt. What could you have done that was bad enough to deserve to die over?" Once again she sat beside him, this time keeping a little more distance.

"Plenty."

She raised her eyebrows, waiting for him to explain.

"I already told you that I was the reason she died."

She studied his twisted red face. "You weren't in the car, right?"

He huffed as though her questions infuriated him. Well, too bad. This was her mother they were talking about.

"I have a right to know."

He took another swig from the bottle and slammed it down on the table. "Why do you have the right to know? Because you knew her? Big deal. Lots of people knew her. Lots of people cared about her. What makes you so special?"

When she realized now was the time to tell him, her heart missed a beat. She opened her mouth, but Holton cut her off before she could speak.

"She was the one who kept everything together. She was the brains. All I was good for was making art." Leaning his head back on the couch, he closed his eyes. "She believed in me."

"She's not the only one, you know," Libby said.

He looked for a minute like he might laugh, but instead his face tightened into an anguished ball and he started to cry. It was such a shocking sight that she had to fight the urge to turn away. Instead she slid over and put her arm around his shoulder. He laid his head against her like a child might do.

"Tess hates me now," he said, his wet eyes dampening the shoulder of her T-shirt.

"She doesn't hate you." Libby looked around for a box of tissues. "I'm pretty sure she's in love with you."

He looked up at her, his droopy eyes now red and wet.

She gave him a sad smile. "You love her too, don't you?"

He wiped his eyes against his knuckles as he shook his head. "When I love someone, God takes them away."

"I know how that feels. But maybe — I don't know — maybe it's not God. Maybe stuff just happens."

Sitting forward, he rested his elbows on his knees. "Nothing happens without him allowing it."

What she wanted to ask was why he would choose to follow someone who would take away the love of his life. It was strange to her that his response wasn't to reject God, but to reject love.

"When I married Adele, I thought I finally

had someone who wouldn't leave me. She was three years younger. I figured I'd have her for life." Tears started to flow down his cheeks again. "Should have had her for life." Without warning, his hand balled into a fist and he slammed it down on the cocktail table with a loud crack.

She jumped up, but she could tell by the defeated look on his face she wasn't in danger. He rubbed his hand. "Lost everything."

"You haven't lost me," she said, knowing how lame that sounded. To him she was just an intern. What did he care if he lost or kept her? It was time to tell him the truth. There would never be a better moment than right now, but she wasn't sure he was sober enough to remember it later. There was nothing to lose by trying, though. "I need to tell you something."

He pulled back and wiped his eyes again.

Her heart pounded against her rib cage as she slipped the adoption papers out of her back pocket and carefully unfolded them before him.

Holton swayed slightly in his seat, fighting to keep his eyes open. "What's that?"

He held the papers close, squinting at them, then closed one eye and held them at arm's length. After a few seconds, the color left him. "What is this?"

He hadn't known about her after all. Adele had never told him. "Your wife was my mother." At the moment the confession left her lips, she felt as naked and helpless as the day she was born.

She had prepared herself for shock, pain, and even anger, but the indifferent expression he wore felt crueler than the worst she had imagined. "It was the only way I could think of to get to know you without —"

He looked down at the adoption papers again, his thick eyebrows finally dipping in confusion. "This is a mistake. It must be another woman with the same name."

"She was born in Belhaven?" Libby asked.

Frowning, he said nothing.

"April 3, 1973?"

The papers dropped from his hand and fluttered to the carpet. "Can't be," he whispered.

She bent to pick them up. He reached for them at the same time and ripped one of the sheets from her hands, giving her a furious look. When she didn't let go, the page tore, and her heart tore with it. Those papers were all she had of her birth mother.

He looked at the partial sheet of paper in his hand, then glared at her.

She reached for it, but he yanked it back.

"Get out of here," he practically hissed.

"But —" she stammered.

"Don't know what your MO is." Balling up the paper he held, he narrowed his droopy eyes at her. "But you can take your little con somewhere else."

She snatched up the rest of the papers before he could rip those too. Fighting to speak, she managed to get out, "I just wanted to know who I am."

"I can tell you who you're not." He reached for the bottle of gin and downed the rest of it in one gulp, then threw the empty bottle at the wall. The loud crash made her jump as hunks of glass fell to the floor.

CHAPTER 21

When Libby finally left, Holton slammed the door behind her, growling as he did. This time he threw the dead bolt so she couldn't get back in. His head swam from alcohol and her bizarre story. Adele keeping a secret child from him . . . it was as ridiculous as a lie could get.

The girl had some kind of nerve, accusing his wife of such a thing. If it were any other woman, he might believe it. But Adele? She had been as close to sainthood as any human could be. He'd never known her to be dishonest about anything. Besides, what would her motivation be? If she'd had a child out of wedlock, he would be shocked, of course, but he wouldn't have held it against her. People made mistakes. He, of all people, understood that, and she had understood that about him.

He looked down at the shards of glass scattered near the wall, and the little gin that had been left in the bottle that was now trickling down the paint. Bending down to clean up, he pricked his thumb on a jagged hunk of glass. He felt the sting on his thumb and then a droplet of red rose up on his skin. Shoving the small wound into his mouth before it could trickle, he tasted copper. After giving the side of his thumb a gentle suck, he pulled it back to have a look.

Satisfied the bleeding had stopped, he bent to pick up more. As his hand touched down on another piece of glass, he thought better of it and stood back up. If things worked out as planned, he would be dead in a few days, maybe weeks, maybe even today. Let them find his dead body in a pile of filth. That's the kind of viewing he deserved.

Holding the wall to steady himself, he slowly stood. As he turned, the picture of Adele hanging crooked on the wall caught his eye. He walked over and straightened it. Framing his hands over her hair, he blocked out everything but her features, and his heart stopped. He was looking at an older version of the intern. Two of them, actually, if he didn't squint. *No,* he thought, *you're just drunk.*

He turned away and scanned the room for a bottle that wasn't empty. Finding

207

none, he walked to the bedroom, opened his closet, and pulled a full one from his stash on the shelf. If only he could down an entire bottle or two in one sitting without his body rejecting it into the toilet, he might finally end the pain.

He carried the bottle to the living room and set it on the now-cracked end table. As he unscrewed the cap, memories flooded his mind — the faded silver marks stretching across Adele's belly and breasts the first time they'd made love . . .

He slammed down a mouthful of gin. No, not the first time; those hadn't been there the first time. He'd asked her about them on their wedding night, and she said that she had let herself go at one point and gained, then lost, quite a few pounds. He'd had no reason not to believe her, and he still didn't.

He remembered, too, the picture of the newborn he'd found hidden behind another photo in one of her albums. She said it was the child of an old college roommate that she couldn't bring herself to throw away. It was clear she didn't want to talk about it and he asked no more questions. The truth was, he didn't really want to know. Even though he still didn't, his feet carried him back to the bedroom to search for it just the same.

Bottle in hand, he knelt on the old carpet and pulled the photo album out from under the bed. It was covered in a thick layer of dust and dog fur. With a quick swipe, he cleared the worst of it, watching strands of fur flitter along a shaft of light streaming in through the window. After the particles settled — and after a good, long drink — he began to tear through the pages, sliding his finger behind each picture. Three drinks and fifteen minutes later, he finally found it.

Holding his breath, he examined the child's face. It had a slightly upturned nose like Libby's, but so did a million other babies. He took another gulp from the bottle, no longer wincing at the burn gliding down his throat. He flipped the photograph around. Within a heart was the name Grace, carefully penned in Adele's unmistakable hand.

Dropping the picture, he ran for the bathroom.

A pounding echoed through the house. Holton opened one eye but saw only white. Opening the other, he could make out the faded linoleum pattern of his bathroom floor, then the commode he was lying beside. He lifted his head and the room

209

began to rotate back and forth like a boat on a rough sea. He laid his head back down, letting the coolness of the floor calm the vertigo.

The pounding continued as he closed his eyes again. He figured whoever it was would go away eventually. Except they didn't. Each knock on the front door felt like a punch to his temple. Unable to take it anymore, he pushed himself up, pausing to vomit one more time on the way to answer it.

A twerp in a suit stood on the other side of the door.

"Go away," he told him, holding his head between his hands, hoping the pressure would keep it from exploding.

"I'm Libby's fiancé."

The smell of the guy's cologne turned Holton's stomach. He slammed the door in his face and started back to the bathroom. The pounding began again. Rufus barked from the porch. Holton sighed and opened the door to let him in, along with another waft of the twerp's cologne.

The man slid his foot between the door and the jamb. "I'm not going anywhere until I talk to Libby."

Hearing the girl's name made Holton's temples pound louder. "You mean Grace, don't you? Hit the road or I'm calling the cops." With that he kicked the guy's foot out of the way, then slammed and locked the door. He desperately wanted to sleep, but then his liver would rid his body of all his hard work and he'd have to start drinking all over again. No, today was going to be the day.

As he made his way to the bedroom to resume where he'd left off, he heard more pounding, this time on the window. If the guy kept on, he was going to break it.

With a grunt, Holton walked to the window to see him holding a rusty folding chair like a bat. It was a threat. He picked up his phone in a threat of his own, but the guy pulled his arms back to swing at the window. The cops would come and arrest this nut, and Holton would be left with a broken front window he couldn't afford to fix. With his luck, it would take him weeks to die and it would storm every day. He decided it was easier just to talk to the moron.

Yanking the front door open, he yelled, "Are you crazy?"

The man threw the chair back into the corner where he'd gotten it with a loud clang. "Where's my girlfriend?"

"Are you talking about that lying — ?" Before he could get another word out, the man drew back his fist and punched him. A

211

jolt of pain exploded in his jaw and he fell to his knees. Holding his aching face, he looked up in disbelief.

"The only thing out of your mouth had better be an address."

Holton felt his face for blood as he jabbed his thumb out toward the studio. "Try the big barn out back. If not, don't know."

Grabbing the doorknob, the man turned around and looked down at him. "Why did you call her that?"

"My wife didn't have any kids."

The man frowned. "Did she show you the papers?"

"Forgery," Holton said, the word vibrating through his skull like a jackhammer. He struggled to his feet. "Hit me again, I'll lay you out." He hoped the kid wouldn't call him on it. There was more to his scrawny fists than met the eye. He couldn't help but wonder if there had been more to Adele too.

"Here I am fighting to keep her, and you're just throwing her away," the man said with a look of contempt. "You're not just a pathetic drunk; you're the world's biggest idiot."

CHAPTER 22

Alison Krauss's latest blared from the clock radio, but it did little to drown out the pangs left by yet another parental rejection. Libby lifted herself up, balled her fist, and punched her tear-soaked pillow. She felt the air squash out of its stuffing, but felt no better for it.

Although she had warned herself time and again that Holton might not react well to the news that she was Adele's daughter, she hadn't been prepared for him to accuse her of being a con artist.

Logic told her that he was drunk, and people who were drunk didn't act the way they might if they were in their right minds. He was going through a lot at the moment, maybe the roughest time of his life. It could have all come down to timing, but even knowing that didn't stop the pain.

There was nothing left to do but put him behind her, just as she'd done with George.

Maybe Adele had other relatives out there somewhere who could fill in the blanks. Or maybe the blanks would have to remain empty. Either way, as disappointing as it was, it was time to stop beating this dead horse and move on.

Caesar purred as he rubbed against her leg. She picked him up, held him against her chest, and stroked him. He rewarded her with a lick on the nose from his sandpaper tongue. "You love me, don't you?" she asked, wiping his slobber away.

He squirmed, wanting to be let down.

She set him free, and in one fluid movement, he extended his front paws and jumped to the floor. "You're rejecting me too?"

A man's voice rose above the music. Leaning on her elbows, she turned off the radio and raised her head to get a better listen.

A tuft of curly dark hair ascended the stairs. Fear paralyzed her for a split second until she recognized Rob's face.

Rubbing her eyes, she tried to erase the evidence that she'd been crying.

Still dressed for work, he tucked his hands into the pockets of his dress slacks and looked around the small apartment. "I called to you, but I guess you couldn't hear me over the music." His gaze finally settled on her. "So this is where you've been staying? It's not at all what I pictured."

"What are you doing here?" she asked, hopeful, realizing he must have talked to Caroline.

"Are you okay?" He kept a tentative distance between them that made her tears want to come back.

"Why wouldn't I be?"

He ran a hand through his hair. "I just came from Holton's house."

Shame filled her. "Oh," she said, averting her eyes. So that was what this was: a pity visit.

"Mind if I sit?" The formality of his question and standoffish body language were almost more than her heart could take.

"Please," she said, pointing to the desk chair. He set it near the bed and took a seat across from her.

He scanned the room, his gaze finally settling on the dying jar of daisies, then the framed picture of himself sitting beside it. A look of sadness passed over him. "What happened over there?"

She bent her knees up on the bed and hugged them as Caesar greeted Rob by dragging himself against his pant leg. Rob leaned down and scratched his back. "Caroline told me you were picking him up. You didn't need to, you know."

Fighting to keep the tears at bay, she said, "I finally told him who I was." When Rob kept his eyes on the cat instead of her, she knew he already at least had a good idea of what happened. He must think her completely pathetic. "He called me a liar and kicked me out." No longer able to fight back the tears, her eyes welled again.

Rob left his chair to sit on the bed beside her. It creaked and dipped under his weight. He rubbed her back as she cried. His touch, his familiar smell, and the fact that he had driven all the way here just for her was as much comfort as anything she could have hoped for.

After a few minutes, she gently shook him off and dried her eyes for the umpteenth time. "Thanks. I really needed that."

"Me too," he said. He was close enough that she could smell the spearmint on his breath. "I've missed you so much, Libby."

She tried to smile. "I've missed you too."

"So what are you going to do now?" His lips disappeared inside his mouth — something he only did when he was nervous. Was it because he wanted her back or because he was afraid that she might want him? One more rejection was all it would take in her fragile state to devastate her. She couldn't take that chance. Not today.

"I guess I go home, find another job, and get back to life."

"Our life or yours?" His eyes were all vulnerability, which told her that he did still want her after all. The fact that someone did made her feel better. Suddenly she wanted nothing more than to marry him. To become Mrs. Robert Beddow right there and then. To once and for all accept the love of the one person in her life who accepted her no matter what.

"I almost bought a house for us," he said.

Her eyebrows shot up and she grinned. "You did what?"

"Caroline said you'd been to it before and loved it. She even offered to loan us the down payment."

Owing Caroline anything was always a mistake. "You didn't —" she started to say.

"No, but I was close. I just wanted to give you someplace to belong, but I figured I should at least ask you before making a decision that big."

Somewhere to belong sounded more than a little nice. "Good call," she said. "Which house was it?"

He described a large house in an affluent neighborhood. Though she didn't remember this particular home, she did know the neighborhood well. A lot of Caroline's friends lived there. Nothing could have been further from her taste. "There's no way we could afford that area."

"Maybe we could," he said. "I never got the chance to tell you that I made partner."

Despite how bad she felt at the moment, this was big for him — huge. She gave him her widest smile and most enthusiastic voice. "That's awesome!"

He grimaced and lifted a shoulder in a half shrug. "Caroline pulled a few strings."

When Rob first got the job, Caroline had hinted that she might have had a little something to do with it. Libby asked no questions because she didn't want to know. He had been so proud, so confident for a change, and she didn't want to ruin it for him. "Did you ask her to?"

He rubbed his hands together nervously. "Not exactly. Sort of. I don't know."

"But you're not happy about it."

"I'm happy," he said glumly.

"Clearly you're not."

He crossed his legs and fiddled with the leather tassel on his shoe. "I guess I wanted to do it on my own. I don't feel like I've earned it."

She didn't understand why, if he had wanted to accomplish it on his own, he had agreed to any help from Caroline, but she didn't have the energy to probe further right then. It was likely to lead to an argument and she was already emotionally spent. "I want to go home," she said. Although she meant nothing more by it than that she wanted to get out of here and to her apartment, the ear-to-ear smile on Rob's face told her that he took it as complete reconciliation. His reaction, in such stark contrast to Holton's, further warmed her heart.

She slid over and laid her head on his shoulder, feeling suddenly vulnerable. "What if you don't really love me? What if you just think you do?" She was fishing for reassurance, as he was constantly doing, but a little ego stroking from the one she loved wasn't such a bad thing now and then, especially when she knew that he'd give it to her freely.

"You're the only girl I've ever loved. Man, Lib, you're the only girl I've ever even dated."

Stunned, she pulled back and studied him. At the beginning of their relationship she'd asked if he'd had other relationships, and he claimed to have just broken up with a longtime girlfriend from high school. She liked the fact that he never talked about her. Now she knew why. "What about Carly?"

His face and neck mottled, and he looked at his lap rather than at her. "I kind of made her up."

She stood and looked down at him. If he'd lied about something as stupid as that, what else had he lied about? "How do you kind of make someone up?"

His eyes darted back and forth, frantically searching hers. "I was just embarrassed to tell you the truth. You'd dated lots of guys. I thought you would think I was a loser. Don't be mad."

If she had known he'd never dated anyone except her, she never would have allowed herself to get serious with him. Maybe he didn't really love her after all. Maybe if he got a taste of what was out there, he would realize that she was nothing special. If they married, he might always wonder. She definitely would. Everyone else in her life had figured out she wasn't worth it. It was only a matter of time until he did too. "If I'm the only one you ever dated, how can you be sure I'm the one for you? You don't even know what else is out there."

When he sighed, his whole body seemed to go limp. "I know."

"You can't know. It's like being a vegetarian and eating your first steak. You can't say a T-bone is your favorite if you've never tried a prime rib. Maybe you'd like the prime rib better."

"I don't have to eat a prime rib to know the T-bone is my cut. You're my cut, Libby."

She shook her head. "You need to pick your menu back up and try a few other dishes. I'm not saying order them all. Just look at them. Smell them. See if one makes you happier."

He held his forehead as though fighting a headache. "A chopped steak or filet isn't going to make me happy. You make me happy."

"We're going to change over the years. I was medium-rare and already I'm well-done. You should try different cuts, different temperatures." Her mind was swirling with the smell of cooking beef, menus, and metaphors.

He stood and crossed then uncrossed his arms, looking flustered. "You can think whatever you want. You can say I don't know what I want, but I do."

"I want you to see other people. Just try," she said, even as she prayed he wouldn't.

"I don't want to see other people. I don't want to order off any menu. I don't want to order another steak. I have the only one in the restaurant that appeals to me. You're well-done, but you *were* medium-rare. What does that mean, anyway?" His voice rose a couple octaves as he began to pace. "You're changing? Good. People are supposed to change. You're supposed to cook the longer you stay on the grill. I don't care if you dry out into jerky. You're my girl, Libby." He stopped pacing and locked eyes with her. "You always will be."

He looked so convincing, so sure of himself. But he didn't know if someone would be a better fit for him. He couldn't. What if he realized it two years into their marriage when he met a type of woman he didn't think existed? What would happen to her then? If she really was the only one in the world for him, then putting himself out there would confirm, not change it. She couldn't take the chance that he was settling without even realizing it. "I'm sorry, Rob," she whispered. "If you don't need to pick up the menu, then maybe I do." She had no desire to date — she'd been there, done that . . . unlike him.

"You want to order steak? Go ahead." His tone became eerily calm. "I'm the same hamburger I always was and always will be. But I'm not well-done, Libby. I'm rare." He tapped his chest. "See the blood dripping from my heart? I'm so rare I'm mooing."

It should have been funny. It was the

stupidest conversation they'd ever had, and they'd had some doozies, but all she felt was hopeless.

"I think you should go home now." She laid her head back down on the damp pillow and closed her eyes.

Listening to the sound of his heavy breathing, she willed herself not to cry again, not until he left. Something clinked loudly, and she looked over to see that he'd overturned his picture.

The last sound she heard was his footsteps pounding down the stairs.

CHAPTER 23

After gathering her belongings from the barn apartment and tidying up, Libby packed Caesar and her suitcase into the Jeep and drove the short distance to Holton's shack so that she could return the key. She considered just mailing it to him when she got home, but she wasn't sure how many copies he had, and with him getting ready to lose his place to foreclosure, he might need it sooner rather than later. Besides, if she was being honest with herself, she wanted to see him one last time, if only through the window.

Maybe it was some small measure of closure she sought, or maybe it was a sliver of hope that he might have sobered and reconsidered his feelings.

Climbing the rickety stairs to his porch, she felt old and weary. She paused midway to look out over the ocean, knowing it would be the last time she would ever see this stretch of beach from this exact angle. Moonlight gleamed off the waves softly rolling in as the breeze carried to her the distinct scent of brine.

She would miss this view, this smell, and even constantly brushing sawdust off herself . . . and, of course, Tess. The thing she would miss most of all, though, was the hope she had once felt here.

The barn key felt cold and small in her hand. Beside the front door hung an old mailbox. It creaked as she opened it, while a peppering of rust rained down. Metal clinked against metal as she set the single key inside and closed the hatch. She half expected Holton to hear her and run out screaming, but the only sound that met her ears was that of the ocean.

She peeked through the window and at first saw nothing but an empty couch. When she looked down, she spotted his hand on the floor. The rest of him was out of view, hidden by the wall she stood on the other side of. She'd started to turn around when movement caught her eye and she took another look. His hand had begun to twitch, then shake violently.

She banged on the window, then ran to the door and twisted the handle. For the first time, it was locked. With all her might she pounded her fist against wood, screaming his name as her heart pounded.

Hurriedly she scanned the small porch. Two rusty folding chairs lay in the corner. Without a moment's pause, she picked one up and swung it hard against the window. The sound of shattering glass filled the air. Using the legs of the chair, she broke away the jagged pieces of glass left behind, clearing the way for her to climb in.

Rufus appeared and was now barking ferociously at her, teeth bared. "It's me," she said, hoping he would recognize her voice. His tail began to wag, and his growl turned into whining, telling her that she was safe.

With a thud, she dropped the chair on the porch and carefully climbed through the window, scraping the back of her thigh on a remaining shard.

Inside, she smelled an awful mix of body fluids and knew before she even saw him that it was bad. He lay on the floor flailing as though possessed. He was covered in vomit, his eyes had rolled back in his head, and the front of his shorts was wet. His color was the dark side of gray.

Not knowing what to do, she ran over and shook him, but he just continued to seize. Panic clouded her mind and she found herself running from the kitchen and back to him again, looking for something but not knowing what.

Calm down, she told herself. *For all you know he does this all the time. Maybe he's an epileptic. Maybe he has pills for this.*

She hurried to the bathroom and checked his medicine cabinet. She found ibuprofen, Tums, and a half-full bottle of Pepto-Bismol, but not a single prescription bottle.

Calm your breathing, she told herself. *Or you're going to end up passing out too.*

She drew in a slow, deep breath and exhaled through pursed lips. *Call Caroline. She'll know what to do. No, Tess — she knows him. She'll know if he has a condition.*

She took the phone out of her front pocket, and with hands shaking almost as badly as Holton's were, she pulled Tess's name up on the contact list and hit Dial.

Mercifully Tess answered on the second ring. "Libby, I'm glad you called. I wanted to tell you —"

"It's Holton," Libby said breathlessly.

"Whatever it is, I don't care. I'm done with —"

"He's having a seizure or something."

"Where are you?"

"His house. Does he have epilepsy?"

"No. Alcohol poisoning is more like it."

"What should I do?"

"Call 911," she said. "I'm on my way. Just make sure he keeps breathing."

The line went dead. Libby watched with horror as Holton's chest arched off the ground, then slammed to the floor over and over. Rufus bayed, looking to her to do something. Holton's color grew increasingly dark, and only when the seizure finally ended was she able to tell that he was indeed breathing, but abnormally slow and shallow.

He's going to die, she thought in horror. She used the hem of his shirt to wipe the corner of his mouth and turned his head to the side in case he should vomit again.

After she called for an ambulance, she knelt beside him, just watching for what seemed like an eternity, as the dispatcher stayed on the phone.

Tires on gravel sounded from the driveway, and she ran to the window to see Tess's truck screech to a halt out front. "Thank you, God," Libby breathed.

Tess jumped out of the cab, not bothering to close the door. Her hair hung loose as she bolted up the stairs, taking them two at a time. Her wild gaze shot to the broken window on her way to the front door.

Libby rushed to the door and opened it.

"I'm so glad you're here."

"Is he breathing?" Tess pushed past her to get to Holton.

Libby covered the phone receiver. "Yes, but it's too slow, and he keeps making these weird rattling sounds."

"You called for an ambulance?"

"The dispatcher's on the phone. They should be here any minute."

Tess looked terrified as she knelt beside Holton and took his hand in hers. "Holt, if you can hear me, you better not die. I mean it. You better not. The ambulance is on its way. Hold on." Tears rolled down her freckled cheeks. "Please hold on."

She let his hand go and laid both hands on his chest, closed her eyes, and started to mumble. It took Libby a second to understand that she was praying.

CHAPTER 24

Libby and Tess spent the night sitting in the intensive care unit waiting room, sipping bitter vending machine coffee and making small talk. It had been hours since they'd last received an update from the doctor, so they still knew nothing more than the fact that Holton was alive and that Tess had been right — the seizures were due to alcohol poisoning.

The artificial lights flickering down on them were starting to give Libby a headache, and it occurred to her that she didn't need to be here. Holton didn't care about her, so why should she care about him?

But one look at Tess reminded her whom she was really here to support. Tess sat beside her with her unruly red hair cascading over slumped shoulders. With half moons under her eyes, she stared wearily at the television screen perched high in the corner of the small, sterile-looking room.

An infomercial for some overpriced shampoo promised to transform even the most brittle hair into a silky, shiny mane after just one application.

Tess looked at her watch, then at Libby. "I wish someone would tell us what's going on already."

"Maybe you should go home and get some sleep," Libby said. "You could always come back in the morning."

"I'm not going anywhere until I know he's okay."

Libby spotted a magazine rack hanging on the far wall and walked over to it. "I thought you were done with him."

"I'm never going to be done with him," Tess practically sighed.

Riffling through dog-eared copies of *Newsweek, Glamour,* and *People,* all with their address labels cut off in neat rectangles, Libby said, "I know you love him, but when's enough enough?"

"I don't love him," she said a little too defensively.

Libby looked over her shoulder, raising an eyebrow at Tess. "Oh, come on."

Tess hid her face in her hands, then ran them through her hair. "That obvious?"

After choosing a two-year-old *Glamour* with a blonde waif posing on the cover,

231

Libby returned to her seat. "To everyone but him."

Tess picked up her coffee cup from the small table beside her chair, took a sip, and wrinkled her nose at it. "He wouldn't notice if a plane crashed into the side of his studio."

"Unless it was carrying booze," Libby said, feeling a little guilty for the joke.

Tess's smile disappeared as quickly as it had come. "I knew something like this was going to happen. I know it's not my fault, but I feel guilty anyway. Like there's something more I should have done to help him."

Unable to focus on the articles, Libby set the magazine down on the table in front of her and picked up her paper cup. It was still warm, but barely. "It's not your fault any more than it is mine. He's a grown man. He makes his own choices."

"My grandfather was an alcoholic," Tess said, studying her as though testing her reaction before continuing. "He was a grown man too, but the addiction turned him into a child. It's a terrible disease."

Libby had heard so many behaviors called diseases, from drug abuse to sex addictions, and the term never rubbed her quite right. Now might not be the right time or place to say so, but she felt safe enough with Tess to speak her mind. She took a sip of her coffee. It tasted like day-old instant decaf.

"I never understood that," she said. "Calling a choice a disease. I mean, if you get cancer, you didn't choose it, but it still might kill you. That's a disease. But drinking or drugging is something a person chooses to do."

Tess gave her a long, hard look. "Have you ever been addicted to anything?"

Libby shifted in her seat, feeling uncomfortable under Tess's scrutiny. "Just chocolate and feeling sorry for myself, I guess."

The joke failed to disarm Tess. "If I told you to stop feeling sorry for yourself, could you?"

She gave it some thought. She probably could have a more positive attitude and outlook if she focused on it hard enough, maybe got some counseling. It dawned on her then that Rob's obsessive insecurity was a sort of addiction too, but a disease?

"I don't understand it either," Tess said, her expression finally softening as she leaned back in her vinyl chair. "I just know some people seem to be wired differently. I could drink every day for a month and not get addicted, while my grandfather would take one sip after two years dry and not be able to stop until he blacked out. I watched him try to quit so many times in so many

233

different ways. I don't know if it's that way for everyone who abuses alcohol, but for him it was definitely a disease."

"What happened to him? Is he — ?"

The sound of laughter rose from the hallway outside the waiting room, and Libby looked up to see a group of nurses carrying frozen dinners and insulated lunch bags as they passed by.

"He passed away last year," Tess said, sounding more thoughtful than sad.

Libby took another sip from her coffee cup. "I'm sorry."

"Don't be. He's in a better place now."

The infomercial finally ended, only to be replaced by another for an ice-pulverizing blender. Tess stared at the TV. After a few seconds, she shook her head as though snapping herself out of a trance. "I'm just glad he had a chance to get his life together and make amends before he died."

"How'd he manage to do that?"

A young man covered in tattoos with sweat stains under his arms walked into the waiting room and sat on the other side of the room. Throwing him a glance, Tess said, "It's a crazy story, the kind that's so over-the-top you hate to tell it because no one believes you."

"Try me," Libby said.

Tess walked her nearly full coffee cup over to the trash can by the door and dropped it in before returning to her seat, oblivious to the dribble of brown that had splashed her white T-shirt. "He walked into church one day — no, stumbled was more like it. You could smell the booze just oozing from his pores. I was there with my parents, and we were all holding our breath." She blushed, then laughed at herself. "I don't mean from the smell. It's just that he had embarrassed us so many times and we thought this was going to be the worst of the worst." Looking deep in thought, she paused. She was quiet for so long, Libby thought she had forgotten to finish the story. Finally she continued. "He walked up to the pulpit. The whole church was quiet as a morgue as we watched him throw himself onto the altar. I remember his hairy knuckles clutching it." She shot Libby a sideways glance and smiled almost apologetically.

"Of all the weird things to stick in my mind, eh? Anyway, the preacher told someone to call an ambulance, but before anyone had a chance to react, Pa-Pa pushed himself up and walked out, straight and steady, like nothing had happened." Tess glanced at her watch. "That was it. He never drank again."

Tess had been right about the story sounding far-fetched. If she hadn't known Tess, Libby would have assumed she was prone to exaggeration, but she was actually more likely to play a story down than up. If Tess said that's the way it happened, then that's the way it probably happened. "He later told us he laid his drinking at the foot of the cross that day and decided that's where it should stay."

"Wow," Libby said. "I guess when you decide to quit, you decide to quit."

Tess picked up the magazine Libby had laid down and began flipping through it. "Maybe, but I think it was more than that."

"Like a miracle or something?"

Tess stopped flipping pages long enough to study a model dabbing her neck with an oversize bottle of perfume. She unfolded the flap at the edge of the page, brought it to her nose, and sniffed. "Yeah, like a miracle."

She offered it to Libby, and she took a sniff. It smelled like baby powder on steroids. "You don't really believe that stuff, do you?"

Tess laughed as she threw the magazine back on the table. "Yes, I believe that stuff. Don't you?"

Libby was quiet for a moment, deciding whether she did or didn't. God hadn't been someone she'd given much thought to. He probably existed. It made more sense than amoebas morphing into humans. But fathers, earthly or heavenly, had never been something she'd been able to count on. "I guess it's a little easier to believe in miracles if you've experienced one yourself."

Tess squinted at her. "Love's a miracle. You've experienced that."

A flash of white caught Libby's periphery, and she turned to see the same doctor they'd spoken to earlier standing in the doorway. She had long brown hair tied into a neat ponytail at the nape of her neck and looked as though she hadn't slept in a week. Tess jumped up. "How is he?"

"Mr. Creary is stable for now." She rubbed the back of her neck as she eyed the chair across from Libby. "Do you mind if I sit?"

Libby wrung her hands as the women took their seats. She didn't know why she was so anxious. Why should she be? He hated her. Still, she felt a knot in her stomach as she waited for the verdict.

The doctor pulled a small pager out of her lab jacket pocket and pressed a button. "You two are family? I'm sorry; I can't remember what you told me earlier."

"She is," Tess said, looking toward Libby.

Libby felt the truth of Tess's words at that

moment. It made no difference if Holton believed she was Adele's daughter or not. He was her stepfather and they would always be family, which was something neither of them had a whole lot of.

"Did someone come by from billing?" the doctor asked, grimacing at her own question.

"Yes," Libby said. "He's not insured, so the lady who spoke to us said a social worker would call in the morning to go over some options."

"I hate to ask," she said apologetically. "We just don't want to shock you with a hundred-thousand-dollar bill."

What little color Tess had left drained from her face. "He can't afford anything like that."

The doctor gave an empathetic smile, sweeping the bangs from her eyes. "We're a nonprofit hospital, which basically means we don't deny anyone treatment for inability to pay."

Libby thought of Caroline. A bill like that would be nothing for her, but to Holton, it was another nail in his financial coffin. He was a believer, so where was his miracle?

"The cost is particularly important because of what I'm proposing." When the doctor crossed her legs, the hem of her green scrub pant leg raised enough to give a glimpse of her Minnie Mouse socks. Libby thought the choice odd, but she tried not to stare.

"Mr. Creary inhaled something into his lungs, most likely emesis — or in layman's terms, vomit. He's at risk until we can clear it. On a positive note, he's been up-front about his drinking problem. He gave me permission to speak freely about it, which is a very good sign that he's serious about recovery." She looked down at her pager again. "Drinking as much as he has for as long as he has, I'm surprised he doesn't have cirrhosis already."

"He's talking?" Tess said, her eyes lighting up for the first time that night. "Can I see him?"

The doctor put her hand up. "Yes, but let me finish. We're going to detox him while he's here."

Tess gasped. Or maybe it was Libby. She couldn't be sure.

The doctor continued without reacting to their surprise. "He's going to be here anyway to treat what's likely to become aspiration pneumonia. I don't know if you've ever heard the term *delirium tremens*?" She looked between them.

Libby shrugged while Tess nodded. The

239

doctor focused on Libby since she was the clueless one.

"When someone is addicted to alcohol and suddenly stops drinking, they can experience some pretty harsh and dangerous symptoms, including depression, seizures, even death. It's painful on every possible level. He's agreed to let us keep him under while we clear his lungs, which will also make his detoxing a lot more comfortable for him." She cleared her throat. "We plan to keep him sedated just for a few days until his body detoxes. You're not going to have another chance to talk to him for a little while, so now's the time."

Libby watched Tess fighting back tears. The doctor put a hand on her back and consoled her with a pat. "It's okay. This alcohol poisoning might have been a blessing in disguise. Now he can —"

"No," Tess interrupted. "I know. I'm not crying because I'm sad. I'm crying because I'm happy." She turned to Libby with an ear-to-ear smile. "He's finally hit his rock bottom. I didn't think he had one." Without warning, she leaned over and wrapped her arms tightly around Libby's shoulders. "He has one, Libby."

Chapter 25

Holton's head pounded, and if he had anything left in his stomach, he wouldn't have been able to keep it down. The nurses kept telling him to get some sleep, but they wouldn't turn off the glaring lights so he could. Beeps and buzzes sounded in every direction. The staff was constantly parading through his room, changing IV bags, poking him for more blood, and studying the bag draining his urine as if it were the most fascinating thing in the world. The blood-pressure cuff around his arm was set to inflate every fifteen minutes, and each time it did it squeezed so hard he was sure his hand would pop off. He would have had an easier time trying to sleep between two rows of winning slot machines while being tasered than in that ICU.

Even if the conditions were ideal for rest, he doubted he'd be able to anyway. His mind wouldn't stop turning over Libby's claim that she was Adele's long-lost daughter. He had known everything there was to know about his late wife, or thought he had. If the girl was telling the truth, then it meant Adele had lied to him. Maybe not outright. It wasn't like he ever thought to ask if she'd given up any children for adoption, but the way he figured it, not telling him something that important was a lie by omission. He just couldn't believe she would deceive him like that. Still, everything else added up.

He stared out the window overlooking the hospital parking lot. More memories that never made sense before began to fit together. He had never understood why every October, like clockwork, Adele became sullen, or why she stared hard at every little girl with dark hair — and the older she got, the older the children she stared at became. More than any of that, there was no mistaking Libby's resemblance.

If Adele did have a child before they'd married, why not tell him? What was she planning on doing if the child came knocking one day? It just didn't make sense.

Whether Libby was right or wrong about Adele being her biological mother, she definitely believed it. The broken look in her eyes when he called her a liar would forever haunt him. He owed her an apology for yelling at her like he did. It wasn't her fault. Besides the apology, he needed to at least thank her for saving his life . . . again. The doctor told him if Libby hadn't found him when she did, he might have suffered brain damage or died. The dying would have been fine; living out the rest of his life having to have someone feed and diaper him, not so much.

He heard footsteps in the hallway and knew immediately by the way she walked harder on her right foot than her left that it was Tess.

She poked her head through the doorway and smiled. Her red hair was a mess, her eyes were bloodshot and swollen, and she'd spilled what looked like a dribble of coffee down the front of her white T-shirt, but she was still a sight for sore eyes. She smiled shyly. "Hey, stranger, how you feeling?"

His hand felt almost too heavy to lift as he waved her in. The clear tubing attached to the IV in his hand hit the bed rail. The bright light shining down on him from the ceiling gave her an odd, almost-greenish hue. Knowing her, she had been worried to death about him. It sickened him to think of how many times over the years she had suffered because of his selfishness and stupidity.

She walked to his bedside, leaned down, and kissed his cheek. Her lips were warm and soft, and she smelled of cherry and faintly of the coffee spilled on her shirt. "You almost died, you know."

Suddenly whatever he'd aspirated tried hard to get out, and a cough seized him. It felt as though someone had set his lungs on fire. With a fist he covered his mouth and turned his head toward the wall, away from her. After a few seconds the spasms stopped, but his chest hurt worse than ever. Everything hurt.

He turned back to Tess, who now had a stack of worry lines etched into her forehead. "Are you okay?"

He tried to smile. "Never better."

"You're lucky to be alive," she said. Her voice was the kind of scratchy that only came from hours of screaming or plenty of crying.

"You sound like my doctor." He grabbed a tissue from the small box on his bedside table, wiped his mouth with it, and dropped it into the wastebasket beside his bed. "She said I could have suffered worse than death. I could have had a stroke, or all my organs could have shut down and I could be on life support right now. If I do this again, I might die — or worse, I might live the rest of my life as an invalid." He studied her green eyes, her strawberry-blonde lashes, and freckled nose, and knew that even then she would still be by his side. The last thing in the world he would ever want to be was a burden — to her or to anyone. But that's exactly what he had turned into.

Tess looked as tired as he felt. "So don't do this again."

"Did they tell you they're going to knock me out for a few days and detox me?"

Her eyes glinted, and he loved her for it. She was always hoping for the best from him. He had held that kind of belief in someone once, and looking at Tess then made him almost remember how good that could feel.

"I'm proud of you," she said.

He suppressed the smile that wanted to form. For the first time in a long while, he was actually kind of proud of himself too. "Some choice. Detox without drugs or with. Which would you choose?"

She wrapped her arms around herself as though she were suddenly cold. "Don't play this off like it's not a big deal. I know what you're doing, and I'm allowed to be proud of you. You can do this, Holt."

He put his hand on hers, knowing that she meant it. "When I was lying on the floor at home, I couldn't even reach for my phone. I thought I was having a heart attack. I've never been that scared in my life."

She held his cold hand between her warm ones. "Me too."

"I thought I was going to see Adele." He'd always heard that when a person was getting ready to die, their life flashed before their eyes, but it was Adele's face that flashed before his. The look of disappointment was not a pretty sight at all.

Tess's grip loosened slightly and she looked down.

"You know what's funny?" he said. "I was more afraid of facing her in heaven than dying. Do you know how ticked off she'd be at me for the mess I've made of my life?"

"Not to mention the way you treated her daughter."

Her daughter. It sounded so strange to his ears. All the years they'd spent trying to have children, and she had one out there all along.

"I didn't know," he finally said. "She never told me." He knew then that he believed Libby. Which made him feel guilty, because his faith in the girl meant less faith in his wife. There was no denying it, though, as much as he wanted to. It was time to stop denying a lot of things. Sweeping everything that didn't suit him under the rug had ruined his life. Maybe the opposite would also be true.

"Sounds like your beef was with her, not Libby. It's not her fault how she came into the world."

"I know," he said. A fresh wave of shame washed over him, making him want a drink in the worst possible way.

Tess glanced around the room, taking in all the machines and gizmos. "Yeah, I wondered about that. She's a good kid, Holt. She just wants to know who she is."

"Makes two of us. I've probably got more questions for her than answers, though."

A middle-aged blonde dressed in blue scrubs walked into the room carrying a glass bottle and a fresh bag of IV fluids. "I need to hook you up now."

Tess's gaze traveled down the front of the nurse, sizing her up as she did any woman who crossed his path. She turned her attention back to Holton. "Guess we'd better say good-bye for now."

"Looks like I'm heading off to la-la land," he said, dreading what was to come. The doctor said he'd be out of it, but what if he wasn't? What if he just couldn't react to the pain and panic he felt? "Guess I'll see you on the flip side," he said.

Her eyes glistened with tears. "I'll be praying for you."

He squeezed her hand. "I'm scared."

She smiled sadly. "Bravery is being terrified but doing it anyway."

"I feel anything but," he said. "Tell the girl I'm sorry and I'll do everything I can to help her when I'm out of here."

She brushed his hair off his forehead and kissed it. "I will."

Suddenly afraid to be left alone with no one there he knew or cared about, he grabbed Tess's hand as she started to leave. "Hey, how about when I come home I take you out for a steak?"

She laughed as she gave his fingers a final squeeze. "We're both broke. Better make it the dollar menu at McDonald's."

He opened his mouth to say he wasn't that broke, but then remembered his boycott on denial. "It's a date," he said instead.

Wiping at her eyes, she said, "Do you know how long I've been waiting to hear those three little words come out of your mouth?" She looked over at the nurse, who was now threading tubing through a machine on his IV pole. "You're my witness. He asked me out."

The nurse looked down at Holton, then back to Tess with a lost expression.

"You don't need a witness." His mind returned to that terrifying moment alone on his living room floor when he thought he was going to die. As much as he hated to admit it, even to himself, he wasn't the island he'd tried to make himself out to be. He needed people. He needed Tess. And he could tell by the look in her eyes that she needed him too. "I'm not going to try and get out of it."

She bent down and kissed his lips softly. "I love you, Holton Creary."

The polite thing to do would be to say he loved her too, but he wasn't quite ready to part with those three little words.

CHAPTER 26

Not having slept all night, Libby decided to crash at Tess's apartment until she was rested enough to make the drive home. The building itself was a typical brick-face, three-story number. Tess's stake of the place was small — only seven hundred square feet or so — but she made it appear more spacious by decorating it in airy monochromatic whites. Artwork hung on every available parcel of wall, but it wasn't until early afternoon, when Libby finally awoke, that she was able to get a good look at it.

The sun shone through the window behind the couch, making the insides of her lids glow red, and the smell of honeysuckle surrounded her. She rubbed her eyes and slowly opened them. It took a moment for her disorientation to ebb as she remembered where she was. The source of the fragrance was a white candle resting on the cocktail table in front of the couch she'd slept on.

Lining the wall across from the couch was a row of small and large boxes, the lists of their contents scrolled across the tops in black magic marker.

Lying on her back, she pushed herself onto her elbows and looked around the apartment. Hanging on the wall across from her was a huge nautical still life, mounted on a rustic wood shelf that appeared to be nothing more than a splintered wood beam, stained walnut. On top of it sat a rusty anchor and an antique wood helm with a circle of tarnished brass outlining its center. Conch shells, starfish, and sand dollars surrounded the two larger pieces, and faux seaweed had been woven throughout all of it.

It was an odd mix, but together it worked perfectly. She had never seen anything quite like it.

On the wall beside the kitchen hung an enormous mosaic of the sea. Sitting up, she stretched long and slow before making her way over to it to have a better look. The mosaic wasn't made up of tiles like others she'd seen. This one was comprised entirely of seashells. The waves were made of blue and purple bits of broken shells, the sky of small white clamshells, and the sun of an assortment of gold and orange miniature conchs. She ran her fingertips gently over the bumpy piece, marveling at the artistry and texture.

"Good morning," Tess said behind her.

Libby startled, a hand flying to her chest.

Tess's long hair hung wild and matted slightly on one side. Her eyes were puffy and her sweatpants inside out. "Sorry, I didn't mean to scare you. How'd you sleep?"

"Like a rock," Libby said. It was her standard answer whenever she slept away from home, regardless of how restless her night might have been. In this case, however, she really did sleep well. As tired as she was, she could have fallen asleep on a brush pile. "Did Holton do this?" She pointed to the mosaic.

Tess hesitated. "No, this is what I do when I'm bored. I know it's nothing to —"

Libby's jaw dropped. "*You* made this?"

Tess's cheeks turned a rosy shade of pink. "Is it that bad?"

She laughed. "That *good*. It's amazing."

Tess looked down. "You really think so, or are you just trying to make me feel good?"

Libby touched one small, smooth shell that had been sanded into opalescence by the ocean. "Have you ever tried to sell one of these?"

Tess shrugged, then shook her head.

"Are you kidding? I would love to have one of these. This must have taken you forever to put together."

"About a month," Tess said, considering her own work as if for the first time.

Of all the fad artwork Caroline's rich friends paid an arm and a leg for, none of it was half as beautiful. How could Tess not know what she had? "I'll bet you could ask four or five grand."

Scrunching her nose like Libby was crazy, Tess said, "In my dreams." She studied the piece again. "But if you're right, I'd sell it in a heartbeat. I'm going to need to pick up some money now that Holton's out of commission. You really think someone would pay for this?"

"I know it," Libby said. "What about the anchor still life? Did you do that one too?"

A stack of dirty dishes sat piled high in the sink of the otherwise-spotless kitchen, and Tess couldn't seem to take her eyes off them. "That depends on what you think of it."

"I think you're every bit as talented as Holton, and that's saying a lot."

Tess's mouth curled up in a tentative smile as her gaze moved from the sink to Libby. "You're being serious, aren't you?"

"Does he know you have these?"

"Believe it or not, he's never been to my place, and honestly, I'd be a little embarrassed to show him. I mean, his work's so incredible. If he hated them, it would just make me want to stop."

"How many of these do you have?" Libby asked, her mind already working to calculate how much Tess could bring in and whether or not she would be willing to help Holton put a stop to his foreclosure. Not that he deserved it.

"This is the only one I have here. My mom has two at her house, and I have three in storage. Plus two more mosaics."

"Sounds like you might need to throw your own exhibition. How many unsold tables does Holton have left?"

Biting her bottom lip, Tess looked to the side. "At least nine. Make that eight, since he smashed the newest one."

That was it, Libby thought. That's what Tess needed to do. Hold her own art show, offering her pieces along with Holton's. If Tess could sell everything, and if she was willing to use the money to help Holton, she could make enough to save his house with maybe some left over to revamp their outdated website and begin again.

Tess combed her fingers through her hair,

grimacing as she caught them in a tangle. "How about some coffee?"

"I'd love it." Libby followed her the rest of the way into the kitchen. It was small, but updated with stainless appliances, freshly painted cabinets, and a neutral beige tiled floor. Tess opened a cabinet above the stove and pulled out a bag of value-brand coffee and a brown paper filter.

As she worked, Libby leaned against the counter, watching her fill the pot from the sink. "So, do you think Holton really wants to quit drinking?"

Tess sighed as she poured the water into the coffee machine. "I'm cautiously optimistic. Like I said before, I watched my grandfather try to quit drinking so many times and fail. I think Holton wants to, and I've never seen him want to before, but it's going to be hard. He's going to have to do the work."

Libby ran a tongue over her gritty teeth, wishing her toothbrush wasn't packed. "What work?"

"AA meetings, exercise, whatever it takes for him, I guess. I think it's different for everyone. I know stress is a big trigger, and with the financial mess he's in, the timing couldn't be worse. But then again, if it wasn't for that, he might not have hit his rock bottom, so maybe it's all been a blessing in disguise."

"Did he say anything about me when you talked to him?" It was a question she'd desperately wanted to ask that morning when they'd first arrived at Tess's apartment, but she was exhausted and wasn't sure she could have handled it emotionally if what he had to say was more of the same.

Tess sighed as the pot percolated and the smell of coffee filled the air. She busied herself getting out the sugar bowl and mugs from the cabinet. "He knows he owes you an apology and a big fat thank-you for saving his life."

She tried to hide the vulnerability she felt. "Did he say that?"

Tess turned around to give her full attention. "He doesn't want to believe his wife would have kept something like that from him, but he sees that you look enough like her to be her daughter and he doesn't think you're a liar. Looks to me like he's still hoping it's a mistake."

A mistake. Good thing life didn't come with a big eraser, or she'd have been wiped off everyone's page long ago.

As if Tess could read her mind, she quickly added, "He thinks you're great, Libby; it's not that. It's just he's put her on this pedestal of sainthood. He doesn't like to believe she may have only been human after all."

"What do you think?" Libby tucked her fidgeting hands behind her to keep them still and to soften the feel of the hard counter digging into her back.

"Once you said it, I went back and looked at a picture of her. I don't know how I missed it before, but the resemblance is irrefutable. He sees it too. You'd have to be blind not to." She pulled the two mugs close to the coffee machine and filled them. A curl of steam rose from each. "I'm sorry, but I don't have any cream. Just some powdered stuff."

"That'll work," Libby said, more interested in the conversation than the coffee.

Mug in hand, Tess led them out of the kitchen to the small dining room, which was just big enough for a tiny table and four chairs.

Libby set her mug on the table as she took the chair across from Tess.

"Are you hungry?" Tess asked. "I think I've got a —"

"Not at all." It was a lie. She was famished, but she knew Tess was low on money and didn't want to take what little food she might have.

257

Tess looked at the watch she never took off. "Wow, it's well after lunchtime. So, what are your plans for today?"

Libby shrugged. She had nothing to go home to. No job. No boyfriend. Not a soul in the world who was missing her. "I guess just driving home and trying to find a job." The thought of going back to Casings only added to her blueness.

"You're not going to stay until Holton's released?"

"When will that be?"

Tess blew the steam from her cup and took a cautious sip. "You know as much as I do. It will take up to a week to detox him. Then I guess it depends on if he develops pneumonia or not."

"Do you think I should hang around?" She wrapped her fingers around the warm mug. Why was she suggesting staying? Holton didn't want her in his life. She was nothing but living proof that his wife had sex with another man. He was sorry — so what. She didn't need to stick around for more rejection just to get the satisfaction of an apology.

"I know he wants to talk to you." Tess reached across the table and laid her hand atop Libby's. "And I think it's obvious that you need to talk to him." The gesture, the words — they were both something a mother would say and do. Why couldn't Tess have been the one to give her life? She wouldn't have given her up. Libby could have grown up here in Nags Head with Tess and Holton, and all of their lives could have turned out so differently. She shook off the thought. Longing for what should have, could have been, had never brought her anything but misery.

"I could always drive back when he gets out of the hospital. It's not like it's across the country." Or he could just give her a call, though she doubted he would. He'd forget about her just like the rest of them. "I think he'd rather I disappear."

There was no mistaking the disappointment written on Tess's face. Libby supposed if the shoe were on the other foot, and Rob were in the hospital, she wouldn't want to be alone either. "What are *your* plans?"

"Well," Tess said, setting her mug back down, "I've been thinking. If my pieces really are worth trying to sell, I may just do that. Though I'm not that good at the selling side of things. I was kind of hoping you could help me. If I get a good price for them, it might be enough to keep us afloat for a while."

Libby loved Tess's artwork, so she certainly wouldn't have to fake enthusiasm. Helping her sell a few pieces was the least she could do to thank her for being so kind. "Sure, I'd love to help."

Tess wrapped her hands around her mug and drummed her fingertips against it. "There's something else I'd like to try and sell."

Libby raised her eyebrows.

"I'll have to show you."

After both of them had showered and dressed, they rode to the barn studio in Tess's truck.

Libby grabbed on to the handrail to keep herself from hitting her head as the truck bounced down the gravel road leading past Holton's shack to the studio. Tess parked beside Libby's Jeep and the two women got out.

Without a cloud in the sky, the scorching sun pressed down on them like a branding iron and she had to squint to see against its glare. They stepped inside the studio, and her eyes fought to adjust.

Tess looked around. "It feels so strange without him here."

"What did you want to show me?"

Pointing to the back of the barn, Tess answered her question. Libby followed her to the door she had never paid much attention to, dismissing it as a closet or utility room. Tess filed through her keys until she came to a small brass one. When she unlocked the door, Libby was surprised to see how large the room actually was. The space was lit by one small, dusty window. Walls of shelves displayed large plastic buckets of chemicals and paint. On the floor stood what looked like some sort of statue covered in a paint-speckled sheet.

Without fanfare, Tess yanked the sheet off, revealing a life-size driftwood stallion that stole Libby's breath. "Did you do this?"

With a smile, Tess ran her hand across the horse's wood mane. "I wish. Isn't it amazing?"

Libby admired the artistry, marveling especially over the fluid bends in the stallion's tail, which appeared in mid-flap. "I've never seen anything like it."

"Holton's been working on this here and there. I'd like to see Henry try to knock this off."

"Wow," was all Libby could say. She had already thought Holton was talented, but this was a masterpiece. It was then she noticed the horse was missing a front leg and part of his thigh. "It's not finished."

Tess's gaze moved to the uncompleted area. "He was still working on it. I told him that he should be doing these instead of the tables, or at least in addition to them."

"No joke," Libby said, imagining the piece in some rich couple's garden or in the front window of a hip boutique. "Someone would pay a lot of money to get something like this."

"That's what I thought too," Tess said. "Too bad it's not finished. I'm thinking this could bring in a lot of money, and a few of these might be enough to get him out of this financial hole he's in."

"What if we could finish it for him?" She had spent the last few weeks watching Holton work. Tess, of course, had spent years. Libby hadn't tried her hand at it herself and doubted she had a creative bone in her body, but Tess was an artist all the way, and she probably had fooled around on the side with this medium. Maybe between the two of them . . .

Tess shook her head and frowned. "I'm no artist."

"Don't even try it. I saw what you can do. You're every bit as good of an artist as he is."

"Even if that were true," Tess said, looking anything but convinced, "I'm not a driftwood artist."

Libby walked around the horse, touching

the smooth individual pieces of driftwood making up the whole. "Do you think he'd be willing to sell it if we could finish it?"

"I think he'd sell his kidney if it would help him keep the shack," Tess said.

Chewing on her thumbnail, Libby considered how the small pieces of wood fit together to form each muscle and joint. Tess would be able to fashion them together, no problem, if she could just envision which piece of wood would work where. Looking at what he had already done, she thought they might be able to do it. "Then let's try. What's the worst that can happen?"

Tess rubbed the back of her neck and looked up at the dusty beams across the A-frame ceiling. "Nothing good ever comes of someone saying that." She laid her hand on the stallion's back. "We could ruin it and he could kill us."

Libby squatted on her haunches and examined the pieces that would need to fit with the thigh that was yet to be built. This was an analytical problem to be solved, nothing more, she told herself. "We could fashion the leg apart from it and then attach it. If it doesn't look right, we won't add it. Just think, if he gets out of the hospital and his financial troubles are behind him, how much easier it would be

263

for him to concentrate on getting healthy."

Tess tilted her head to the side as she considered the stallion. Finally a small smile pulled at the corner of her mouth. "I think that would make all the difference in the world."

"Let's at least try."

Tess studied her. "After the way he treated you, why do you want to help him?"

She was startled by the question. She'd always had a picture of how the perfect family would be if such a thing existed. They would be supportive, loving, and most of all there for each other no matter what. *No matter what,* she repeated in her mind. When the going got rough for her parents, they deserted, and wasn't that what she had almost done? She couldn't change what was done to her, but she could show them what love was supposed to look like. More than that, she could show herself. "Isn't that what families do for each other?"

"That's what they should do," Tess said, "but it doesn't sound like that's been done for you."

The validation in that statement made Libby want to cry. "You know, I've spent my entire life wishing for a certain kind of family, but maybe it's time to start making the best of the one I've got."

"Be the change you want to see?" Tess asked.

"I guess." Helping Holton might not win him over, but at least she could feel good about herself. If she couldn't have the parents she wanted, she could at least be the daughter she had always wanted to be.

CHAPTER 27

With Libby on one side of the heavy mosaic and Tess on the other, they carried it into the gift store where they hoped to sell it. Libby's shoulders ached in protest. The thing had to weigh a hundred pounds. They started at Southern Seas Gifts and Collectibles since Tess said they were the most likely to sell wall art. The place was full of antique desks, mermaid bookends, and plenty of Henry's knockoff driftwood tables, all reasonably priced but shoddy work compared to Holton's.

"Let me do the talking," she said to Tess.

The owner was a middle-aged woman with curly brown hair that hung wild down to her waist. She was dressed in a long tie-dyed skirt, matching tank top, and a hemp necklace. "Tess, it's been a long time. Where's Holton?"

Tess looked to Libby, obeying her orders to let her speak for the both of them.

"Holton's in the hospital with pneumonia," Libby said.

The woman's shapeless eyebrows knit together into a look of concern. "Oh no. Is he going to be okay?"

"We hope so. He's in the ICU."

"Oh, goodness," she said.

Tess pressed her lips together tight, as if not speaking required great effort.

Libby's arms were starting to cramp from holding the heavy piece.

The woman looked at it but could only see the back, since the front faced Libby's chest. "What have you got there?"

Tess and Libby set the mosaic down gently on the floor and turned it around so the front faced outward.

The woman gasped. "It's beautiful. Wow, he's really outdone himself. When did he start working with shells?"

Tess opened her mouth to speak, but Libby shook her head, silencing her.

The woman reached out her fingertips and ran them over the surface of the rolling waves. "What are you asking for it?"

"Well, it is one of a kind," Libby said.

It was obvious the owner was more than a little interested by the way she pinched nervously at her chin.

"What do you need to get out of it?" she

asked, and the slight difference in the wording of the question from her first inquiry of price didn't go unnoticed by Libby. It was a classic negotiation technique. Not how much do you want for it, but what's the least you'll accept. Having Caroline for a mother and having to listen to her negotiating deals over the years had actually taught Libby something useful.

"We've already had an offer of five, but under the circumstances, I think we could do better," Libby said as her toes curled around the toe straps of her sandals.

The woman jerked her head back in surprise. "Five thousand?"

Libby casually nodded. She could see Tess's eyes grow large, and her foot began to tap against the brick floor. She slid her own foot on top of Tess's to still it.

"Gosh, I don't know," the woman said as she eyed the piece with a hungry look. She was definitely on the hook. All Libby needed to do was reel her in. "That's a lot of money. Most of my customers couldn't afford anything like that."

Libby shrugged and bent down to pick up her end of the mosaic. Tess frowned but followed suit.

"Wait," the woman said. "Let me make a call. I've got a customer who's always

268

complaining I don't have anything unique enough. Cost has never been an issue for her. Let's see if she's willing to put her money where her mouth is. You mind if I take a few pictures to send her?"

"Not at all," Libby said.

The woman held up her iPhone and clicked a few shots from different angles, then disappeared behind a closed office door.

When she was out of earshot, Tess practically squealed. "Five thousand? I would have taken five hundred."

Libby placed a finger over her lips to quiet her. "That's the mind-set you and Holton need to get out of," she whispered. "What you do is worth paying for. You both are exceptionally talented. You should get paid for that."

Tess bent over the piece and looked at it, then stood back up and shook her head in disbelief. "I'll bet if we'd had you all along, we would have been living on the Riviera by now."

Libby had never thought of herself as a salesperson, but maybe she had the gift after all. "Do you know how much Holton owes on his house?"

Tess shook her head. "I don't know the exact figures. But I'm pretty sure his mortgage hasn't been paid in months — maybe more than a year — and he owes back property taxes too."

Libby tried to guess what the mortgage on his place would be but couldn't imagine. The house itself couldn't be worth much, but the land might be worth a small fortune. "Any way we could find out?"

"Well, I have to go to his house to pick up Rufus. I could do a little poking around."

The woman emerged from the office with a poker face. "My client is definitely interested, but she doesn't want to be in it for more than forty-five."

Libby squinted at her. "I just told you I had an offer of five already." She bent down to pick up her side of the mosaic, trying her best to look irritated, but inside her stomach flip-flopped.

"Wait," the woman said. "Five-fifty and not a penny higher."

Libby's stomach stilled as she stood. It was all she could do not to laugh in relief. "She'll never find another piece like this because one doesn't exist. Fifty-three and I need the cash today."

"Fifty-one and you've got a deal," the woman said.

When Libby slid her hand out to shake, the woman finally allowed herself to gush.

"It's beautiful. When Holton gets better, tell him I want as many of these as he can produce. I'll need them on a smaller scale, though. I could move a sixteen-by-twenty for, say, two to twenty-five a lot easier."

"Holton's not the artist," Libby finally admitted now that the deal was cinched. She tilted her head toward Tess.

"You, Tess?" the woman said. "I had no idea."

"Me either," Tess said with a shy smile. "I've also got a still life. Want to have a look?"

They drove away from Southern Seas $7200 richer and two pieces lighter. Tess was practically floating on air. "I could kick myself for not selling those sooner. Last week I was combing my couch cushions for change to buy a bottle of ketchup. How much do you think we could get out of the stallion if we can really pull this off?"

It was a question Libby had given a lot of thought to. "I'm thinking fifteen to the right buyer."

Tess jerked her head in Libby's direction. "You're kidding."

"Nope. But finding that right buyer is going to be the trick." She remembered then the small driftwood statuettes in Holton's bedroom and asked Tess about them.

271

"Yeah," Tess said, flipping on her blinker as she approached a red light. "I remember those. He made them forever ago."

"I think we can probably get a hundred apiece for those, easy. There had to be two dozen of them, which would bring in another $2400."

"Wow," Tess said. "This is really adding up." When the light turned green, she made a right and pulled onto the shoulder of the road. As a blue convertible whizzed by them, she turned to Libby. "Thank you. I couldn't do this without you."

Libby smiled, liking the way helping Tess was making her feel. "We're not there yet."

"Hey, if you don't find your real father, I'll adopt you."

"I don't have such a good track record with the whole adoption thing," Libby said. "But I could definitely use another friend."

CHAPTER 28

Libby and Tess picked up Rufus from Holton's place on their way home from selling Tess's pieces. Never had a dog been so glad to see a human. As soon as Tess opened the front door, he took off running down the stairs and over to the first patch of vegetation he saw.

His business taken care of, he rushed to Tess, who now stood at the bottom of the stairs, then to Libby, jumping up on his back paws and lavishing her hand in slobber, whining all the while.

"Okay," Tess said. "Calm down already."

Turning to Libby, she said, "Would you mind taking him over to my place? I left the door unlocked. I'll poke around here a bit to see what I can find out about Holton's financial state; then I'll pick up some dog food at the store." She clapped her hands together happily and jumped up and down like an excited child. "I get to go grocery shopping! I'm bringing us home two of the fattest, juiciest steaks they have." She bent down to scratch Rufus behind the ears. "Make that three."

Libby couldn't help but smile at Tess's enthusiasm. "Sounds great," she said. She had never seen anyone that excited about a trip to the supermarket, but she supposed that after being broke for so long, spaghetti every night was probably getting old.

A seagull made the mistake of landing on a hill of sand near Rufus and almost became toast when he lunged at it. With a squall and a frantic flap of its wings, the bird managed to escape by the skin of its beak, leaving Rufus with nothing but a feather hanging precariously from the corner of his mouth.

Libby glanced up at Holton's shack and the front window she'd broken to get to him. One of the early responders must have taken pity and taped it up with plastic to keep out the elements and wildlife. She thought of the mess still festering inside. "Do you think we should clean up the place before we go? I hate for him to come home to that."

Tess glanced up at the window, then back to Libby. "Absolutely not. Let him clean up his own filth. It'll be a good reminder for him."

Although it seemed a little harsh, it made a certain amount of sense. He probably had no idea how bad off he'd been when she found him. One look at the mess he left behind ought to paint a stark-enough picture for him. "When did you get all tough-love?"

Tess laughed. "I've picked up a few things at the Al-Anon meetings I've been going to lately." She glanced over at Libby. "You might want to start coming with me. I think they'd help you, too."

"He's the one with the problem," Libby said, shielding her eyes from the sun. "He should be the one to go, not us."

Tess pulled her sunglasses off the top of her head and slid them on. "That's the thing. It's not just the alcoholic who's sick. It's everyone around him too. It's hard to explain. You'll just have to come with me a few times to see."

Libby wasn't planning on sticking around long enough to join any groups. As soon as she helped Tess sell the pieces and Holton was out of the hospital, she'd have her talk with him and be off to start her new life — or rather, start her old life over. The thought of going back home to the same pointless, boring life, without Rob to buffer it, overwhelmed her with sadness.

Inside Tess's place, she locked Caesar safely in the bedroom and let Rufus have free rein over the rest of the apartment. With Tess out shopping, she and the animals had the place to themselves, which was good since she needed some privacy to talk with Caroline. Hopefully she'd be willing to help Libby put together a gallery showing.

Libby was the world's worst hostess, but Caroline could throw together an event everyone, including the local press, would be talking about. Knowing that her help always came at a price, Libby hated to ask, but truth be told, she missed her mother, and this was the perfect excuse to call.

As Rufus lapped thirstily at the bowl of water she'd given him, she sat cross-legged on Tess's couch and dialed her mother's number. For a change, Caroline picked up on the first ring.

"I've been by your apartment twice in the last two days, and it's obvious you haven't been there."

Libby leaned her head back on the couch and stared at the ceiling. It took everything she had not to yell at her mother for once again invading her privacy. "I know. Something came —"

"Well, when *are* you coming home?" Caroline interjected. "I'm tired of doing all the planning for your wedding by myself. I need you here."

Glad Caroline couldn't see her roll her eyes, Libby said, "For the last time, there isn't going to be a wedding. Rob and I broke up."

"Nonsense. No girl breaks up with a man after he makes partner. You didn't know he was promoted, did you?"

"Yes, Mother. All thanks to you."

"You're welcome," Caroline said, either missing or ignoring the sarcasm.

Libby picked up a round, decorative pillow from beside her and laid it on her lap. "I'll be home in a few days, but right now I need to do something to help Holton." She filled her mother in on Holton's overdose and subsequent hospitalization, his financial problems, and her plan to throw a gallery showing so that he and Tess could sell their artwork and dig themselves out in one — hopefully, wildly successful — event.

"Let me get this straight," Caroline said. "I'm supposed to not only plan your wedding alone, but now you want me to throw another party in the meantime to help out a man who is probably going to drink the money away anyway?"

277

Libby's blood pressure shot up so fast it felt as though her head would blow off her shoulders. "I should have known. You insist on going all-out on a wedding when Rob and I broke up, but you refuse to help me throw a party that I actually want. I wish for once you would do what I need instead of what you want." Before Caroline had a chance to answer, Libby hung up.

Her phone rang, and Caroline's name popped up on the screen. She ignored that call and the four that followed it. She didn't need Caroline anyway. There was no reason Libby couldn't manage this on her own. It might not be the extravagant affair Caroline could have pulled off, but it didn't have to be. All they needed was a place to show art and some people there to buy it.

She wished she'd actually had the guts to make her mother listen for once, to understand where she was coming from, to see her heart.

After pacing the floor out of sheer boredom, then washing up the dishes in the sink, she glanced down at her phone. She should probably call Rob and warn him that Caroline was still planning the wedding as if nothing had changed between them.

She dialed his number, and after half a dozen rings it went to voice mail. She left a short message asking him to call her, adding a casual "if you want to" at the end. It was strange for him not to answer. He always answered her calls, but that was of course when they were together. Now she was nobody special to him. Just a girl he used to date.

She heard a muted mew and walked to Tess's room to check on Caesar. He was lying in the window, curled into his orange-and-white tail, just as content as could be. As she closed the door behind her, her phone rang. She hurried to the couch, where she'd laid it, moving so fast she tripped over the pillow she'd dropped. Throwing her arms out for balance, she was able to avoid a tumble, and luckily only Rufus was there to see the spectacle.

The screen showed Rob's name. She answered and pressed the phone to her ear. "Hello?" she said breathlessly.

"Hi, Libby. I saw you called. Everything okay?" His voice sounded so warmly familiar it made her heart ache.

"Oh yeah, fine," she said, trying her best to sound bored.

"What did you need?"

His curtness caught her off guard. She'd always been able to call him for no reason in particular, but things had changed, and she'd been the one to change them. "Oh, um —" Forgetting her original reason for phoning him, she frantically searched her mind for a legitimate-sounding excuse for the call. "Yeah, I'm throwing together an art auction to benefit Holton. I was hoping you could go."

There was a long pause, followed by, "I'm not sure. I'm pretty busy with my case and, you know, trying out new menus. When is it?"

The thought of him dating made her want to throw up. She held the decorative pillow by its corner and swung hard at the armrest of the couch. "I'm not sure just yet, but I can —"

"Just let me know when you've got a date. Listen, I've got to run."

Before she could even say good-bye, he'd hung up. It shouldn't upset her. She'd been the one to break up with him, after all. But she held the pillow to her face and screamed her pain into it anyway.

CHAPTER 29

The studio was a sauna, and having to work the steam box didn't help. Libby pulled the ponytail holder off her wrist and fastened her hair back. Fanning herself gave the back of her damp neck a slight tingle, but it was about as effective as a wet wipe on a forest fire. Giving up, she instead rubbed at the indentation the rubber band had left on her wrist.

Tess looked at the horse sculpture missing its front leg and held a piece of driftwood up to it. "What about this one?" A streak of sawdust ran down the slope of her nose and perspiration beaded across her hairline.

Libby looked at the driftwood, then at the horse. Eyeing the contours of its shoulders, she shook her head. "I think he should be prancing. We need one smaller piece and one longer. We can fasten them together with screws."

Squinting at the piece, Tess placed a finger

over her mouth, deep in thought. "You've got a good eye. I can totally see that." She riffled through the pile of driftwood and pulled out a piece that was nearly as tall as she was. "We don't necessarily have to use two pieces, though. What if we use this one? We could steam it and bend it at the knee."

Libby considered it. "It's worth a try."

The steam box Holton had handcrafted resembled a narrow plywood coffin with a wallpaper steamer hooked to it via a steel pipe. Tess began carving a horse's hoof out of a small hunk of sun-bleached wood. Libby raised her eyebrows. Of course Tess could carve wood; what couldn't she do? Tearing her gaze off the ease and speed with which Tess worked, Libby opened the steam box and was hit in the face with a plume of scorching mist. She jumped back, swatting the steam away.

"Easy," Tess said. "Holton got a second-degree burn doing that."

Libby patted her face, glad her eyebrows were still where they should be. The sting quickly wore off and she got back to business. Wearing thick leather gloves several sizes too large, she placed the driftwood inside the box.

Several hours later the timer finally went off, alerting them that the wood was ready to be molded. After carefully removing it, Libby carried it over to the worktable and cinched it with the vise. With a few turns of the clamp's screw handle, it was secured to the table. Together, she and Tess pulled and prodded the wood around the mold Tess had fashioned and held it in place with several C-clamps.

"What do we do now?" Libby asked, wiping the dampness from her brow.

Tess leaned her head to the left, then right, working out the kinks. "It has to set overnight, so all there is left to do is wait and say a prayer."

CHAPTER 30

In his entire life, Holton had never slept so much yet felt so unrested. Even so, if the ICU wasn't costing him so much, he might have asked to stay a few extra days just to get a little more time clean before having to face his problems and the temptations of the world. At least his wallet was happy that the doctor had cleared him to go.

He had been sedated through detox, and the worst — physically, at least — was behind him. Unfortunately, the craving for alcohol was as strong as ever. He couldn't imagine a day when he wouldn't obsess about it. Of course, the Antabuse the doctor prescribed him ought to help. As long as he took it every day, even if he succumbed to temptation and had a drink, the medication would make him so sick he'd wish he hadn't.

The way he figured it, that drug was going to be his lifeline in the coming months.

The stuff wasn't cheap, but if he could scrounge up the money for gin, he could certainly come up with the cash for the medication. He wished he didn't have to use that or any crutch, but until he got his sea legs, he needed all the help he could get. Apparently no one got through life without a little help now and then, not even him.

As he held his breath, the nurse removed his Foley catheter with one gentle but highly unpleasant tug. He looked down, relieved to see she hadn't accidentally yanked his bladder out along with it.

As soon as he was able to use the bathroom, she said he would be allowed to leave.

He guzzled cup after thin, plastic cup of water, and soon enough he had proven that his plumbing was in working order. The nurse grinned at him like a proud parent who'd finally succeeded in getting her toddler potty trained.

When she left, he studied himself in the mirror above the sink. He couldn't believe how much he'd aged in the last few days. His eyes were as bloodshot as Rufus's, and his hair seemed twice the salt and half the pepper. Touching his scraggly cheek, he decided that the five o'clock shadow he normally wore had morphed into a near eclipse. Tugging at his chin hair, he debated asking the nurse for a razor. They'd probably charge him fifty bucks for it. He grabbed his cell off the counter and dialed Tess's number.

She answered cheerfully. "Is it time?"

Nodding as though she could see him, he sighed. "Ready or not."

"You're going to be fine," she said.

He sat on the edge of his hospital bed, and the blue gown rose above his furry calves. If only he could feel the way she sounded. He wasn't going to be fine — destitute and homeless was more like it.

"I can be there in twenty minutes."

"I'll be ready." Looking down at his feet, he realized he had on ugly green socks that didn't belong to him. One hung halfway off his foot like a flipper. Another *ka-ching* dinged in his head.

The discharge nurse brought him in a stack of papers to sign, reinforcing his thoughts of the enormous bill he was going to be receiving. One stupid bender had at least doubled his debt. Bankruptcy was something he never thought he'd resort to, but now it looked as though he had no other option.

It made him sick to think of how much money he'd drunken away since Adele had passed. He closed his eyes, intending to pray, but then remembered that he and God weren't exactly on speaking terms.

Maybe like others had said over the years, God had his reasons, but Holton didn't care what they were. A flood of anger washed over him. He reached for his plastic cup and slammed down the last of the water as though it were a shot of gin, but the bite wasn't there, nor the feeling of fire gin always sent down his throat on first swallow. And worst of all, it did nothing to dull the pain.

He gathered what few belongings he had into the plastic bag they'd given him and waited for what seemed like forever, watching the hand on his watch tick away at the speed of a snail. Forcing his eyes off the watch face, he focused on doing something productive with his time and read the information the doctor had given him.

She listed all the things that could happen if he went back to drinking, including cirrhosis of the liver, pancreatitis, heart attack, depression, and death — to name a few. She included the website and phone numbers of some local Alcoholics Anonymous groups.

Just thinking about attending a meeting made him want to drink. This wasn't going to be easy, and he wasn't sure he could do it. *One day at a time,* he told himself, but then decided he'd better focus on a minute at a time for now. He'd work up to the day thing later.

A woman called into his room from the intercom and told him that his ride was out front and that someone would be right in to bring him down. They must have been anxious to see him go, because the second she clicked off, a man in scrubs rolled in a wheelchair and asked if he was ready.

He wasn't sure that he was, but he knew the question was rhetorical. "I'm fine to walk," he said, grimacing at the wheelchair.

The man scratched at his tight goatee and told him the wheelchair was required by hospital policy. Holton had never felt so conspicuous as he did being wheeled out of that room, down the hall, and into a crowded elevator. Everyone who happened to look his way gave him a sympathetic look. He couldn't stand the unwarranted pity.

He was rolled off the elevator, through a drafty vestibule, and finally through an oversize pneumatic door that led outside. His eyes struggled to adjust from the artificial light of the hospital to the ultrabright summer sun. It took him a few seconds to spot Tess's truck even though it was parked right in front of him.

"There she is," he said, pointing straight ahead.

Before the man could even put a brake on the wheelchair, Holton hopped up and grabbed his bag from him. "Thanks for everything," he said.

The man tried to open the passenger door for him, but Holton beat him to it. "Got it. Thanks again," he said, climbing into the truck as fast as he could.

Tess sat at the wheel looking radiant and smelling of flowers instead of tangerines. Her red hair hung in long, flowing curls. She flashed him a smile.

He squinted at her. Her freckles were all but concealed, her lips were a rosy shade of pink, and her lashes were black rather than their normal strawberry blonde. "Are you wearing makeup?" he asked. He'd never seen her so much as powder her nose.

The blush of her cheeks grew darker. "Maybe."

It occurred to him then that she had taken the time for his benefit, and it made him more than a little uncomfortable. He shouldn't have promised her a date. What if he couldn't stop drinking? What if he decided that he didn't really want to, after all? If he got involved with her romantically, it would only put pressure on him to succeed.

Pressure made him drink. He couldn't let her down again. "I know I promised you a date, but I don't think I'm feeling up to it today."

"You did? I don't remember that." The smirk remained on her thin, glossy lips, but the glint had faded from her eyes.

He threw his plastic bag full of clothes behind the bench seat and buckled up. "Whew, then I guess I'm off the hook."

She turned the wheel, cutting a hard right out of the parking lot. "You want to be off the hook? Then consider yourself off." Her smile was gone now, replaced by a scowl, which made her look even more beautiful. He realized then that he wasn't entirely sure he wanted to be off the hook.

"Relax," he said. "I just meant today."

Sunshine streamed in through the glass, highlighting all the slobber and noseprints Rufus had made since she'd last washed the truck. The fact that she hadn't taken time to also gussy up the truck relieved him. She adjusted her rearview mirror before turning onto the highway. "So how are you feeling?"

"Like I need a drink."

She took her eyes off the road long enough to look at him. The car veered to the right, crossing onto the shoulder. He pointed back

290

at the road and she straightened out the wheel.

"I'm just being honest," he said. "You asked."

Her expression softened. "I'm really proud of you, Holt. You've so got this."

There was no doubt in his mind she believed that, but he wasn't quite there yet. "Did Libby go home?"

"No, she's waiting to talk to you."

The tires hit a pothole and he had to slap a hand onto the dash to keep from whacking his head on the door. "I see you haven't gotten the suspension fixed yet."

"I haven't had a chance to check my couch cushions for change."

She was joking, of course, but he couldn't find the humor in it. He hadn't been able to afford to fix Adele's car either, and look how well that turned out.

Once again, because of him, someone he cared about couldn't afford to have her basic needs met. He pulled the visor down to block the worst of the sun. "She could have gone home and just called from there. Did she stay this whole time?"

"She sat at your bedside more than one night when you were under," Tess said, slowing to a crawl at a stop sign.

Guilt bit him hard as he thought of how

he had treated Libby and all the kindness she had shown him. The weight of it was almost too much to bear. A bottle of gin would numb it right up, but since that wasn't an option, he guessed he'd better face it. It had been a long time since he really had to deal with his emotions. He didn't even know how to begin. "She's a special young lady."

"Yes, your stepdaughter is," Tess said, the affection for the girl obvious by her tone.

He stared out his window past a smear of what had to be dried dog slobber at a group of teenagers milling about in bathing suits in front of a surf shop. "Has Rufus been staying with you?"

"Me and Libby. I've had her at my apartment this week."

"She must have been bored out of her skull." Tess didn't so much as own a TV. He didn't know how she could stand it.

She flashed a Cheshire grin as she flipped on her blinker to pass a VW Bug. "Not exactly."

"What have you two been up to?"

"Saving your butt."

He studied her profile. He could barely make out the freckles bridging her small nose, and there was a small, almost heart-shaped beauty mark on the side of her neck he'd never noticed before. "What do you mean?"

"You'll find out tomorrow night," she said. "On our first date."

CHAPTER 31

All nerves, Libby sat on her bed and rubbed vanilla-scented lotion onto her heels, then slipped on black pumps. She had never given a decent party, and here she was throwing an art show that was supposed to draw out some of Nags Head's social elite?

She wouldn't feel half as anxious if Tess hadn't sunk so much of her newly earned money into the show. They'd both underestimated how much decent wine cost, and they'd ordered cases of the stuff. Not to mention the added expense of renting the hall, advertising, catering, and waitstaff.

Although she'd hoped the local papers would do full articles on the art show, she'd only seen a brief mention in one. Hopefully the one well-placed ad in the largest local paper would be enough to bring in a crowd. If they sold all of the pieces that night, it would be a success, but she knew they could just as easily sell nothing. That would not only hurt Tess's wallet, but probably Holton's morale at a time when he could least afford it.

She'd texted Rob that morning to tell him about the event, and he said he'd try to make it, but he couldn't promise. It was just as well, she told herself. Her heart couldn't take much more.

Looking in the mirror, she found herself fretting more than a little herself over her appearance. Rob probably wouldn't make it, but just in case, she wanted to look her best — if only to show him what he was losing. A sickening thought hit her. What if he brought a date? Her insides twisted as she imagined a woman hanging on his arm and laughing at every goofy thing he said. One who liked a little clinginess in her man. One who hadn't told him time and again that he needed to get a life.

It was unlikely he'd have a date already, she assured herself. It wasn't like he was a Casanova — not that he couldn't be with his good looks and sweet personality, but it took him until college to get the nerve to ask out just one girl. It would probably take him another ten years to get up the nerve to ask out another.

Forcing him and the imaginary trollop from her mind, she leaned into the mirror and brought the crimson pencil to her lips. She carefully outlined them and filled them in with fire-engine red. It was a color Caroline had given her and was always trying to coax her to use. Men loved the color, she'd always said. Until now, Libby couldn't have cared less what any man thought as long as she was happy with the way she looked.

She wondered then if her mother would bother to show up. She might, just to see Libby fail. Hopefully she would drag along a rich boyfriend who would buy something out of obligation, if nothing else. Caroline wouldn't, of course, because in her mind, it would be akin to giving a drug addict money to buy heroin with.

She ran her fingers through her freshly straightened hair, then pinched a tiny clump of mascara from the corner of her lashes. Satisfied with her face and hair, she backed up from the mirror and stood on her tiptoes to check her dress. It was a basic black number, which flattered her petite frame. She wished she had packed something with a little more pizzazz, but the dress was elegant and appropriate and would do the trick.

She touched her collarbone, wishing she'd accepted the pearls Caroline had tried to give her several years back. She'd said she wasn't a pearl person and never would be, but apparently her mother had been right about her tastes changing over time.

Libby pulled into the gallery parking lot as the setting sun painted the blue sky with cotton candy and orange cream. The catering truck and a few other vehicles were already there. When she walked inside, the place smelled like bread and bacon and looked twice as drab as the day she'd booked it. She had been so desperate to get a place that she had let herself see it through rose-colored glasses.

Besides its dark, musty feel, it was even smaller than she remembered. If there were a considerable crowd, they'd be in trouble. Of course, that would be a good problem to have, and probably an unlikely one.

Two waiters busied themselves by taking hors d'oeuvres out of a tray the caterer had brought and arranging them on silver platters, while the bartender uncorked wine. The owner had her back to Libby as she fooled with what looked like a stereo system built into the wall. Soft music began to play. The woman turned around, and her face lit with recognition as her gaze fell on Libby.

"How does everything look?" she asked.

Libby tried not to focus on the woman's

hair. It looked like she had gone to a lot of trouble to get it to resemble a bird's nest. "Good," she said, forcing herself to smile. "Have you gotten many calls about the art show?"

The woman nervously glanced at the door, then back to her. "Well, I did get one call tonight asking if we could postpone it an hour."

One call. Libby's stomach dropped. This wasn't only *not* going to help Holton and Tess; it was going to be a huge embarrassment to them all.

The woman played with her oversize string of orange beads circling a nearly nonexistent neck. "She was very insistent. I finally had to hang up on her." Something about Libby's expression made her flush. "I don't normally hang up on customers. I must have told her half a dozen times that the time was already advertised and we couldn't possibly —"

"Don't worry about it," Libby said. "It was just my mother. She's like that."

The woman placed a hand on her chest to show her relief. "Bless your heart, honey. I've got one of those too."

The sound of a car pulling into the parking lot made her breath catch. *Here we go,* she thought. Libby smoothed her dress.

After a minute or two, the door opened and in stepped Holton and Tess looking nothing like themselves. Gone were the frayed cutoff shorts, sweat-stained T-shirts, and sawdust in their hair. Tess looked amazing in a burgundy cocktail dress that would be right at home at one of Caroline's parties. She wore her hair in a partial updo with large ringlets cascading all around her face, and she smelled like roses.

As beautiful as Tess looked, it was Holton who stole the show. It was the first time Libby had seen him clean-shaven and with his hair combed back out of his face. He looked more *GQ* than beach bum. She hadn't spoken with him since he'd kicked her out of his house, but judging by his inability to look her in the eye and the way he fidgeted, she could tell he was contrite. She decided to let him off the hook and be the one to speak first. "You two look amazing," she said, approaching them.

He waved away the compliment while Tess beamed, grabbing hold of his arm. "You clean up pretty good yourself, girl." She frowned as she glanced around the gallery. "Quite a crowd we've drawn."

Libby felt her face grow warm. "It doesn't start for another fifteen minutes. Besides, the people who will come to something like this are always fashionably late."

"Where's the artwork?" Tess asked.

Libby pointed to the back of the room, then followed them as they headed toward it. The display was simple, with a single light shining either above or below each piece. Tess's mosaics and still lifes were first in line. Holton stopped in front of the first, which was a small mosaic of a seagull. With a frown, he turned to Tess. "Thought you said this was a show featuring our work?"

"It is," Libby said, feeling as proud as if she'd created them herself. "Tess did these."

His jaw hit the ground. "What? When?"

"Impressive, aren't they?" Libby asked, watching Tess blush.

"Of course I'm impressed," he said. He looked at Tess as if he were seeing her for the first time. "I had no idea." He brushed a strand of hair from her forehead, and she turned into his touch. "This what you've been doing with all those shells you pick up?"

She looked down at her feet and nodded. He hooked her chin with a finger and guided her face up so that her eyes met his. "Honey, this is incredible."

Her smile melted Libby's heart, and she hoped it was doing the same to Holton's.

Going from piece to piece, he shook his

head in wonder and lavished Tess with praise. By the time they got to Holton's pieces, his and Tess's fingers were intertwined and he looked genuinely happy for a change.

The first showing of Holton's portion of the exhibit was a shelf displaying all his smaller horses. His face turned white as he picked up the first one — a mare nuzzling her colt. "I didn't make these to sell. These were gifts to Adele."

Libby gave Tess a horrified look. She'd never considered that.

He set it back down on the shelf and picked up the galloping horse beside it. He ran his finger gently over its spine and tail, looking like he might cry.

Despite what Tess had said about him needing the money, they should have asked his permission before selling them. Of course they meant something to him, or he would have sold them long ago. "I'm sorry," Libby said, feeling on the verge of tears herself. "We didn't know. We were just trying to get you out of debt. We should have asked."

Tess began to gather them from the shelf, but Holton set his hand atop hers to stop her.

"It's okay," he said, putting them back. "If

301

I'm ever going to be able to let the big things go, I guess I better start with the small." He looked between her and Libby. "It's okay, girls. You did good."

Libby studied the mare nuzzling her colt and thought of Adele. The thought of this piece going home with anyone else but her was unfathomable. "I'll be your first customer. I love this one."

Tess frowned at Holton as a look passed between them. He nodded at her and turned to Libby. "It's yours," he said, picking it up. "I'm sure she must have thought about you every time she looked at it. She'd want you to have it."

Libby gently took it from his hands and held it against her heart. "Thank you," was all she could manage to say.

"Speaking of your mother," he said, practically choking on the word, "I have a surprise for you. I'm guessing your grandmother will want to meet you."

Grandmother? It was overwhelming to think of being in the presence of the woman who had given birth to, nursed, and raised her own birth mother. "I have a grandmother," she said to Tess, as though she hadn't been right there to hear it. Caroline had been a change-of-life baby, and her parents had died when Libby was still an infant. Her adoptive father's parents didn't come around after he left, so she never really had grandparents before. It was almost too much to wrap her heart around.

Tess's smile seemed forced. "She might have the answers you're both looking for."

Holton lifted his hand, still attached to Tess's, and glanced at his watch. "Well, we better get out there."

"Wait," Tess said. "You haven't seen our signature piece."

He raised a thick eyebrow at her, looking more debonair than ever. "Let me guess — you also paint Rembrandts on the side."

With a Mona Lisa smile, she narrowed her eyes at him. "Go look for yourself. It's under the velvet sheet."

He scanned past his driftwood tables to the back of the room and took in the sculpture draped in black. There was no mistaking the shape of the horse beneath it. "That looks like the stallion, but it can't be. It isn't finished."

"It is now," Libby said, holding her breath.

He walked back to it, his eyes filled with trepidation, and slowly lifted the sheet. "What in the world?" The leg Tess and Libby had fashioned was a perfect match. It was no masterpiece in itself, but the driftwood horse as a whole was, and the grafted leg blended right in.

When he turned around, his mouth was scrunched tight, and his chest rose and fell in quick succession. Libby thought she might faint. He didn't just look upset; he looked like he was barely containing fury. "Who did this?" he demanded.

Libby opened her mouth to accept full blame, but a squeal escaped instead of words. With head held high, Tess stepped forward. "It's my fault. I just thought that it was your finest piece, and I know you wanted to finish it, but you were in the hospital. You can be mad if you want, but we were just trying to help you get out of this mess."

He walked up to her. "I can't believe you did this."

Tess's voice began to break up and her lips quivered, but whether it was from fear, sadness, or anger, Libby didn't know . . . until Tess jabbed a finger an inch from his nose.

"All these years I've been standing by your side, watching you waste away your talents drinking, and now you've got an opportunity to turn it all around. So what if you weren't the one to finish it? So what if you have to share a little of the glory or criticism? So what if you needed help? And so what if the person you needed it from was me? You have no right —"

Before she could finish her sentence, Holton silenced her with a kiss.

CHAPTER 32

Forty-five minutes after the art show was scheduled to begin, the air was not full with the sound of chatter, clinking wineglasses, or money changing hands — just soft jazz, the smell of hors d'oeuvres, and the murmuring of the waitstaff. Tess, Holton, and Libby were still the only ones present not being paid to be there. They stuffed their faces with finger foods, made small talk, and tried to ignore the whispers of the staff.

Libby bit into a small square of sourdough topped with brie and apricot preserves. At least the food was good. Her heart ached for Holton, who, despite his smile, had to be more than a little disappointed that he might never get out of the financial hole he had dug himself into. She knew she shouldn't feel guilty — his predicament was his fault, not hers — but the art show had been her idea, and she'd managed to get everyone's hopes up for nothing.

The gallery owner wore a look of exaggerated pity as she ambled over to them, her long skirt swishing between her ankles. "You never know how these things are going to go. I thought for sure you'd have a nice turnout."

Libby tried to keep the melancholy she felt from bleeding through her voice. "I'm sorry we wasted your time." She slid her gaze to Holton and Tess. "Yours too."

Holton dug his hands into the front pockets of his dress pants and shrugged. "Hey, you tried, and that's a lot more than I can say for myself. Thanks for giving me a shot. I didn't deserve it."

Tess draped one arm over his shoulders and the other around Libby's. In that instant, Libby felt what other girls who had two parents probably took for granted.

"I think we're going to be okay," Tess said. "Thanks to you, Libby. Now I know my pieces will sell, and there's no doubt in my mind that stallion of Holt's is going to bring big bucks from the right buyer. You should feel nothing but proud."

Just then the front door opened and they all turned around expectantly, only to see Henry. He wore a suit jacket and tie along with a pair of black shorts and flip-flops. They let out a collective sigh.

"Here we go again," Libby said. As if the night weren't a big-enough disaster, Holton's nemesis was going to revel in adding insult to injury.

Henry tucked his hands into his pockets as he looked around the room. "Quite a turnout you got here."

Holton's nose flared. "Haven't you done enough?"

Tess's hands balled at her sides. "Let me handle this."

"No." Libby put on her sweetest smile. "Allow me." She knew why he was there and wasn't about to let him have the satisfaction. She might have no control over how the evening turned out, but handling this slime bag was within her power. "Henry!" she exclaimed, throwing a quick wink over her shoulder to Tess and Holton. "I'm so glad you made it."

He expelled a haughty laugh. "Really? It was lucky I even knew about the thing since my invitation seems to have gotten lost in the mail."

Skin crawling, she intertwined her arm with his. "We didn't send out invitations, silly. This is a public event." She looked him over slowly, as if taking time to admire his ridiculous outfit. "Wow, look at you. That's really cool."

When he grinned sheepishly, she knew she had him. "Seriously?" He lowered his voice and leaned his head toward her. "I was actually going for goofy."

She giggled and tossed her hair, Caroline style. "Well, you failed. I'm talking movie-star cool."

He looked down at the blond fur on his legs, then back to her.

"You want to see what we're selling?"

His eyes glinted with amusement as his gaze fell on Holton. "Looks like nothing."

Holton took a sip from his water glass, clearly trying to look as though he wouldn't just love to knock Henry's head off his shoulders.

"Well," Henry added, "I wouldn't take it personally, man. It's just that there are so many talented artists out there to choose from." He ran his hands down the front of himself, indicating he thought he was one of them. "People these days want value."

Holton's mouth flashed open, and Libby shook her head to silence him.

She grabbed a glass of wine off the bar and handed it to Henry as she led him back to the exhibits. "I was so afraid we weren't going to sell a single piece —" she exhaled in feigned relief — "but you're here now."

He cleared his throat. "I'm just window-shopping."

When they reached the back room, his gaze glinted with jealousy as he eyed the display. Although he was winning this price war against Holton, he had to realize he'd never match the man in creativity. It was no wonder he was so bent on forcing Holton out of business.

Henry tried to be inconspicuous as he stepped forward with his back to her, snapping pictures with his cell phone. When he saw that she had caught him, he smiled and shrugged.

"What do you think of the stallion?" she asked, pretending not to care.

He rubbed his dimpled chin. "I think it's going to be hard to copy."

Good, she thought. *Maybe you'll have to actually create something original for a change.*

"But," he added, as though reading her thoughts, "I'll get it. I always do."

She fought the urge to stomp his foot with her spike heel. "You know —" she leaned in as if to share a secret — "something told me you were a good guy at heart. I'm always hearing how cheap and heartless you are, but here you are, supporting the competition. That takes a big man." She gave his arm a gentle squeeze. "Thank you, Henry."

His eyebrows dipped in confusion as lines etched across his forehead. "Yeah, I'm that kind of guy."

Tilting her head, she smiled at him. "I can see that now."

He brought his middle finger up and smoothed his eyebrows. "Hey, what do you say when this thing's over, I take you out for a drink?" He looked like a lion eyeing a gazelle as his gaze wandered over her.

She forced herself to grin at him. "Business before pleasure. Let's find you something to take home first."

Arm in arm, she led him down the corridor, stopping in front of each piece to deliver the sales pitch. When they reached Tess's ocean mosaic, she paused in front of it. "This is my favorite. I could just stare at it all night."

Henry glanced sideways at Libby. "Is that right? How much are they asking?"

"Four."

Slipping his hand into his pocket, he reached for his wallet. He opened it and slid out four crisp hundred-dollar bills. "I'd like to say that at least it's for a good cause, but let's face it —" he glanced back at Holton with a look of contempt — "lost cause would be more like it."

"That's so sweet," she said with an extra

dose of saccharin, "but it's four *thousand.*"

His face turned shades as he shoved the money back into his wallet. "No wonder he can't sell anything."

She gave him a look of exaggerated pity. "What's a few thousand for a successful guy like you?"

He stared down at his flip-flops. "I'm kind of saving for . . ." His gaze darted around the room as though he were trying to find something to spark an idea.

"Oh, I see." She gave him a knowing look. "I think I have something in your price range." She led him to the miniature horses and picked up a reclining colt. "This is only three hundred." Her gaze shifted to him. "You can afford *that,* can't you?"

He closed his eyes for a split second as if in resignation. "Yeah, what the heck. It's for charity, right?"

Charity. This guy had some nerve. "You're a sweetheart." She held out her hand to take the money. The gallery owner was supposed to handle the payments, but Libby wasn't going to take a chance Henry would stiff them. "Would you like me to wrap it for you?"

He shoved it into his pocket. "So, how about that drink?"

"Hey, guys," she called to Holton and

Tess, "Henry bought the first piece."

They both blinked at her without reaction.

His eyes began to roam over her again. "So, how about that drink later?"

"I don't drink," she said. "But thanks for supporting a local artist." She gave him two quick pats to the back of his shoulder.

His expression hardened as he realized he'd been had. He almost knocked shoulders with her as he stomped past her toward the front door. When he reached Tess and Holton, he sneered at them, then turned back to her. "If I were you, I'd start keeping better company." He gave Holton a slow once-over. "You lie down with dogs, you wake up with fleas."

Libby joined Tess and Holton. "I hope you and your fleas have a good night, Henry."

Tess leaned into her shoulder, giving her a side hug as they watched Henry storm out.

"Don't go away mad," Holton called after him.

"Just go away," Tess added through laughter.

"You're definitely your mother's child," Holton said. "She'd be so proud of you." He looked over at her, then the floor. "*I'm* proud."

"Thanks," she said, feeling giddy despite the night's flop.

Tess looked toward the front of the gallery, which was still empty. "Well, should we call it?"

The owner materialized from a closed door as though waiting for this moment. "If people aren't here by now, they probably aren't —"

The sound of tires rolling into the parking lot — lots of tires — turned everyone's heads toward the door. They all exchanged surprised glances.

Rows of headlights lit up the front windows. The waitstaff, who were all standing around in their penguin suits and looking on the verge of falling asleep, perked up.

The door opened and in strolled Caroline, wearing a shimmery cream pantsuit with a faux mink collar. The room filled with her expensive perfume.

"You made it," Libby said, trying not to look as relieved as she felt.

Caroline scanned the room and cleared her throat disapprovingly. "Good grief, you weren't kidding when you said you needed my help. Showing the art at a morgue would be less depressing."

The gallery owner scowled at her, but Caroline was oblivious as usual.

"Who's in all those cars?"

"They're friends," Caroline said. "I told

you I'd be here."

Libby didn't bother to argue, even though she knew Caroline hadn't said any such thing.

Caroline turned to Holton and Tess, who were looking at her as if she were an alien. "I'm Elizabeth's mother. I gather you're Holton and his help?"

"Assistant," Tess said indignantly.

Holton put his hand out to shake. "It's good to finally meet you. You have one incredible daughter here."

Caroline looked down at his hand but made no move toward it. "Of course I do. I'm glad you realize that." She glanced around the room. "Where is the artwork? I need to see how it's displayed before I usher these people in."

Tess raised her eyebrows at Libby but led Caroline to the back room without comment. Afraid of what her mother might say, Libby followed.

Caroline eyed the showing. "The pieces are lovely," she said without emotion. "But the display is —" she huffed in annoyance — "well, hideous, to put it nicely."

"That's putting it nicely?" Libby asked, horrified once again by Caroline's bedside manner.

"Well, it's too late now to do anything

about that. We'll just have to make do." Her heels clicked sharply as she strode over to each piece and looked down at the prices. You could have heard a pin drop as Caroline crossed her arms and tapped her long red fingernail against the elbow of her jacket. "Change this overhead music to classical. Tilt the up-lights so they're aimed at the sides of the tables instead of the centers, and double the prices."

"What?" Tess blurted. "We've already doubled what we normally charge. We're going to price ourselves out of selling anything."

Caroline made a disgusted noise. "Do you want my help or not? My guests are used to paying top dollar, and we're not going to offend them by leading them to believe these are less than the very best. And the very best has its price."

Tess stood there with her mouth parted until Caroline bugged her eyes out at her. "Do it."

When Libby frowned at her rudeness, Caroline put on a smile that seemed to pain her and added a "please" to her demand.

To Libby's shock and joy, by the end of the night, all the artwork had been purchased, and an informal bidding war ensued over the stallion. Caroline eventually outbid a silver-haired man for a price that made Libby dizzy. Finally conceding to defeat, the man threw his arms up. "Way to go, Caroline. You managed to drive up the price of a piece I was trying to buy for *you.*"

She laid a hand on the side of his tightly clipped beard. "I appreciate that, Charles, but I'm more than capable of purchasing my own baubles."

Libby opened her mouth, prepared to chastise her mother for her flippant description of Holton's beautiful sculpture, but the sound of the front door opening stole her attention.

She glanced over, expecting to see one of the guests returning from carrying a piece out to a vehicle, or one of the waitstaff coming back in after a smoke break. But it was Rob who stood in the doorway, overdressed in a tuxedo. By his side was a beautiful young woman with short black hair, a red suede miniskirt, and legs up to the ceiling.

Libby tried to look away before he saw her gawking. Her heart began to beat wildly and she had to take Caroline's arm to steady herself. Caroline looked over to Rob and his date. "What does he think he's doing? Who is that girl?"

Libby drew in a sharp breath, unable to speak.

Rob spotted them and waved nonchalantly. The woman followed him over like a lost puppy. "I'm sorry I'm late," he said. It was shameless the way he could just stand there next to that woman as if he didn't know he was thrusting a dagger into Libby's heart.

Caroline glared at his date until she finally excused herself, mumbling something about the bathroom and needing some air.

Before she was even out of earshot, Caroline dug a hand into her narrow hip and laid into Rob. "What do you think you're doing? You're marrying my daughter in a matter of weeks and you show up here with that strumpet on your arm? After everything I've done for you."

Embarrassed beyond belief, Libby sputtered, "For the last time, we're not getting married."

Rob's eyebrows knit together and his lips thinned. "She's not a date. She's my friend's wife. He had to park the car across the street because the lot's full. And for your information, I quit Smith and Johnson, so my days of owing you are over."

Caroline and Libby gasped at the same time.

"It's okay," he said, gaze fixed on Libby. "I'm making some changes."

Caroline grabbed his arm, her long fingernails digging into his jacket. "Have you lost your mind? How are you going to support my daughter?"

Libby grunted in frustration. "We're not getting married."

Closing her eyes as if she could no longer stand the sight of them, Caroline said, "I need a drink." With that, she finally left them alone.

"Hey," Rob said with a sweet smile that made Libby's heart flutter.

"Hey," she said, unable to stop herself from smiling back. "Thanks for coming."

Conversations, laughter, and music swirled all around them, but she heard only Rob's voice.

"I would have been here sooner," he said, "but Toby's sense of direction is even worse than mine, and the stupid GPS kept taking us in circles. I think he bought one of the first ones they made and hasn't updated it since."

"It's okay." She stared past his long lashes into his eyes. Her only thought was that those beautiful eyes used to be hers to look into whenever she wanted. "Thanks for coming. It was a long trip to make. You quit your job, huh?"

"Like I said." He glanced around. "I'm making some changes."

Neither of them said anything for a moment. Silence had always felt comfortable between them until now. To fill the void, she said, "Caroline is still planning the wedding."

He shook his head. "I guess we'll show up and see how she handles it when we refuse to walk down the aisle."

"Yeah," she said glumly. Feeling suddenly self-conscious, she touched her hair.

"You look beautiful."

"Look," she said, "I'm sorry about telling you to date other people. I've been crazy jealous thinking that you might be."

His gaze fixated on her left hand. "You're not wearing my ring."

She touched her bare finger, feeling guilty.

"It's okay," he said. "I'm glad you're not. The next time I slip that ring on you, I want you to be as sure as I am."

Her throat tightened until she could barely breathe. If she could take back the stupid menu conversation, she would have at that moment.

He reached for her hand, and she took hold of it tighter than she ever had before. "I know now what you were looking for," he said, "because I'm looking for it too. We need to be fully ourselves before we can be fully us."

His words shouldn't have cut her as much as they did. Just as she'd told him to do a hundred times, he was growing up. She just wondered now if he was growing away, as well.

As usual, he intuitively picked up on what she was feeling. "I'm still sure about you," he added. "I just have to be sure about me now. You know what my counselor said?"

"You're seeing a counselor?"

His frown told her he had already mentioned it. Maybe she was more like Caroline than she thought. "He said that I've been trying to control things I can't. Like hanging on so tightly to our relationship because I'm afraid to lose you."

"You're not losing me," she said.

"Apparently I have all this subconscious guilt about losing my sister and it's bleeding into our relationship. He thinks that's why I've been so paranoid. He said when I come to terms with the fact I had no control over Heather's cystic fibrosis, I'll be able to relax around you and trust that what's meant to be, will be."

Libby glanced around and saw a waitress staring in their direction. When their eyes met, the woman quickly looked away. She thought about the fact that Rob was seeing a counselor and was actually taking what he had to say seriously. "That makes sense."

Rob's face lit up. "Yeah, he said my lack of trust has nothing to do with you. He said the real person I don't trust is myself. It fits, don't you think?"

It did, and she nodded.

He looked around the crowded room. As a waiter passed with a tray of stuffed mushrooms, Rob picked one off and put it between his lips so that it stuck out like a tongue. Speaking around it, he playfully asked, "Want a bite?"

And with that, she knew that despite his changes, he was still Rob and they were still okay. She stepped into his arms and took a bite. As she swallowed the spicy spinach-and-cheese concoction, he kissed the top of her head. "I've missed you, Libs. I know you don't believe me, but I don't want anyone else."

"Me either," she said, trying to catch the tears against her fingertip before they turned her eyeliner into sludge.

Caroline raised her wineglass in their direction, and Libby's heart swelled with affection. Maybe Caroline wasn't crazy about Rob. But at least she accepted that her daughter was, and she actually wanted for Libby, at that moment, what Libby wanted for herself.

After the pieces were paid for and carried out to cars and the food and wine were nearly gone, Caroline thanked everyone for coming, one by one, and handed out Holton's business cards like the perfect hostess she was.

From across the room, Libby watched Holton approach her mother. They spoke for a minute, and Caroline wrapped her arms around his shoulders and gave him a quick hug before she composed herself, smoothed her jacket, and strode away.

Libby caught up with her. "Mom, you saved the day."

Caroline closed her eyes and shrugged in a dramatic show of feigned humility.

"Next time, though, could you not refer to the artist's masterpiece as a bauble?"

Caroline twisted the diamond tennis bracelet around her wrist, her expression resuming its usual stony appearance. "Next time, could *you* please give me decent notice? We could have had twice the crowd if I'd had a little more time. And for the love of pete, never book this awful place again."

Libby quirked an eyebrow at her. "You

could have just said, 'You're welcome.' "

She quirked one back. "And you could have just said thank you."

When the guests had all left, Tess disappeared into the gallery owner's office to collect the money and receipts, and Libby was left alone with Holton.

He kicked at the wood floor. "I'm sorry for the way I treated you."

Not knowing what else to say, she simply answered, "Apology accepted."

He rubbed his nose, scratched his cheek, and kicked at the floor some more. The overhead music cut off, adding to the uncomfortable silence. "Thank you for saving my life," he finally said. "Again."

"You're welcome." She brushed imaginary lint off the skirt of her dress as her insides churned.

"Your mom's pretty great," he said, glancing out the front door to the parking lot, now nearly empty.

"She's a little rough around the edges," she said, cringing anew at Caroline's rude behavior earlier that night.

"She loves you a lot."

Libby had already begun to realize that herself, but she wondered what made him say so. "How do you figure?"

His expression finally relaxed as he chuckled. "She drove over two hours with an entire entourage, spent a small fortune, and spent the entire night telling everyone how smart, pretty, and brilliant you are."

Libby felt her lips pull up into a smile. "She did?"

"And all to help a man she's never met. A man who she has to be terrified is going to steal her daughter away from her. If that ain't love, I don't know what is."

"She's not afraid of losing me," Libby said, though she was no longer so sure.

"Are you kidding?" Holton locked eyes with her. "Know what she said to me over there?"

If she had to guess, Caroline had probably offered derogatory remarks regarding his alcoholism, choice of occupation, and outfit. She shook her head.

"She said that you were the most precious thing in the world to her and if I hurt you, she'd hurt me."

Libby laughed even as she felt like crying. "I just wish she'd accept me for what I am instead of what she wants me to be."

He let out a long breath aimed at the floor, then looked up at her. "I've learned that if you want others to accept you, you need to accept them."

CHAPTER 33

Holton stood looking out at the ocean as the sun slowly took its place among the clouds. He glanced up, trying to predict the day's weather. The sun shone red, which told him that another scorcher was on its way. Thin, white clouds haloed in gold loomed above, sure to be burned up before ever having a chance to spill water. That was fine by him. The last thing he needed was bad weather to put a damper on an otherwise-beautiful day.

A seagull landed on one of the dunes and Rufus wagged his tail and barked playfully. The bird kept one eye on him as it pecked at something in the sand. "Leave him alone, you old mutt."

Taking the admonishment as beckoning, Rufus trotted over. Holton ran a hand over his short, soft fur. "What would I do without you, you crazy hound dog?"

After licking his hand, Rufus tore off down

the beach without looking back. Drying his palm on his shorts, Holton watched him disappear toward the mansion, then began his walk in the opposite direction.

At 9 a.m. sharp, he would go down to the bank and catch up on his mortgage and the rest of the bills. Only now that it was lifting did he realize just how much his debt had been weighing him down. It dawned on him that he hadn't even thought of having a drink yesterday. Not once. Not even with a room full of wineglasses clinking around him. Not even before the room filled with the sound of clinking wineglasses, for that matter. That in itself had to be some kind of miracle. God had given him two in one day — neither of which he deserved. "Thank you," he mumbled to the sky, not having the nerve to look up.

He walked to the edge of the ocean and slipped off his tattered flip-flops. The cold water ran over his feet, leaving behind a tiny piece of seaweed sprawled across his big toe. Bending down to pick it off, he noticed a piece of wood bobbing along the froth. Before the ocean could reclaim it, he hurried over to grab it.

It was a long, thin piece, no thicker than his thumb, but it was a perfect shade of white. He ran his hand over its smooth, wet surface.

"Whatcha got there?" Tess's voice rang out from behind him.

Panicked, he whipped his head toward her. "Please tell me I didn't stand you up again."

She smiled, looking tired but content. He could still taste her kiss from the night before, and guilt filled him. What right did a man like him have to be this happy?

"No, I just felt like taking a walk and thought I might join you this morning." Gone was the makeup she had hidden behind for the past few days, and he was glad. Seeing her freckles, strawberry-blonde lashes, and the natural blush of her cheeks was the best part of his day.

He stood. "Quite a night we had."

"Quite a stepdaughter you have."

He opened his mouth to tell her that he didn't think Libby was his stepdaughter after all, but he decided the girl should be the first to know. "Do you ever imagine," he asked instead, "what the driftwood might have been as you're collecting it?"

Tess blew a strand of hair from her eyes and shook her head. "Not really. I think it's far more interesting to imagine what it could become."

That was the difference between them. He was always looking at the past, and she, the future. Then again, she didn't have a leash of regret tugging at her throat every time she tried to take a step forward.

He held up his latest find. "This, for instance. It used to be part of a tree. It was full of leaves, squirrels jumping from it, birds nesting in it, maybe fruit weighing it down. Then one day it broke off and somehow found its way into the ocean. Now look at it." He ran his finger gingerly down its gnarled, twisted surface. All the color and weight had been leached out. "It's just a dead piece of driftwood now."

Tess pulled at a string dangling from her cutoffs. "Remind you of anyone?"

He dipped his eyebrows at her.

She hooked her thumbs into the belt loops of her jean shorts. "Not to get all super-spiritual or anything, but I always think it's amazing how God can take something broken, tossed around by the sea, slammed against the rocks, and turn it into something beautiful again. I always figured that's why you chose this medium to work with."

He had never given it much thought, but she was probably right about why he was drawn to driftwood. What he wouldn't give to be half the man she saw him as. "Deadwood, that's me."

Looking into her green eyes, he felt a longing he hadn't felt, hadn't allowed himself to
feel, in a very long time. It seemed almost
sacrilegious to even think it, but the truth
was she had always gotten him in a way even
Adele hadn't. His wife had been the love of
his life, but maybe true love wasn't a one-
time shot. Maybe like this branch-turned-
driftwood, hearts could be repurposed.

He started to walk and turned to make
sure she was coming. When he looked back,
a smile lit her face and she joined him. They
carried on in silence for a few moments,
listening to the ocean thunder and seagulls
screech all around them. Without a word,
he slipped his fingers between hers. Her
hand felt so small in his, and he had an
overwhelming desire to protect her from
whatever life may throw at them. But the
truth was, he was the only thing she needed
to be protected from. When he let her hand
drop suddenly, confusion and pain filled her
eyes, but she said nothing. She was, after
all, used to being disappointed by him.

"I'm going to give up furniture making,"
he said. It had never been his passion. He
had only gotten into it because it had helped
him and Adele make ends meet. "We'll leave
that crumb for Henry the Hack."

Tess's smile told him that she liked that idea too. They walked in silence along the surf for a time, each of them lost in their own thoughts. He looked down, surprised to find her hand had found its way back into his, and he couldn't help but smile inside. Despite everything he did, she refused to give up on him.

"Are you mad at her?" she asked, looking at the sand rather than at him.

He glanced at her, surprised by the off-topic question. "Mad at Libby?"

"Adele."

He knew he had every right to be angry, and at first he had been. He'd always put Adele on a pedestal, and finding out she wasn't quite the saint he'd made her out to be rocked his faith in her. But the more he thought about it, the more he understood why she did what she did. And maybe if he could forgive her for something so big, she could look down at him from heaven with a little forgiveness too. "Not really."

"That was a pretty big secret to keep."

"Huge," he agreed.

"But you forgive her?"

He sighed. "If we want to be forgiven, we have to forgive. You know as well as anyone how much forgiveness I'm going to need."

"Wow," she said with a smile. "It's been a

long time since I heard you talk like that."
She leaned into his shoulder and he kissed
the top of her head. It was hot from the sun
beating down on them, and once again she
smelled of tangerines.

"What is that?" he asked, sniffing her.

She pulled away, looking self-conscious.
"What is what?"

"That smell." Why did everything he said
always have to come out wrong?

She glanced over, looking unsure.

"It's nice. Like tangerines."

Her face relaxed again. "If you like it so
much, maybe I'll use this shampoo more
often."

The last thing he wanted was for her to
change her life any more than she already
had just for his sake. She might start thinking it implied some kind of commitment,
and he wasn't about to sentence her to that
fate. He shrugged. "Use what you like."

She frowned but said nothing. When they
reached the pier, she started up the stairs
and he followed, trying to keep his gaze
from riding the sway of her hips. To keep
his mind from going where it ought not, he
focused on the feel of the worn wood
against his feet.

The tall sea grass bowed in the wind as
they passed, like weeds of worship. He

smiled to himself, thinking that might make an interesting name for a piece. He loved a good metaphor as well as anything. And wasn't that what humanity was, really? Nothing but weeds in God's garden, waiting for the day they would be changed into flowers.

It never ceased to amaze him how inspiration came at the oddest times, from the strangest of places. Tess kicked off her flip-flops, sat at the edge of the pier, and dangled her feet over. Only when she pointed her painted toes downward did they graze the water. Her thin but shapely legs looked so graceful, like a ballerina's. He thought she would probably like to hear that, but instead of saying it aloud, he just took a seat beside her.

"You've got a good smell too," she said.

"What, like sweat and sawdust?"

"Yeah, that," she said, dipping her big toe cautiously into the water. "And Irish Spring."

"You know what kind of soap I use?" He barely even knew the name. Green package, white lettering, bottom shelf at the Rite Aid.

"You know when you were gone for a week to Roanoke Rapids? I bought a bar of it, just to smell."

He tried not to let his surprise show.

"That trip was four years ago." She cared about him, he knew that, but he had no idea she had it that bad and certainly not for that long.

Tucking in her lips, she turned her head to hide her blush.

"I didn't know," he said, feeling guilty again. "I'm sorry." He looked out at the ocean as far as his eyes could see as she laid her head on his shoulder, letting him know all was forgiven.

"Think God can forgive a believer for murdering somebody?" He hadn't meant to ask the question. Didn't even know he'd thought it until it came out of his mouth.

Looking up at him, sunlight shone across her face, lighting her eyes like emeralds. "Are you asking about murder or unintentional manslaughter?"

"Is there a difference?"

"Of course there's a difference. You didn't kill her, Holt."

"I told you?"

"That you messed up her brakes? Yeah, you told me. About a dozen times. Like I said, you talk when you're drunk."

She knew. All this time, she knew and she didn't hate him. "Do you think she forgives me?"

Tess leaned back on her arms and watched

the waves roll in. "I think when we die, we shed this world like an old skin. I don't think she gives a hoot how she died. She's just glad to be in paradise. Besides, it was an accident. You don't even know for sure if the brakes malfunctioned. For all you know, they were working perfectly. It could have been a hundred other things that caused that accident."

She was probably right about Adele moving on to bigger and better things instead of wasting eternity worrying about him, but there was no doubt in his mind what caused the accident. "What about God?"

She raised her thin eyebrows at him. "You're seriously worried about God forgiving you for accidentally putting air in the brake line?" She leaned her head back and closed her eyes, basking in the sun. "Yeah, Holt, I think he can forgive that. You've got bigger fish to fry with God than being a second-rate mechanic."

He watched a minnow zigzag between rocks, followed by the rest of the school. "You're talking about my drinking."

"Not to mention the anger, the unforgiveness, the —" She seemed on the verge of rattling off a laundry list she'd been mentally keeping, but he cut her off.

"Anger and getting drunk, yes, but unforgiveness? I don't think I'm guilty of that one."

She gave him her infamous you-can't-be-serious look.

"Are you talking about Henry?" Henry was an idiot, a hack, and a jerk, but he was also barely a man. He'd mature in time and probably look back on the follies of his youth, like most of them did, with a fair amount of shame and embarrassment. "He's not worth being mad —"

"I'm not talking about Henry, you goof. I'm talking about you."

He rubbed the heels of his hands over his gritty eyes. "I don't deserve forgiveness. If I'd done what I said I would do and took her —"

"None of us deserves it. That's why it's called grace."

Grace, he thought, finally registering why Adele must have given Libby the name. She hoped one day to receive it.

"If we confess our sins, God is faithful and just to forgive them," she said, kicking at the water and sending a tiny wave into the air. "Even you, Holt."

He wanted to believe that; he did. But he knew he shouldn't be getting drunk, and yet he did it anyway. Sinning before he knew what sinning really was — that was one thing. Sinning when he'd already been redeemed couldn't be forgiven so easily. Shouldn't.

"I hope Libby stays," Tess said, mercifully changing the subject.

"Me too." She was a good girl and he would like her regardless of their familial relationship.

Tess leaned back and lay flat against the pier, staring up at the blue sky and a small red-and-white Piper Cub plane. It was too early for it to be out if the pilot was hoping to attract attention. What little crowds they had on this relatively remote beach wouldn't be out for at least another hour or two. "Holt," Tess asked, turning her head to look at him, "when did you know that you loved her? Adele, I mean."

He turned his head so she couldn't read more into his expression than was really there. Women always had a way of doing that. Interpreting every blink, squint, or bend of mouth into something life-shattering. There was no way to answer that question without setting off a land mine. He let out an annoyed sigh. "Please don't," he said.

She sat up and frowned at him. "Don't what? Ask you a question?" Lines etched into her forehead as a scowl formed on her face.

"I knew when I knew."

She stood, glaring down at him. "Why can't you talk about her to me?"

He ran a hand through his hair, then pushed himself up. "Because it always turns into an argument."

"Because you act all weird about it. I'm just asking you a question."

A question without an answer that would satisfy her. "When did you know you loved Mr. Pugsley?"

Her unexpected laughter was music to his ears. "The moment my mommy gave him to me."

Wrapping his arm around her shoulder, warm from the sun, he said, "Look, Tess, I loved her, but that doesn't mean I can't love anyone else." Inside, he cringed. There he went leading her on, knowing full well he would eventually let her down again. The right thing to do was to go back to the way things used to be and act like he didn't care. Let her find someone who wasn't a blight on God's green earth. Except that he couldn't go back; not anymore, not when he had fallen in love.

The smile she wore looked pained. "I knew I loved you the day you took me out on your sailboat the first time."

That would have been a couple months after Adele's funeral. He had seen her walking down the beach collecting bits of shell and had waved to her from the water. She swam out to him and they'd spent the afternoon together. He'd only wanted a little company back then. Now . . . Well, he found himself wanting a little more.

Her eyes were fixed on him, glinting with fear and hope. "You've been looking behind you for so long. It's time to start looking up."

"You mean ahead," he said.

She grinned and shook her head. "No, I mean up."

He followed her gaze to the sky and that Piper Cub plane flying above. It dipped sharply, exposing its white banner in full. It read in big black letters, "Holton Will You Marry Me?"

He felt his stomach drop and couldn't remember even how to breathe for a second as his mind whirled with all the reasons he couldn't and shouldn't, but as she looked into his eyes, he couldn't conjure a single one. She loved him. He loved her. He looked up to heaven for a sign, and the plane did a somersault, turning the question upside down . . . and he had his answer.

"I can't," he said.

With a pained expression, she closed her eyes.

"Tess, I can't let a woman propose to me."

Before she could open her eyes again, he lowered himself to one knee.

CHAPTER 34

Early the next morning, Libby heard a beep outside Tess's apartment. She took one last look at herself in the mirror and rushed out to meet Holton. It was late enough to be light, but still early enough to be cool. Today she was going to meet her grandmother, and she couldn't be more nervous or excited.

She waved through the passenger window, then climbed aboard. The truck was old enough to be classified as an antique, but there was nothing classic-looking about it. The outside was dinged as though it had been parked in the middle of a driving range. The windows were in desperate need of some Windex and the floor was covered in napkins, crumpled receipts, and empty soda bottles. Thankfully Holton had a Christmas-tree air freshener hanging from the rearview mirror, which at least made it smell clean.

The nursing home where her maternal

grandmother, Elsie, lived was a good hour's drive away, which gave them plenty of time to talk, though neither of them seemed to be able to bring themselves to begin. She had so many questions, but she knew he probably had more than a few of his own. She couldn't imagine what he must be feeling, finding out the woman he loved had kept her child a secret from him.

The tension was thick, much thicker than Libby's skin, as she tried to brace herself to hear the answers she had been seeking since the day she found out she was adopted. They drove with the radio tuned to a classic rock station playing Journey's "Faithfully." Holton hung his elbow out the open window. The morning air blowing in through it was a comfortable seventysomething degrees, and Libby decided to roll her window down too — in order to avoid seeing all the dried dog slobber as much as to enjoy the breeze.

An empty Mr. Pibb can rolled back and forth on the floor every time Holton had to brake or speed up. With her foot, Libby slid it under the seat and tried to muster courage enough to speak.

Holton hit the radio control and the cab fell silent. "There's something I need to tell you."

The seriousness in his tone made her stomach cramp. He wanted her to leave and give him some time alone with Tess. No, worse than that — he did some investigating and found out her biological father was a serial rapist. That's why Adele didn't disclose his name or tell anyone. She didn't want her daughter to know she was the offspring of a monster.

"It's possible that I'm your father," he said, throwing a nervous glance at her.

She jerked her head toward him. "What?" She couldn't possibly have heard him right.

He stared ahead at the road, stone-faced. "Adele and I . . . well, we have a sordid past."

Her mind filled with confusion, and once again it felt as though her world as she knew it was being turned upside down. She studied his profile. His nose was nothing like hers, but the shape of his chin, maybe. His eye color, definitely. But it couldn't be. Adele would have told her own husband about the child they shared.

Libby pressed her palm to her forehead as though checking for fever as she looked out the window at the couples strolling down the sidewalk.

She'd just come to terms with the fact that Caroline was the only parent she would ever know, and she was starting to be okay with that. Holton was mistaken, maybe even hoping it was true. He liked her; she knew that he did. And she liked him too, especially now that he was trying to be her father despite its impossibility. She turned to look at him again. There was a resemblance, though. More than just their eye color. Something about the way he moved. The way he spoke with his hands. She'd told Caroline and Rob as much. But they were right; it was just wishful thinking. She just wanted a father, and maybe the idea had started to grow on him too. It was sweet, but it wasn't reality.

He white-knuckled the steering wheel and stared past a crack in the windshield at the road ahead. "It drove me crazy finding out that my wife had a daughter she never told me about." He scratched the stubble on his cheek. "We were so close. I thought I knew everything there was to know about her. Adele and I dated for a short time in high school. I was three years older — a senior when she was a freshman. I'm surprised she even gave me the time of day. She was a Christian girl, a real goody-two-shoes, and, well, I was a typical teenage boy trying to experience everything as fast as I could. I pressured her into doing something she didn't want to. I led her to believe I loved her when I didn't. Not yet." He threw Libby another glance as though gauging her reaction.

Keeping her expression neutral wasn't easy, but she didn't want him to temper the truth, whatever it might be, to spare her feelings. With her thumb she anxiously rubbed the leather seat to the right of her so hard she was threatening to wear a hole in it, but her left hand, the one he could see, sat calm and still at her side.

"She broke up with me after figuring out what I was about. I was too stupid to realize back then just what I was losing, and when I finally got around to apologizing, she'd moved away. The next time I saw her, she was a woman and a college graduate. She turned up at one of my art shows. I apologized for what I'd done years earlier and she said she'd forgive me if I agreed to go to church with her, which I did more to get a date than to clear my conscience, I guess. Eventually we started dating, I got saved, and we got married. We tried to have children, but it just didn't happen for us."

A myriad of conflicting emotions filled her, from anger at Holton for pressuring a young Adele into having sex, to elation that she might actually have a father after all.

Trying to process the news, she gazed out her window, barely registering the hordes of tourists trailing jet skis, bikes, and boats behind them. It all made sense why Adele wouldn't have told him about her. She was a pregnant teen who knew she wasn't ready to be a mother. She'd already realized he was a jerk and had broken up with him. Why she didn't tell him later made sense too. How did you tell a man you never thought you'd see again that you gave up his child for adoption?

"They have paternity tests we could take," she said. Her voice sounded distant and strange as though someone else were speaking. "We could know for sure."

He said nothing as he flipped on his blinker and prepared to pass a semi. She sneaked a glance at him, feeling way too vulnerable.

He rubbed the back of his neck. "There's a verse in the Bible that says faith is being confident of what we hope for and sure of things we can't see." He reached for her hand and gave it a brief squeeze before returning his grip to the steering wheel. "Libby, you're Adele's daughter, and as far as I'm concerned, you're mine too. Adele just wasn't the type to sleep around, if you know what I mean. I doubt if it could have been anyone else. If we took a test and found I wasn't biologically related, then what? You go searching for another dad? I want to be that man. I *am* that man."

This was something Libby had never expected and hadn't prepared herself for. "But what if it confirmed it? You would never have to wonder."

He tucked his lips in and drummed the steering wheel with his thumb for what seemed like forever, then finally said, "I know I've been horrible to you. Why would you want a nasty drunk for a father? But, Libby, looking at you, I see her. I loved her and I already love you. You bring out the best in me. You, me, and Tess — we kind of already feel like a family, don't you think?"

Despite her best efforts to keep them at bay, tears rolled down her face. It was so much more than she'd hoped for. "I think so too," she said.

When he turned to smile at her, she saw that his eyes were wet too. It was all too much, and yet just right.

"Can you tell me about her?"

He looked ahead at a large green-and-white reflective highway sign and flipped on the blinker, preparing to take the next exit headed west. "I brought you something that can tell you more about her than I ever could." He reached behind the seat and slid his arm around, feeling for something. After a few seconds, his hand emerged holding a book bound in blue leather. He handed it to her. "I'm probably the last person in the world that should be telling anyone about God, but I guess I'm starting to make peace with him. I was so ticked that he took her from me. I thought he must really hate me to do something like that, and that's when I started to drink. I mean, if God stops loving you, you must be pretty worthless, right? But looking at you and seeing your selflessness despite everything I've done . . ." His Adam's apple rose and fell as he swallowed. "I see him in you, Libby. If he didn't think there was hope for me, he wouldn't have led you here."

The cover of the book was tattered and peeling and the gold lettering on the front had all but worn away, but it was clear that it was a Bible. She had hoped he was giving her a photo album, a journal, even a college yearbook.

"That was her prized possession," he said. "You can't know your mother without knowing her God. That's who she was more than your mother, my wife, or anything else."

Libby cracked the pages in the middle and

was delighted to see lots of handwritten notes and scribbles. "Is this her handwriting?"

He glanced over and nodded. "I used to love to read what she wrote in the margins. Even after years of marriage, I could never learn enough about her."

"Why do you think she didn't tell you?" It dawned on her then that he wasn't the only one who had a right to be angry at Adele. If she had told him as she ought to have done, they might have been able to have a relationship sooner. He could have been at her graduation, taught her to drive, or any of the things she'd missed out on by not having a father.

She wanted to ask him why he wasn't angry, but there was too much else to talk about. The rest of the ride flew by. They couldn't talk fast enough, and by the time they arrived at the nursing home, she actually felt like she was beginning to know Adele, Holton, and even herself just a little bit better.

CHAPTER 35

Libby's sandals tapped steadily against the tiled floor as she followed Holton down the long hallway of Hillbridge Oaks Retirement Home. The walls were painted a color that reminded her of tobacco-stained teeth, and the place smelled of Lysol and ammonia.

They approached the receptionist sitting at the front desk. She wore her hair in what could only be described as a mousy-brown beehive. "May I help you?" she asked flatly.

Holton looked at Libby, then stepped forward. "I'm here to see my mother-in-law, Elsie Davison."

"What floor is she on?"

"Last time I was here was five years ago." He studied his feet, looking ashamed of himself.

The pinched look on the woman's face gave away her contempt. She probably saw it all the time. She typed something into her ancient-looking computer and looked over the screen at them. "What floor *was* she on?"

Jangling the change in his pocket, he said, "She wasn't on a floor. She was in assisted living, but I don't remember the apartment number."

Again the woman typed, then studied the screen they couldn't see. "She moved to Two North about a year ago."

"What kind of floor is that?" Libby asked, hoping it wasn't the Alzheimer's unit.

"It's our subacute floor."

"What's that mean?" Holton asked, looking alarmed.

The woman looked at the phone as though willing it to ring. "It's for residents who need nursing care."

"What's wrong with her?" Libby asked.

"I'm sorry, hon, you'll have to talk with the nursing staff." She pointed to the elevator at their right. "Take that to the second floor, turn left, and follow the corridor until you see the sign." The phone rang, and she snatched it up. "Hillbridge Oaks. How may I direct your call?"

Libby and Holton had started toward the elevator when the receptionist called to them. She had her hand placed over the receiver. "She's in room 223."

"Thank you," Libby called back.

As they stepped off the elevator, the acrid smell of bleach hit her. Several patients were lined up along the hallway, sitting in what looked like adult-size high chairs. One lady, who looked like she was in her thirties, leaned to the side while a string of drool trickled from the corner of her mouth.

"This place is depressing," she whispered to Holton.

He approached the nurses' station, where a woman sat typing on a computer. She glanced up at them. "May I help you?"

"I'm here to see Elsie Davison," he said. "I'm her son-in-law."

Behind the station, a nurse filled a pitcher of water and set it on a medicine cart. "You're Elsie's first visitors since she's been with us," she said happily, as though they should be proud of the fact.

Libby felt ashamed, though she knew there was no reason she should be. She hadn't even known she had a grandmother until yesterday.

"Can we see her?" he asked.

"Let me make sure she's ready," she said, and started to stand.

Libby quickly interjected, wanting to get a true picture of the care her grandmother was getting there, rather than some staged version. "That's not necessary." She grabbed

Holton by the hand and started up the hall. They followed the room numbers until they came to room 223.

The door stood partially open. She took a deep breath. Part of her was brimming with excitement to be meeting more of her family. Part of her was petrified that her grandmother either wouldn't be in her right mind or else wouldn't believe that she was who she said she was.

She looked at Holton for moral support. His shoulders were slumped, and he picked at his bottom lip. No doubt the fact that he hadn't come to visit his mother-in-law since her daughter died weighed on him. And it should, she thought. It was awful leaving her without so much as bringing her flowers on Mother's Day or taking her out to eat once in a while.

Libby rapped her knuckles lightly on the door. A surprisingly young voice told them to come in.

Holding her breath, she slowly pushed the door open. A young woman in pink scrubs appeared surprised to see them. "Oh, I thought you were one of the nurses."

"Nope, just family," Holton said.

The nurse looked at the elderly woman with tight white curls lying in the bed with her eyes clamped too tightly shut to be sleeping. She was covered with a white blanket, but even through it, Libby could see by her thin outline that she was petite like her.

"Nice to meet you," the nurse said to Holton with a warm smile. "I'm Beverly. I work with Elsie a lot." She turned her attention to Libby. "And you are?"

The question hung in the air for an uncomfortably long time. "Her granddaughter," Holton finally said.

Elsie's eyes sprang wide open, and Libby jumped in surprise.

The nurse looked at Elsie with obvious affection. "I just helped her to the commode and she's had her breakfast." She turned to Elsie. "Haven't you, sweetheart?"

Elsie rolled her eyes. "You can go now," she told the woman. It wasn't the sweet, shaky voice Libby had expected.

"She's a firecracker," the woman said to Holton as though they were sharing an inside joke.

When she left, Holton just stood at the foot of the bed with his hands shoved in the front pockets of his shorts, looking like he'd rather be anywhere but there.

Elsie pushed herself up to a sitting position. "She's a sweet girl, but she treats me like a child. She insists on walking me to the bathroom every single time. She's afraid I'm going to fall and break a hip."

"It's good to see you," Holton whispered, his eyes roaming everywhere but at her.

"Is it?" she said. "I wish I could say the same." She turned her attention to Libby. "Come here, young lady. My eyes aren't as good as they used to be."

With her heart in her throat, Libby walked over to the bed. Feathering from Elsie's mouth were too many wrinkles to count, but her skin was almost the color of porcelain, just like her daughter's, just like Libby's. "Come closer," Elsie said, reaching her fingertips toward her.

Libby leaned into her soft touch.

Elsie gasped. "Oh my word, you look just like her."

"You know about me," she stated rather than asked. If Elsie had known about her, then why didn't she try to find her? Because, like everyone else, she decided Libby wasn't worth the effort?

Elsie smiled. "I can't believe it's you, Grace. I can't believe he found you."

"Actually, she found me, Mom," Holton said, sounding more at ease. "And her name's Libby now."

She glared in his direction. "You lost the

right to call me Mom when you deserted me."

Libby sat on the edge of the hospital bed. "I came to find her, but I got here too late."

Elsie took Libby's hand and pressed it against her heart. A soft, steady beat pulsated against her palm. A scowl suddenly pinched Elsie's features and she glared in Holton's direction again. "Don't just stand there staring at us like some Peeping Tom. Give me and my granddaughter some privacy."

"I'll be in the hall," he mumbled.

Elsie picked up the plastic cup from her bedside table and flung it at his back. It landed several feet short. He looked down at the cup, then walked out of the room and closed the door behind him.

"Go on, leave," Elsie yelled. "It's what you do best."

Libby stood to move the lump of blanket out of her way, then sat again beside her grandmother. "You hate him."

The scowl Elsie had been wearing melted away. "Oh, sweetheart, I don't hate anyone. I'm just angry. He's the only family I've got in the world —" she smiled apologetically — "except you. If someone did that to you and didn't even pick up the phone to call you once in a while, you'd be mad too."

Did she seriously not see the irony? "You're mad at him for abandoning you, and he was just your son-in-law. I'm not mad at my mother or you for abandoning me."

Elsie's eyes grew wide. "She didn't abandon you, sweetheart. She gave you a better life."

Libby felt a rage welling up from a place she didn't know existed. "A better life? How did she know who I'd end up with? I could have been adopted by a child molester for all she knew."

"She was just a child herself."

"*You* weren't," Libby said, on the verge of hysteria. Until that moment, she hadn't felt mad at her birth mother for giving her up, so why now? Why take it out on her poor grandmother? She felt guilt and fury at the same time, wanting to scream at her but afraid to lose the only piece of Adele she had left. "Why didn't you make her keep me?"

Elsie's lips quivered like a child's. "It was her choice, Grace."

"You could have raised me. You could have given me a good life, and I could have grown up knowing her."

The tears forming in Elsie's eyes angered Libby more, because they made her feel guilty when she wasn't the one who had abandoned anyone. She'd been given away like old clothes to Goodwill, but here she was anyway, reaching out when no one did the same for her. She'd turned eighteen two years before her mother's passing, so why hadn't Adele tried to find her then? She was worth trying to find.

"Why didn't she look for me?"

Elsie's damp, milky eyes searched hers frantically. "I don't know, honey. Maybe she was afraid you would reject her."

Libby closed her eyes. "Why didn't you?"

She felt Elsie's hand stroke her hair. "The same reason, I guess. She loved you, Grace. I love you. We did what we thought was going to be best for you. After the nurse came to take you away, I sat beside her in the hospital bed, just like you're doing now. I held her for hours as she cried herself to sleep."

Libby laid her head beside her grandmother and let her hold her just as she'd done with Adele all those years ago.

"I'm so sorry," Elsie said over and over. "She loved you. She loved you."

After what seemed like forever, Libby ran out of tears. Letting out one last ragged breath, she dried her eyes and sat back up. "I'm sorry for —"

Elsie touched her lips to quiet her. "You have nothing to be sorry about. But, honey, neither did your mother. She did what she thought was best. She made a mistake getting pregnant, but she did the most selfless thing I've ever witnessed a human being do. She gave up the part of herself she loved the most, all so you could have parents who could take care of you the way you deserved."

Libby considered what Adele must have gone through. Though it hurt like crazy, she believed Elsie. She believed she had been wanted after all.

"I wish I could have known her," she said.

"I wish you could have too, and I wish she could have known you. She would have been so proud." Elsie tucked in her lips as tears welled again in her eyes. "I'll tell her all about you when I get to heaven, okay?" Her sad smile melted Libby's heart. "How did you find the old boar?" She glanced at the door Holton was presumably on the other side of.

"My mother gave me the adoption papers, and I found Holton on the web."

"Phooey," she said, batting the air with her small hand. "Web. Web. Everyone's talking about it. Sounds like something meant to trap its prey." She patted Libby's hand.

"It doesn't matter. You're here now. I prayed to the good Lord I'd get to meet you before I passed, and here you are right on time. Do you know that you're my only grandchild? I always thought there'd be more, but it wasn't to be."

"I'm so glad to finally meet you," Libby said. She couldn't believe the depth of love she already felt for a woman she'd just met. She had so many more questions for her, but before she could voice the first, Elsie began to answer them.

"Adele came to me one night and told me she'd made a mistake." She chuckled. "As though that sort of thing happened because she forgot to tie her shoes. Once she'd made up her mind to put you up for adoption, there was no reason anyone needed to know. She stayed with my sister until she gave birth to you." A sad look passed over her. "People can be so judgmental. Especially when you're the preacher's daughter."

Libby's grandfather had been a preacher, and this pleased her, though she couldn't say why. She supposed it would have pleased her finding out he was a spy or a plumber just as much. She was just so happy to have a family history. Every word Elsie said now was another piece of her puzzle put back into place.

"Why didn't she ever tell Holton she had a daughter?"

A look passed over her after a moment that said things were finally falling into place for her, too. She touched the top of her white curls as if just considering her appearance. "She hadn't told me who your father was, and quite frankly, I didn't ask. But inside, I guess I always knew it had to be him. She thought she'd never see him again."

Libby felt a surge of disappointment, then relief that Elsie could neither confirm nor deny Holton's paternity. He wanted to be her dad, and that was more than she could say for any other man in the world.

"She didn't like him much the first time they dated," Elsie said, turning on her side and leaning on her elbow. "You wouldn't believe what a turd that man was." Her lips puckered as if she'd just sucked a lemon. "Her father and I couldn't stand him. The worst part was, he was running around town with as many girls as he could scrape off the bottom of his shoe, but he was so jealous when your mother so much as talked to the grocery boy."

Libby scrunched her nose in disbelief. Holton had more than his fair share of faults, but she couldn't see him being the jealous type.

When Elsie waved her hand, Libby spotted a small bruise on her elbow — the kind the elderly seemed to get from everything that touched them. "That boy was so clingy he was breathing in her exhaled air."

She laughed at that. It was just so hard to imagine. He was as aloof as anyone she'd ever met. "Huh."

"But after he'd grown up a bit, he was much better and began to love your mother fiercely, and more importantly, Jesus. Even so, he's always had an artist's temperament through and through. I always thought that's why she didn't tell him, but now I think maybe she didn't believe he could ever forgive her for giving away his child." Her milky eyes searched Libby's with a childlike vulnerability. "Your adoptive parents — they were good to you, weren't they?"

Libby decided not to complain about all the things she'd missed growing up not having a father or about how controlling Caroline could be. It would serve no purpose other than making Elsie sad. Besides, she was realizing that though Caroline might not have been what she wanted, she had probably been just what she needed. "Yes, Grandma, I've had a good life. My adoptive mother is a good woman. What about you?

Are they good to you here?"

"Say that again," Elsie said, her eyes filling.

"I had a good life?" Libby repeated.

"No, call me Grandma again. I've waited all my life to hear that."

"Grandma," Libby repeated, wiping at her eyes. "Grandma," she said again, both of them laughing through tears.

Suddenly Elsie laid her head back on the pillow and scrunched her eyes closed.

Alarmed, Libby jumped up and shook her. "Grandma, are you okay?"

Elsie's fake snore was too loud and sudden to be real. Either she had some sort of narcolepsy or else she was faking. The smirk on her lips hinted at the latter.

"I know you're not sleeping," Libby said with a frown.

Elsie opened one eye, then the other, and grinned. "I never could fool your mother either."

It was an odd thing to do, but Libby decided she didn't care if the woman was getting senile or was just eccentric. She had a grandmother, a father, and a mother. Just like other girls. And suddenly miracles didn't seem so hard to believe in. "Come home with me," Libby said.

Elsie smiled. "Oh no, honey. This is my

363

home and these people have become my family. Besides, tonight they're serving banana pudding, and those little darlings from the elementary school are coming to sing to us. I couldn't miss that."

Sadness filled Libby. "Are you sure? I can learn to make pudding, and I'm not too bad of a singer."

Elsie pulled out her upper dentures and gave them a perturbed look before sliding them back in. "I'm sure. Thank you for making this old woman happy. Will you come back and see me again?" she asked in a childlike voice.

"Every week," Libby said.

Elsie's smile was radiant. "Would you send your father back in here?"

Your father. No two words had ever sounded sweeter. Except maybe, "Yes, Grandma."

Libby emerged from Elsie's room with red, swollen eyes and a smile. "She wants to see you," she said.

Holton's whole body sighed. "How mad is she?"

"She'll be fine," she said, not sounding too sure. "Go ahead and get it over with."

He pushed open the door, feeling like a

little boy as he put his hand up in a half wave.

"Come closer. I'm going blind," Elsie said. Her eyes were puffy, telling him she'd been crying too. He wanted a drink so badly it scared him. How was he ever going to get through this sober?

He walked to the edge of her bed.

"You still drinking?" she asked like an accusation.

"Nope. Quit. For good."

She raised her eyebrows. "Why?"

He dug his hands into his pockets, wondering if he should go with the long answer or the short. "Almost died."

"Isn't that what you wanted?"

He looked down at a nick on the linoleum tile beside his foot. "Not anymore."

She studied him for an uncomfortable moment. "Because you've got someone who needs you again." The sound of laughter came from the hallway and he thought of Libby, hoping it was her laughter he was hearing and that she wasn't out there crying her eyes out over the sins of her parents.

"You know I thought you went to pot because Adele wasn't around to take care of you, but now I think it's because you stopped having someone to take care of."

He sneaked a glance at her. She was sitting up with her pillow lying across her lap.

"The problem is you're still trying to take care of her."

"What's that supposed to mean?" he asked, sounding as defensive as he felt.

"She's gone," Elsie said flippantly. "Let the dead bury the dead."

If a man had said that to him, he would have knocked him upside the head. Adele deserved more. "This is your daughter you're talking about."

She crossed her arms over her flannel nightgown. "No, I'm talking about your wife. Your *late* wife. It's time to move on. You make up to Grace what your little back-seat car romp did to that girl. You know Adele would have wanted you to."

"She should have told me."

She narrowed her eyes at him. "You say that as if I didn't know the man you used to be. What would you have done if she had?" Before he could answer, she did. "Offer to marry her out of obligation and then prance around like a peacock, proud of how you did the right thing? You would have left my teenage daughter at home, with no money and no life, while you were out chasing skirts. You would have resented her, and she would have felt like nothing to you but a burden. You've spent enough time in denial.

366

Get real with yourself for once in your life."

Holton had no response. Elsie was right, and they both knew it. He would have felt trapped. He would have resented Adele. He resented her back then just for trying to get him to go steady with her. "I'm a different man. I'm going to be a good father to Libby."

Elsie stared him down. "You better be."

CHAPTER 36

Holton entered the church meeting room and took a seat in the back. The place was drab with its avocado walls, faded carpet, and musty smell, but then, as far as he knew, they offered the space for free, so no one really had a right to complain. The room was full of chatter and laughter rising from men of all walks of life — nose-ringed punks, guys with neck tattoos who looked like they just got out of prison, suits, grandfathers, and even a few frat-boy types. There were even two men dressed in the green scrubs he'd seen doctors wearing. It was the most diverse of the three meetings he'd been at, and he liked that. It reminded him that anyone could struggle with alcoholism.

The kid beside him looked like he needed a note from his mother to be there, and the guy on the other side looked like he was one heartbeat away from a toe tag. The old man caught him looking and put a hand out. His skin was so transparent, Holton could have counted his veins. "Alvin."

Holton gave his hand a pump. "Holt. Nice to meet you."

"Any friend of Al is a friend of mine."

He wondered if one day he'd talk the way these guys did, all the AA lingo and mantras. That was fine, he supposed, so long as he stayed clean.

After a few minutes, the speaker took the floor — just another guy in recovery like the rest of them. Holton shifted in his metal folding chair, trying to get comfortable.

The thirtysomething guy had obviously just come from work, because his suit jacket and tie rested on the chair behind him. "Hello, everyone. I'm Tom, and I'm an alcoholic. I'd like to welcome you to the evening meeting. We would like to give a special welcome to new attendees and have you introduce yourselves."

This was Holton's third meeting but the first at this location. Apparently everyone here was regular enough to know that he wasn't, because a roomful of eyeballs all focused on him expectantly.

He had no intention of speaking when he chose this location, but with all attention on him, he didn't feel he had much of a choice. So he stood and said, "I'm Holton, and I'm an alcoholic."

Voices all around him rang out, "Hi, Holton."

"This is only my third meeting, and I'm already working on step eight. You know, making a list of everyone I've harmed and being ready to make amends. I don't know if it's normal to get through them so quickly, but . . ." He wanted to add, *but the sooner I get through the steps, the sooner I can be done with all this meeting stuff.* He shrugged and waited for someone to acknowledge or admonish him, but no one said a word.

Sometimes, he thought, they took the rule of no cross talk to an extreme so that even when someone needed a "go on" or an "attaboy," he got only uncomfortable stares. "That's all," he blurted out, cringing under their scrutiny. "Talking about it is just making me want to drink more." He turned to leave, not intending to come back. He didn't need this pressure.

"Where you going, Holt?" the old man asked.

When he looked around to see that everyone's attention was still on him, he felt his face catch fire. "I think maybe I'm better off doing this on my own."

"Really?" another man said from behind him. "You can be a drunk on your own, but you can't stay sober that way. If you could have done it on your own, you would have." He turned around to see Roberto, the owner of Ark Antiques, behind him, and he couldn't contain his surprise. He had no idea.

"That's right, I'm an alcoholic too, Holt. Stay and tell us your story. You'll feel better. I know I did."

Holton just stood there, feeling in stupefied limbo — wanting to leave, but not wanting to at the same time. He knew, from the few meetings he'd attended, that he wasn't alone in his alcoholism, but the men were all people who weren't quite real to him. Roberto was someone he saw every week. He had known Adele. He was real.

Holton looked around and cleared his throat. "I've been drinking since my wife died five years ago. Right or wrong, I blamed myself for her death."

The boy to the left of him pumped his fist. Not knowing what else to do, Holton acknowledged it with a half nod. "I guess I was mad at God for what I'd done. I worked on her car, and I'm pretty sure I screwed up the brakes because she hit another car head-on at sixty miles an hour. He walked away; she didn't. The cops said she could have fallen asleep, but I knew the truth."

He looked around at their faces, expecting to see disgust, but found nothing but sympathetic expressions at best, indifference at worst.

The speaker nodded for him to continue.

"She was everything to me. We didn't have children to dote on, only each other." He shook his head. "Well, I thought we didn't have children, but it turns out —" He paused, realizing he was revealing more than he planned to.

The speaker leaned forward in his chair, resting his arms on his legs. "It's safe, Holt. What's shared at the meeting stays at the meeting."

Holton looked over his shoulder at Roberto, who nodded reassurance.

"It turns out that I have a daughter. A grown daughter that my wife never told me about. When I found out about her, I wanted to drink more. I mean, how could she keep my own child a secret?" The anger he thought he'd already let go of flashed in him again but dissipated just as quickly. "But she's incredible. I mean, she's the kind of daughter we all dream we'll have. She's smart, funny, beautiful, talented. And the thought of letting her down after she's been let down so much already . . ." He had to will himself not to choke up. If he wouldn't let Tess see him cry, he sure wasn't about to break down in front of this motley crew. "Well, I know you're supposed to quit drinking for yourself, but I hope it's okay that it isn't just for me. I want to be clean for her, and for my fiancée." He cringed at the term. It sounded ridiculous coming from someone his age, but he knew if Tess had been there to hear it, it would have made her day.

Heads were nodding approval at him, and he took this cue as his chance to finish and sit down, but before his butt could hit the chair, he stood up again. "But that's not all."

"Please go on," the speaker said.

"It's not just them either. God gave me an amazing wife, but instead of being thankful, I thumbed my nose at him when he took her home. And in the midst of my drinking and cursing him, is he getting even with me? No, he sent a woman to help and love me, all while preparing the way for my daughter to find me at the very moment I'm about to commit suicide via the bottle." He had to pause and clear the lump from his throat.

"My wife — I thought she was a saint. The woman didn't lie, didn't steal, didn't drink, didn't even cuss when she stubbed her toe. I mean, I thought she was about perfect, but when my daughter showed up, I realized she wasn't any more perfect than I am. I think that's the moment it began to niggle into this wet brain of mine that maybe I didn't deserve to die. Maybe I was no worse than her or anyone else." He looked around the room at several faces smiling like they understood. "Guess that's all."

When he sat, another man stood. "Thanks for sharing, Holton. My name's Gary, and I'm an alcoholic."

"Hi, Gary." Holton added his welcome to all the others chiming out.

"My wife left me and I blamed my drinking on that, but looking back, I didn't drink because she left. She left because I drank. My stinking thinking has always gotten me in trouble, but today I'm celebrating twenty-five years clean thanks to you guys, my higher power, and a whole lot of prayers."

The room erupted in applause and Holton added his to the mix. *Wow,* he thought, *one day at a time could really add up.*

Several more men shared their stories, and then the main speaker stood again. "In closing this meeting, let me remind you that the opinions expressed here are strictly those of the individual. Remember also that the things you hear and share here are spoken and shared in confidence. Let them be treated as confidential. If you listen with an open mind, if you try to absorb what you see and hear, you are bound to gain a better understanding of yourself, your problem, and a way to better handle that problem. Would those who care to please help me close this meeting with the Lord's Prayer?"

When they finished, the men gathered around refreshments, and Holton slid a crumpled piece of paper out of his front pocket. The paper still had the straggly edges from where he'd ripped it out of his notebook. On it were scrawled three names.

Elsie was the first. The best he could do for her was to make it a point to call and visit regularly.

Libby was next. The way he figured it, if he hadn't been a jerk to Adele, the three of them would have been a family from the get-go. He couldn't do anything about that now, but he intended to work on being the best father he could for whatever time they had left together, and that would have to be enough.

Last but not least was Tess. He didn't know what would ever make up for all he'd put her through, but he planned on spending the rest of his life trying.

CHAPTER 37

Libby struggled to lug Tess's suitcase up the stairs to the apartment above the studio. Tess followed behind, struggling even more with an armful of hanging clothes. "It's going to be a tight squeeze," she said. "I'm sorry to impose this on you."

Climbing the last stair, Libby's muscles begged for a break as she set down the suitcase. The place looked twice as small with Tess's belongings now crammed into it. "I'm the one with an apartment just sitting empty," Libby said. "If anyone's imposing, it's me." The polite thing to do would be to go back to her own place and leave Tess and Holton to a little romantic privacy, especially now that they were engaged, but she couldn't bring herself to say good-bye a moment before she had to.

Tess wiped the perspiration from her brow and laid her armful of clothes on the bed with a grunt. "The only thing you've imposed is a little function and happiness around here."

Libby felt herself blush. "I don't know about that." It was nice to think of how far Holton had come in the short time she'd been there and how his and Tess's relationship had finally bloomed, but she doubted she had much to do with any of it. Pulling the damp hair off the back of her neck, she fanned herself with her hand. As tired as she was getting of the blistering heat, the end of summer also meant the end of her time here, and she wished that could go on forever.

Caesar peeked his head out of his kitty condo and meowed a hello.

Tess rubbed at the mark left on her wrist by one of the clothes hangers she had carried in. "That cat's got more living room than we do." Glancing around the room full of boxes and clothes, a look of contentment passed over her. "It'll be tight, but it'll also be fun. Besides, it's just until the wedding."

The wedding. What an interesting day that was going to be. Libby couldn't wait to see Holton all gussied up as they walked down the aisle together . . . or Rob waiting beside the altar. And no matter what kind of over-the-top monstrosity Caroline turned the ceremony into, it was going to be perfect.

When Tess grabbed a stack of clothes off the bed and busied herself putting them away in an unoccupied crevice inside the closet, Libby walked to the bathroom and splashed cold water on her face in an attempt to cool down. The cold rivulets of water trickling down her cheeks felt heavenly against her overheated skin. She grabbed a hand towel off the ring. As she pressed the terry cloth to her face, she caught sight of herself in the mirror and smiled. This was a different woman from the one who'd arrived here just weeks earlier. Never in a million years did she imagine this finale when she found Holton lying blue on the floor.

"You know," she said to Tess as she walked back out of the bathroom, "people say that men make plans and God laughs. I always thought that meant he was sitting on his throne, getting his jollies by throwing marbles under everyone's skates." She stopped to pick up a pair of socks that had fallen out of a clothes basket and tossed them back in.

Tess closed the dresser drawer and looked over her shoulder. "Wow. And now?"

"Now I think maybe his plans really are better than the ones we make for ourselves."

Tess tilted her head and smiled. "Sounds

378

like someone's been reading her mother's Bible."

She shrugged like it was no big deal, but it was and they both knew it. Even bigger than a wedding, which she had thought a few short months ago was as big as life could get.

"I forgot to tell you," Tess said, then paused to look at herself in the mirror. She slid her braid over her shoulder and brushed a few stray hairs from her forehead before continuing. "Holton texted while you were in the bathroom. He has something he wants to show us."

Libby raised her eyebrows in question.

Flopping backward onto the bed with a loud sigh, Tess lay right on top of her clothes. "All I know is he's been working like a madman on a new piece. He hasn't offered me so much as a peek."

Whatever it was, Libby couldn't wait to see it. She hadn't seen much of her father since he took her to meet Elsie, but she was beginning to understand the focus great art required of its creator. Besides, she knew it kept him from drinking. Whatever worked for him was fine by her.

"He was like that with the stallion too," Tess said, staring up at the wood ceiling. "He's always been weird about showing new things he's trying until they're finished."

"I can understand that." Libby moved a T-shirt out of her way and sat beside Tess on the small bed. It was just a twin, which meant one of them would need to sleep on the floor. She'd insist on it being her. The way Tess rubbed at the small of her back after a long day of bending over told Libby that despite her youthful body, middle age was catching up to her. "My curiosity is definitely piqued."

Tess sat up suddenly, making the mattress spring under her. "Guess we'll find out together." She slipped her cell phone out of her pocket and looked at the time. "I guess we better get going."

The three of them sat on the bench seat of Holton's truck as they drove with the sun glaring in at them through the windshield. Libby looked down at the floor, free of the usual soda cans, crumpled napkins, and coating of sand that normally covered it. Even the windows, which were usually smudged with fingerprints and dog slobber, were sparkling. "Hey, it's clean," she said.

Gripping the wheel, Holton took his eyes off the road long enough to throw her a glance. "That's what happens when you get a woman. They start cleaning stuff." He shook his head as though this were a bad thing.

Tess playfully smacked his thigh. "And when you get a man, they start repairing stuff." She turned to Libby. "Guess who surprised me by having my suspension fixed?"

"Way to go, Holt," she said. She almost asked if he did the work himself, but stopped herself just in time. That would have been a thoughtless question. Of course he didn't.

When they came to a stop sign, he slowed to a stop behind a primed Corvette. "Libby, I was thinking," he said, looking to Tess as though he needed help, "that maybe, you know, you could, if you wanted . . ." He licked his lips nervously. "With me being, you know —"

"He wants you to call him Dad," Tess blurted, then slapped a hand over her mouth as though it had acted against her wishes. Her small princess diamond sparkled in the sunlight.

"Thanks a lot," he mumbled.

The Corvette in front of them revved its engine and rolled forward as Libby felt her breath catch. She had spent most of her childhood pining to have someone to call Dad, but she had resigned herself to the fact that it wasn't meant to be.

"Sorry," Tess said, sounding miserable. "You were just rambling on. I figured you needed some help."

A car beeped behind them, and Holton glanced into the rearview, looking startled, before setting off again.

The thought of saying the endearment out loud made Libby feel vulnerable and afraid. *He's not George,* she reminded herself. *He's not going to abandon you.* But even if he did, she'd read enough to know that God wouldn't. And that thought, more than anything, helped her relax. "Dad," she said, cautiously trying it out. She'd grown so used to calling him by his first name that the word felt a little strange on her lips, but she knew in time, it would become as comfortable as their relationship.

Letting her know she'd done well, Tess reached over and gave her arm a gentle squeeze.

"So, Dad," she said, trying out the word again, "what's this surprise you're taking me and Tess to?"

He turned onto Main Street and parked out front of a small store with a For Lease sign.

Tess turned to look out Libby's window, and her eyes grew wide with understanding.

"Is this what I think it is?"

Holton drummed his thumbs against the steering wheel. "So, what do you think? Gallery material?"

He didn't wait for an answer. Instead he pulled the keys out of the ignition and climbed out. He walked around to open the passenger door.

"Thanks, Dad," Libby said as she stepped onto the sidewalk and back into the heat.

"You don't have to wear it out," he said with a wink in his voice.

"Holton Bartholomew Creary," Tess admonished.

Flecks in the sidewalk glinting like shards of crystal in the sunlight caught Libby's eye. "Your middle name is Bartholomew?"

"No. It's Samuel. She thinks she's being funny." He gave Tess a look that said he wasn't amused, though his tone said otherwise. "There's a lot of quirks you're going to learn about Tess if you hang around here long enough. Like when she's sick, she sleeps with a stuffed bear."

Tess narrowed her eyes at him.

"And," he laughed, "its name is Mr. Pugsley."

"*His* name," Tess said. "And you'd better not be talking smack about the Pugs." She looked up at the turquoise awning covering the storefront's doorway and touched the whitewashed stone admiringly. "Wow, this is nice," she said to herself before turning her attention back to the conversation. "He's got his eccentricities too. Believe me."

Libby laughed. "Oh, I believe you." Before getting sober, he was nothing but.

Holton paused in front of the oversize front window. An array of local band flyers were taped haphazardly over the bottom half of it.

She almost said out loud that the adhesive ought to be fun to scrape off, but she stopped herself in time. This was a time to celebrate his accomplishment, not bemoan how much work it was going to be.

"I figure this will be the perfect spot for a display." He reached over and took Tess's hand as he slid a key into the dead bolt. With a quick turn of hand, they were inside and out of the heat of the sun.

The place had an old bookstore kind of aroma, but she knew the wonderful smells of glue and sawdust would soon replace it. They walked across a polished oak floor that possessed just enough scratches to give it character. The wall across from the front window was brick, and it looked like it had once been exposed to the elements. "It's got a nice artsy feel to it," Libby said to no one in particular.

"That's what I thought too," he said, scanning the open room. "Tess, if you're up for it, I'd like for you to plan the layout."

She threw her arms around him enthusiastically.

He chuckled. "I'll take that as a yes."

Tess grinned over his shoulder at Libby, and she couldn't help but grin back. Their dreams were beginning to come true, and she felt so lucky that she was there to see it.

Holton locked eyes with her. "Lib, I'd like . . . if you would have time . . . You know, you're so good with numbers and all the marketing —" his face reddened — "but I know you have your own life, and . . ." He rubbed a smudge on the floor with the tip of his flip-flop.

She decided to put him out of his misery. "Are you asking me to go into business with you?"

"If he isn't, I am," Tess said. Libby could practically see her wheels turning as she eyed the walls, ceiling, and nooks, mentally setting up shop.

"That's what I'm asking," he said, daring a glance up.

Excitement filled her, but she did her best to keep it from bubbling over for now. It wasn't just her decision to make. A few weeks ago it would have been an impossibility, but now that Rob was job hunting, here was as good a place as any to begin again. "I'll have to talk to Rob. It would mean living here full-time, and I don't know if he's going to be okay with that." She thought of all the promises she had made to him that this whole living arrangement was just for the summer.

Holton slid the key back into his pocket and started walking toward the back of the store. "Of course. That goes without saying. Just tell him that his future father-in-law would really appreciate him sharing you with your daddy."

The way he said *daddy* made her want to cry, but she'd done far too much of that already this summer. She wanted this so badly, not just because she knew he needed more time with her but because she had fallen in love with his art, Nags Head, Rufus, and most of all, him and Tess. "I'll crack my knuckles in his face when I —" she held up two fingers on each hand, making air quotes — " 'ask' him."

"That's my girl," Holton said, finally looking at ease. She noticed then that he wasn't wearing either of the two pairs of frayed Bermuda shorts he rotated between, but a new pair of khakis.

"New shorts?" she asked, her voice echoing through the empty space.

He leaned over and kissed Tess's cheek. "Women," he said, "always got to try and make everything look presentable."

Tess gave him an incredulous look. "Yeah, right. He bought those himself."

He walked to the back of the room and waved them over. "I have an idea for the front display."

Libby noticed then that there was a shrouded shape in the far corner. When he pulled off the covering, Libby gasped. An enormous driftwood tree stood before her. Its trunk was as thick as her body; its long, twisted branches were made of varying shades of light and dark wood, each flawlessly worked into the braided trunk that supported them. She couldn't imagine the time and effort it must have taken him to steam so many pieces to get them to bend like that. At the end of each of the branches hung a brightly colored scarf, like the drooping branches of a willow tree. The brilliant colors of the canopy made a striking contrast to the deadwood supporting them.

She glanced at her father, once again awed by his talent. Never would she have thought to add the scarves, and if he had tried to explain the project to her, she would have thought he'd lost it, but somehow it didn't just work; it was brilliant.

He shoved his hands into his pockets. "Think the color is too much? I've never tried to do anything like this, but I guess this place used to be a fabric shop, and I found a box full of those things in the back. I was just messing around, but —"

"Jubilant," Libby said, surprised to hear the word spring from her lips. "It makes me feel jubilant."

With an open mouth, Tess brushed by them both to have a better look. The tree stood a good foot taller than her. Holton hit the overhead lights and they shone through the scarves, casting an array of colors across her face. "Oh, Holt," she breathed. "Now that's what I'm talking about. It's amazing."

He exhaled as though he'd been holding his breath, and the worry lines in his forehead were suddenly replaced by crow's-feet feathering from his smiling eyes. "It didn't even dawn on me that though there were hundreds of scarves in the box, there were only nine different colors." He gave Tess a knowing look, but whatever she was supposed to know had obviously eluded her because she furrowed her brow in confusion.

"The tree, of course, is the Tree of Life,

and since mine is just a shadow of the real thing, the driftwood reminds me that without God, it's all just deadwood. The scarves . . ." His eyes lit up with passion. "I'd like to think those were his contribution to my effort. Each color represents a fruit of the Spirit — red is love; gold, joy; blue, peace; purple for patience; pink for kindness; white, goodness; green, faithfulness; turquoise, gentleness; and —" he let out a long sigh and licked his lips — "silver is the tough one: self-control."

Libby didn't know what the Tree of Life was, but she would try to find out when she had a little time to herself. There was so much she needed to learn — about art, God . . . everything, really.

"And what a great reminder for whoever buys it," Tess said, running her fingers admiringly down the trunk, "of what we should be striving for."

Holton cut his eyes toward her. "This one's not for sale. I'm the one who needs the reminder the most. Besides, it'll look good in the front window. Don't you think?"

"Definitely," she agreed. "I don't see how anyone could pass by that in the window and not stop."

"Well," he said, "if you're both still on board, I'll go ahead and make this thing official then. You girls want to come with me to sign the lease?"

Libby reached up and touched a gold scarf. It was soft and silky and held in place by a single piece of what looked like clear fishing line, threaded through the point of its fold. She could just imagine a soft breeze blowing on the scarves, making them flow and flitter. Maybe she'd suggest keeping a fan on it for the effect. "I would, but Rob's coming to take me to dinner, and —" she waved a hand over herself — "I'm not exactly dressed to impress." She still wore the stained T-shirt and dusty shorts she'd thrown on to help Tess move in. No doubt she smelled awful, and her hair had been so soaked with perspiration, no amount of dry shampoo would get it clean.

Her stomach clenched at the conversation she was going to have to have with Rob. He'd done so much changing in recent weeks, but he didn't sign up for a life in Nags Head. If he said no, she didn't know what she would do.

"Penny for your thoughts," Tess said, looking concerned.

Libby forced the worry away and smiled. "I'm excited for you guys."

Worry lines once again etched themselves in Holton's forehead. "Just for us?"

"Say a prayer for me. This may be the most important conversation Rob and I have ever had," she said.

Holton gave Tess a worried glance, then turned to Libby. "Already have."

CHAPTER 38

The moon was full and high, casting a rippling gold path over the ocean leading to the beach. Across the sky, the black silhouette of a bird glided by with outstretched wings. Libby and Rob stood hand in hand looking out at the water. "Thanks for dinner," she said.

"Thanks for keeping me company." He slipped his warm fingers through hers. "You're cold," he said, his eyes full of concern.

Trying to look good for their date, she'd worn an embroidered cotton spaghetti-strap dress that stopped just above her knees. In the coolness of the ocean breeze, she regretted the decision. "Maybe a little."

He slipped off his blazer and draped it over her shoulders. Grabbing the lapels, she tightened it around her. The lining felt silky and warm against her bare arms. "That's better," she said as she snuggled into it.

"Thanks, babe."

Dinner had been a nice, relaxing time of laughter and hand-holding, but now anxiety was doing a number on Libby's full stomach. She had yet to tell him of Holton's offer. What if Rob didn't want to live in Nags Head? What if she would have to choose between the father she'd just found and the man she loved?

She blew out a breath of nerves and turned to him. "There's something I need to ask you."

When he turned his face toward her and away from the light of the moon, soft shadows masked his expression. "Me first."

She held her breath and nodded. He rubbed her left finger nervously. "I'd like for you to start wearing my ring again."

She didn't know if he could see the tightness of her smile. "If you still want me to —" she started to say.

"My feelings haven't changed and never will."

"You didn't let me finish," she whispered. "Holton and Tess are opening a gallery."

"That's great," he said, sounding genuinely pleased.

A white-haired couple passed by them, arm in arm, and they paused to admire the older couple's affection. She could tell by

Rob's expression that he, too, was imagining the two of them in fifty years. "I could love you like that," she said. "That long, I mean."

His smile lit up the dark beach. "I think I finally believe you."

Her gaze meandered over his short curls down to his deep-brown eyes, and her heart swelled for the hundredth time that night. "It's about time."

A breeze kicked up sand, and they both tucked their chins in until it died down. "I'm a little slow, I guess," he said. He slid behind her and wrapped his arms around her waist.

She watched the waves lap at the shore. "So beautiful," she said.

"Yes, you are." He squeezed her tighter as his breath warmed her ear. "I love you, Libby Slater."

"I love you, too." She turned around to face him. Moonlight reflected off his eyes, making them sparkle.

He traced her jawline. "I can't wait to marry you."

Her stomach tightened. "That's what I wanted to talk to you about."

"Should I be worried?"

She laid a hand on his cool cheek. "This gallery they're starting — they want me to help run it."

"It's here," he stated rather than asked. "It's in Nags Head."

Trying to read his thoughts through his eyes, all she could see in them was her own reflection. He pulled away from her and walked to the surf.

"What are you thinking?" she asked, but she could barely hear her words against the roar of the ocean.

He sat down on the sand and leaned his elbows on his bent knees.

Taking a seat beside him, she covered her bare legs with the skirt of her dress. "Please talk to me."

He shook his head. "You wondered why I was so freaked out about you coming here. This is why. You said it was just for the summer, but I knew this was going to happen."

She wrapped an arm around his waist and laid her head on his shoulder. "You could find a job here," she offered. "Nothing has to change."

"It already has," he said.

They sat quietly as the waves rolled into shore and back again. She had prepared herself for this. He wasn't one to embrace change easily.

"What if I said I've just been offered a job

back home?" he asked the ocean rather than her.

"Have you?"

He turned to face her, and she could see that his eyes were glistening from more than just the salt air. "Yeah. I wanted to surprise you."

She felt her own eyes welling up. So that was it. She wouldn't be staying in Nags Head after all. She loved Holton, but her place was with Rob. It wasn't that far of a drive. She could always come down every week if she wanted to, but of course, it wouldn't be the same. She'd be the weekend daughter, treated more like a guest than family. She'd go home and then what? Go back to her city apartment and get another accounting job? The thought was nauseatingly depressing. "Did you already accept?" she asked, praying he had waited to talk to her first.

"No," he said. "But I'm going to."

Her stomach dropped and she sat up, distancing herself from him. "I'm glad I've got a say in where we live. What about what *I* want?"

He turned his attention back to the ocean. "Do you even know what that is?"

Of course she knew. She wanted him, but she wanted him *here*. "What's wrong with

Nags Head?"

He ran his fingers through his hair. "Nothing, Libby. I just figured out what I wanted. This whole time, I've been trying to be successful, for you, for Caroline, to prove myself to —" He sighed. "I don't even know who to. I was offered a job as a public defender. I want to do this. Need to do it." He turned and locked eyes with her. "For me."

She let his jacket slip to the sand as she wrapped her arms around herself, needing the hug more than the warmth. "I didn't see this one coming. Why public defender?"

"I want to be more than some lawyer with a McMansion on a man-made lake. I want to make a difference in this world. I want our future children to be proud of me. The way you are of Holton."

Even though her heart felt like it was ripping in two, she was falling in love with him all over again. He hadn't said *his* children. He'd said *our* children. And that said everything. "I'm a little surprised, but I guess I shouldn't be. That's always who you've been." It made sense. She hadn't really thought about the altruistic man she'd known in college slowly changing over time into one obsessed with making partner. Hadn't even taken the time to question his motives. "I'm proud of you, but I'm going to miss Nags Head," she said, wiping the wetness from her face.

He picked his jacket off the sand and laid it back over her shoulders. "You should stay," he said, his voice cracking with emotion.

She turned to him, confused. "What?"

"I've never seen you so happy. You've got a father here, a grandmother, Tess; and besides, this is a great opportunity. You hate being an accountant. As much as I want you near me, I don't want you resenting me —"

"I won't resent you. It's my decision."

Even though he sat shoulder to shoulder with her, staring out at the ocean, he seemed miles away. "I don't want you to spend the rest of your life wondering *what if.*" He leaned over and kissed the tip of her nose. "I don't want to wonder that for myself either."

She wiped at her eyes, but fresh tears kept replacing the ones she rubbed away. "Where does that leave us?"

"It's only a two-and-a-half-hour drive," he said, rubbing his thumb over his own eye. "I'll come down every weekend I can."

If their love wasn't so strong, she might have thought it was all lip service, a losing game that nobody wanted to call. But they would make it through this. She was his cut of meat, after all. "And on the weekends you can't come to me," she said, "I'll come to you."

He slid his hand into the back of her hair. She thought he was getting ready to kiss her, but he just stared into her eyes. "You don't know how much I love you, Libby."

"I know," she said, burying her face in his warm neck.

"I'm only going to sign a one-year contract," he said. "We can survive anything for a year."

"We can," she agreed, feeling better. She looked up at him. "And after the year?"

He licked his lips. "Maybe you'll be ready to come home."

She didn't need a year to know that Nags Head was where she belonged. It was the first place she'd ever lived that felt like home. "And if I'm not?" she whispered.

"If you're not . . ." When he paused, she felt her heart stop. "Then Nags Head is as good a place as any to start a law firm. When I took the job in Casings, I knew you didn't want to live there."

She tried to laugh but couldn't. "What gave it away?"

Raising an eyebrow at her, a smile pulled at the corner of his mouth. "You saying every day that you hate Casings, probably."

"Once more for old times' sake, I hate Casings."

He slid his fingers between hers and brought her hand to his lips, kissing the place on her left hand where his ring should be. "But you said wherever I was, was where you belonged. Now it's my turn. Wherever you end up, Libby, that's where I belong."

She squeezed his hand. "One year," she said, resigned.

"One year," he repeated.

CHAPTER 39

On the day of what was to be Libby and Rob's wedding, Caroline must have called a hundred times fussing at her for not being at the church early enough. She had long since stopped reminding her mother that she and Rob were postponing the wedding.

Besides the fact that they would be in different towns for the next year, they knew that the only chance they had of their eventual wedding being what they wanted was if they simply told Caroline about it via invitation. The trade-off would be that they had to pay for everything themselves, but it was a small price to pay to ensure they'd have their day, their way . . . someday.

Caroline's last text message said that someone had better be getting married after all the time and money she'd put out.

Libby texted back: Don't worry, someone will be.

Caroline texted again: Where are your

bridesmaids? No one is here except the guests and the preacher!

They're there. Don't worry. Everything is going as planned.

Just not your *plan,* she thought with a smile. She set her phone down on the dashboard of Rob's car and looked at him. "She's going to be so ticked."

He flashed her a mischievous smile as he turned into the church parking lot. "Strangely enough, I'm okay with that." He lifted her hand to his lips and kissed the place just above where her engagement ring sat once again. "Are you sure you don't want to just get this over with today? We could have a double ceremony."

It was tempting. She couldn't wait to be his wife, but neither of them felt any reason to rush to the altar. So many changes were going on in each of their lives. There was still so much they were learning about themselves and each other. "Our day is going to be our way," she said and found herself once again making mental plans. Plans she wouldn't let Caroline hijack this time.

The parking lot of the church was packed. No doubt people who might not have felt like attending were there if only to see what was sure to be a spectacle. Most of the attendees already knew that Libby and Rob were not getting married. Caroline seemed to be the only person in denial. Libby felt a little sorry for her mother, but it was her own doing. It's not like they hadn't told her a hundred times in a hundred different ways that they had made other plans. But if it was a wedding she wanted, it was a wedding she was going to get. There was no sense wasting it all.

Rob opened her door, and she stepped out of the car and into the sunshine. It was a perfect seventysomething degrees with not a cloud in the sky. They couldn't have asked for a more beautiful day not to be getting married. "How do I look?" she asked him, glancing down at the yellow chenille dress she'd picked out for her bridesmaids. It was a good thing she and Emily were about the same size. He held his key out in the direction of his car and pushed the button that locked the doors with a beep, then turned his attention back to her.

His expression told her more than his words ever could. The look on his face made her feel like the most beautiful woman in the world. "Amazing as always," he said. He looked pretty amazing himself in his light-gray suit and bow tie. "I guess we better get in there. You have a father to give away."

And so Libby stood at the end of the aisle on the arm of the man who was everything a girl could hope to have in a daddy. She wasn't in the white gown as she had always thought she'd be. That honor was Tess's today. But as she smiled at Holton, she realized that everything in her life had brought her to this moment, and even if she could, she wouldn't change a thing.

Holton straightened his already-straight vest. "I guess it's time to walk me up front so I can watch my bride walk down the aisle." He was so handsome in the tux Caroline had picked out for Rob. He released some of his anxiety in the form of a heavy breath, then smiled at her.

"Thanks for making Rob your best man," she said.

"Do you know how much I love you, Libby?"

She leaned into his shoulder and gave his arm a squeeze. "I do," she said and laughed at the irony of it.

At the end of a long aisle of pews decorated with white silk and matching roses, they waited for the harpist to give their cue to start walking. Libby glanced at the groom's side of the church and saw Elsie sitting along the aisle. Elsie pushed her false teeth at her as a greeting.

Behind them, someone shrieked. She turned around to see Caroline, wearing an extravagant opalescent gown fit for a queen . . . and a look of horror. "Elizabeth, you are not getting married in that bridesmaid dress!"

Elsie whispered, loud enough for anyone close to hear, "Need me to trip her?"

Libby wagged her finger, then looked over to her father. "I guess that's our cue." She intertwined her arm in his and started up the aisle as the sound of harp music directed everyone's eyes to them.

"Elizabeth!" Caroline called again.

Holton threw a look over his shoulder and laughed. "We'd better walk fast."

A NOTE FROM THE AUTHOR

I hope you've enjoyed *Driftwood Tides*. Learning to forgive has been a theme in all my novels, and this one is no exception. We all need to extend forgiveness because we all need it ourselves. Many of us know someone — or *are* someone — who is dealing with a trauma that leads away from living up to the name we are called by. Sometimes, like Holton, we can feel our sins are too big and too bad to forgive, so we give up and simply continue along that path.

But the truth we need to remember is that Jesus already paid the price for our sins. *All* of our sins. Grace is granted anew each and every morning. No, we don't deserve it, but yes, it is ours for the taking. One of my favorite passages from the Bible says it better than I ever could: "I am convinced that nothing can ever separate us from God's love. Neither death nor life, neither angels nor demons, neither our fears for today nor our worries about tomorrow — not even the powers of hell can separate us from God's love. No power in the sky above or in the earth below — indeed, nothing in all creation will ever be able to separate us from the love of God that is revealed in Christ Jesus our Lord" (Romans 8:38-39).

DISCUSSION QUESTIONS

1. Do you think alcoholism is a disease or a choice — or some of each? What advice would you give someone who has a Holton in the family?

2. Did Adele make the right choice in giving up her baby for adoption? What other options might she have had?

3. How do you feel about Adele's choice not to tell Holton about the baby after they were married? Why do you suppose she never told him?

4. How might Holton and Adele's marriage have been different if he had known about Libby? Would it have weakened or strengthened their relationship? Are there some secrets that are better left undisclosed between a husband and a wife?

5. Tess has been a friend to Holton for many years and knows both his strengths and weaknesses. What made her decide she wanted to marry him? Was she wise to stick around so long, or should she have followed her sister's advice to make something better of her life?

6. Rob struggles with feelings of insecurity and paranoia, which he comes to realize stem from something in his past that he couldn't control. Is there anything like that in your life? How have you learned to cope with it?

7. Caroline is not the mother Libby wishes she'd had, but eventually Libby realizes Caroline was the mother she needed. What changed her perspective? In what ways were your parents what you needed, even if they weren't always what you wanted?

8. Tess compares Holton's life to the repurposing of driftwood. In what ways have you seen the brokenness of someone's life used for good?

ABOUT THE AUTHOR

Gina Holmes is the author of the bestselling and award-winning debut novel *Crossing Oceans; Dry as Rain,* a finalist for the 2012 Christy Award for excellence in Christian fiction; and *Wings of Glass,* named one of *Library Journal*'s best books of 2013.

Gina founded the influential literary website Novel Rocket, regularly named as one of *Writers Digest*'s best sites for writers. She holds degrees in science and nursing and currently resides with her husband and children in southern Virginia. She works too hard, laughs too loud, and longs to see others heal from their past and discover their God-given purpose. To learn more about her, visit www.ginaholmes.com or www.novelrocket.com.